MW01139859

THE
DISPATCHER

By James Robert Fuller

A Myrtle Beach
Crime Thriller

Book V

I don't want to mention who the book is dedicated to … just yet!

The dedication appears at the end of the story.

Don't peek!

THE MYRTLE BEACH CRIME THRILLERS

By *James Robert Fuller*

Paradise: Disturbed – Book I
The Scale Tippers – Book II
The Falano Findings - Book III
The Combo – Book IV
The Dispatcher – Book V
Dancing Dead – Book VI
(Coming Summer 2021)

FOLLOW THE SERIES AT:
MYRTLEBEACHTHRILLERS.COM

Contact the author at:
RONWING44@GMAIL.COM

Paradise: Disturbed

Much to our collective delight we finished reading "Paradise Disturbed." Wonderful twists and turns with the backdrop visits of the murderer to some of our favorite golf courses, tourist attractions and restaurants. This is a must read for any murder mystery fan, especially locals familiar with Myrtle Beach. What a plot! Weaving a diabolical serial killer into a golf course theme, along with the Alligator Adventure scenario, is a stroke of genius. Plus the repartee that goes on between the two FBI agents adds just the right touch of humor!... Bob and Judi Kiernan.

I enjoy the dialogue between FBI agents, Ron Lee, and Tim Pond. The constant ragging on each other makes me laugh. Great characters… John Coughenour

Poor Ernie! I loved that character…and I loved the book!... Bill Jackson

I just finished Paradise Disturbed, which I had a hard time putting it down. I thoroughly enjoyed the story. I can't wait to start The Scale Tippers… Tere Harper

I'm having a hard time putting this book down! I absolutely love it!... Linda Bolt

Paradise Disturbed was so much fun in a terrifying way, that I read it almost in one sitting and immediately passed it on to a golfer friend.

These books are great for escaping from the pandemic for a few hours... Nancy Bracken

I have read Paradise: Disturbed and love the fast pace you set. The two agents are great together and the creep factor was really good on this one - can't wait to get to the next one... Mary Patten

The Scale Tippers

All I can say is I really enjoyed the 1st book of your new series... and then, the second was even better. I had to throw away a couple of shirts due to salivating down the front of myself while reading all of Agent Ron Lee's donut adventures... Joe Saffran

The books are gripping, I can't put them down. Everything stops until I finish. My wife is still waiting for me to mow the lawn...when is the next one?... Gary Whittaker

Lay off the donut comments!... Ron Lee

I have read the 2nd book and thoroughly enjoyed it. I can't wait to read The Falano Findings. They are great!... Tere Harper

I have read all four of the Myrtle Beach Crime Thrillers and Scale Tippers is my favorite. I know the locales used in the story and I love stories that involve the Mafia!... Tim Graham

The Falano Findings

I just finished The Falano's Findings and all I can say is... I loved it! Looking forward to whatever comes next!... Tere Harper

*Loved all three of the Murder Mystery Series! The Falano Findings, brings you savage, intense, brutal, murders; however softens the tone with wit & humor brought on by the antics of the donut toting, I.R.S. Special Agent Ron Lee, and his partner Agent Tim Pond. A real page turner...*Joe Saffran

I read "The Falano Findings" and was hooked immediately and couldn't put it down.. I can't wait for "The Combo". I am an Horry County and Myrtle Beach native and J.R. Fuller really brings life... AND DEATH to the area... Sig Buster, III

"Falano Findings" was his best yet. Looking forward to the next one. Now my favorite author!... Gary Whitaker

I'm not much of a reader, but I couldn't put Paradise Disturbed down and read it in record time. Same thing happened with Scale Tippers and The Falano Findings. They pull you in and won't let go! I can't wait for the next one !!... Paul Reilley

The Combo

Been waiting for "THE COMBO" ever since I finished "FALANO." When it finally arrived it didn't disappoint. It took off where "The Falano Findings" left off and the race was on for the rest of the book. Now I'm waiting with bated breath for "The Dispatcher"... Sig Buster, III

All four in the Murder Mystery series have been enjoyable to read ! The Combo, like the others grabs you and won't let go until the end. If you think know how the book will end, you better keep on reading because you will be wrong! Can't wait for the next book to come out ... Paul Reilley

"Loved it!" ... Joe Saffran

"Quite a storyline! The Mamba was a great character and the twist in the story was perfect." ... Alex Harvey

"That cartel is never going to let up, is it? Loved the story and I love Ron and Tim. Keep those donuts coming! ... Agnus Cosart

THE DISPATCHER

A Myrtle Beach Crime Thriller

Book V

Authored by

JAMES ROBERT FULLER

FIRST EDITION

NOVEMBER 2020

ISBN: 978-1-71664-474-0

PROLOGUE

He was a patient man. After all, he waited well over a year before exacting his revenge.

His looks belied his 72 years of age. Most would think he was in his upper 50s, especially when he wore a hat that hid his balding head.

An athlete, he had played football and baseball in high school. He stood five-ten and weighed only 22 pounds over his high school weight of 168. Running and daily exercising kept him in extraordinary condition for his age.

Known as a people person, his early career activities included two years on a cruise ship as the shore excursion manager.

Numerous customers marveled at how, after just a brief interview, he could match them to activities that fit their enjoyment level.

When he announced he was leaving, the cruise line begged him to stay, even offering him the position of cruise director. But he declined, saying he had other fish to fry.

His knowledge of computers made him in demand wherever he went. Those in need of such a qualified person considered him one of the brightest minds in the always growing and oh-so diverse technology field.

Now retired, he had three hobbies: golf, fishing, and now, his newest… killing.

Tomorrow was Friday, and a woman, a frequent attendee of the organization who had laughed at him, was his next target.

Being a supposed people person, it was unfortunate he didn't recognize the difference between good-natured ribbing and humiliation.

This inability to differentiate between the two, turned his normally pleasant demeanor to despair. In a short

1

time, his despair turned to outrage. Hate soon followed and hate fostered revenge. Revenge had already left three women dead in its wake.

Seven more women held what he called a "dispatch ticket."

Tomorrow, he would punch Nancy Bracken's ticket.

CHAPTER 1

Friday, June 28, 2019 – 9:00am

There were four of them. All young, each successful. They weren't filthy rich, but money wasn't a concern.

Three had a spouse, but none had started a family.

They always enjoyed flying first class, five-star hotels, and the finest restaurants, but there were no yachts, second homes in the Hamptons, or a slew of Mercedes in their driveways.

Having known each other since they were young boys growing up in the streets of Detroit, they appreciated what they had accomplished, but they didn't flaunt it.

As happens, they grew up and went their separate ways. Although scattered across the northeast, they remained in constant contact. Their successes left them with an abundance of free time on their hands. Yet even though they were hundreds of miles apart, three or four times a year they would get together to share one unique interest.

They loved to rob banks.

Now they were in Myrtle Beach, South Carolina, where summer arrived, ready for bear, in mid-April. Hot wouldn't describe it. Neither would boiling nor sizzling. The temperature read 97 on the digital sign in front of the Bank of America. The humidity index was nearing 80. Breathing was a chore. There was only one word to describe this kind of heat: miserable.

"Damn, it ain't even 9:00 in the morning yet!" wailed the man sitting in the passenger seat of a stationary ambulance. "Nothing, short of hell itself, could be this fucking hot at 9:00am."

None of his three companions disagreed, but all stayed mum.

The heat, for the sixth straight day, was scorching the earth. Worms, driven from the dry earth in search of moisture, lay roasted on sidewalks. Birds attempting to pluck an insect morsel from the water-deprived ground found the concrete-like dirt a challenge they could not overcome.

Nary man or beast dare venture outdoors on a day like today, except for these four men parked two blocks from the bank on North Oak Street. Four men who remained calm and collected. This wasn't their first rodeo. In fact, it was their tenth.

It was 8:54am, and they were waiting for the bank to open. They weren't waiting to open an account, cash a check, make a deposit, or seek a loan. They were there to make a withdrawal. A large withdrawal, somewhere, they estimated, in the neighborhood of a quarter million dollars.

Since neither of the four had an account with the bank, the term 'withdrawal' is a misnomer. Stealing would be much more accurate.

Being professional bank robbers, they would ply their skills, hoping that no one would attempt to use force to state their objection. Those who did object faced certain death.

Over the years, they had encountered only one objection. A foolish guard tried to be a hero. Nick shot him dead. Although Nick had pulled the trigger, the law, through guilt by association, considered each a murderer.

All were unscrupulous, fearless, and loyal, but they were also intelligent, cautious, and independent.

Their leader was Nick Jonas, a 27-year-old with a Northeastern degree in economics, and a street degree in the art of robbing banks. He was meticulous, leaving no stone unturned when planning a heist, and this heist was no exception.

Nick's right-hand man was Daniel Lucas, age 27, and also a Northeastern graduate. Daniel's degree was in Chemical Science, but his street degree was in things that went "boom!"

Artie Silverman and Aaron Moore were the remaining members of the team.

Artie graduated from Pitt with a degree in Computer Science, but he had a fascination with guns, especially powerful guns, like AK-47s, which he was now holding.

Aaron was the wheelman. He had been driving cars since he was 11-years-old. Now he was sitting behind the wheel of an ambulance. An ambulance they had stolen from Grand Strand Medical Center 30 minutes earlier. The plan was to return it no later than 9:30am.

Aaron, a graduate of Clemson University, earned a degree in chemistry. He never used the degree as he had intended. Instead, he followed his interest in older cars. He formed an antique auto reconstruction company and made himself a rich man by the age of 26.

Robbing banks was their hobby. A needed distraction from the hum-drum of running a business. And they were damn good at it.

Nick, being the Picasso of the group, devised the plan, and it was always a work of art.

This foray had them flying into Myrtle Beach on Wednesday, June 26th, accompanied by their wives, and in Aaron's case, his long-time girlfriend.

Nick decided that they would stay through the Fourth of July weekend, and rob not just one bank, but two.

His escape plan was to use the cover of an estimated 200,000 Fourth of July tourists returning to their homes on Saturday, the 6th. During the week, they would rob a Bank of America on Friday, and then pull off the biggest heist in South Carolina history on July 3rd.

Soon after landing, each man, using an alias, rented a nondescript car. They then drove to their respective reserved room at the Marriot Resort and Spa, located less than a half-mile from the Grand Strand Medical Center.

They would enjoy two days in the sun with their ladies, but on Friday morning, the plan would go into motion.

After removing the license plates from their rented cars, the four men would drive to the Medical Center and park. Each had a facial disguise and wore the uniform of an EMT employee. Each carried a large black leather duffel bag. Inside one duffel bag was a golf club travel bag. It had a dual purpose. First, it would hold the money taken from the bank, and second, when full, would double as an ill person under a gurney's blanket.

Nick's plan had Aaron securing an ambulance from a pool of vehicles that were always ready for the next emergency.

Upon stealing the ambulance, the others would gather in the back, while Aaron drove them, under modest speeds, to the downtown bank.

With business completed inside the bank, the three men would load the gurney into the ambulance. After all were inside, Aaron, with lights flashing and siren wailing, would careen them back to the hospital.

During the high-speed return trip, the three men would equally distribute the money into the four satchels.

As Aaron approached the hospital, he would turn off the lights and siren so as not to draw attention from the hospital staff. He would park the ambulance in the pool area, where all would exit and return to their rented cars.

The last step of the plan was exiting the hospital property. They would take dissimilar routes to their hotel's parking lot. There, they would reattach the license plates. Minutes later, they would join their families on the beach. The entire undertaking would take less than an hour.

They had used the ambulance scenario two years earlier, in Knoxville, Tennessee.

It was 9:00am when an ambulance pulled up to a Wells Fargo bank in downtown Knoxville. As soon as it stopped, the rear door flung open and three men, dressed as paramedics, scrambled out. They pulled a blanket-covered gurney from the vehicle and rushed into the bank.

Once inside, the blanket, stripped from the gurney, would reveal the hidden firearms used to overwhelm the bank's security force.

Now in control, the thieves went about looting the vault, stacking the money on the gurney so that when covered by the blanket, it resembled a body.

After locking all the bank employees inside the plundered vault, they wheeled the gurney out to the ambulance. Once all were inside, Aaron whisked them away with lights flashing and siren wailing.

It was a thing of beauty.

They were hoping it would go just as well here in the blistering heat of Myrtle Beach, South Carolina.

All would go as planned. But one of them would put a blip on the law's radar. That blip spelled death to many.

CHAPTER 2

Her doorbell rang at 10:15 that morning.

Nancy Bracken, a 75-year-old widow, peeked through the door's spyhole to see who it was. It was a man, his position such that she could not see his face, but the patch on his jacket's arm indicated he was from the postal service.

She opened the inside door and felt the oppressive heat waft over her.

"Yes, may I help you?"

He looked familiar, but she couldn't place where she had seen him before. He was no spring chicken, that she could tell, but his stature and his eyes looked familiar.

"Mrs. Nancy Bracken?"

"Yes, that would be me."

"Package for you, ma'am. It's quite heavy. Should I bring it in for you?"

"Yes, please do," replied Nancy as she swung open the screen door and let the man, now carrying a 3x3 box, into her home.

"Where would you like me to sit this ma'am?"

They had walked down the short foyer and entered Nancy's living room.

"You may put it on the coffee table."

The mailman placed the package on the table and while holding a box cutter, asked, "Would you like me to open it for you, ma'am?"

"Why, that is very nice of you. Thank you."

Extending the box cutter's blade, he sliced the tape across the box's seam and opened the two flaps.

"There you go, ma'am."

Nancy walked over to the box, and staring into it, saw there was nothing but a single item lying in the box.

"I thought you said this box was heavy…"

"You shouldn't have laughed at me, Nancy. It wasn't right."

The box cutter flashed through the air and cut Nancy across the throat, severing her left carotid artery. Blood spewed everywhere as she sank to the floor with arms flailing and eyes bulging. She was dead in less than 20 seconds.

Straddling her body, he bent down and applied a second cut that severed her larynx.

"You won't scorn me any longer, Nancy."

Reaching into the box, the killer collected the book that lay inside, and walked across the room to where Nancy had accumulated shelves of books, knick-knacks, and family photos. He slid the book between two others that were, along with a dozen others, held up by matching book-ends. The book-ends, presented to Nancy when she left the bench, depicted a hand holding a gavel.

Nancy, a five-year retired federal judge, was the fourth victim of a revenge-seeking insane man.

He had baffled local law enforcement up to this point. The pseudo-mailman had waited more than a year before beginning his revenge. He knew the trail would be cold and memories would have faded. Connecting the dead would be difficult for those trying to catch him.

But after killing Nancy Bracken, he would now have to deal with the FBI. He didn't know it, but the odds were no longer in his favor.

CHAPTER 3

Friday, June 28, 2019

It was 9:15 when FBI Agent Tim Pond approached the intersection of Route 17 and 29th Avenue. Although the light was green, all traffic had stopped as a shrieking ambulance, barreling westward on 29th, turned north onto 17. With its red lights flashing, it headed toward the Grand Strand Medical Center.

Someone must have had a heat stroke, thought Tim, as traffic resumed movement.

He was just about to creep out into the intersection when he applied the brakes because of the fast approaching screams of police vehicles coming toward him and from behind.

He watched as three southbound police vehicles, with blue lights volleying back and forth, turned left onto 29th Avenue. Two others, driving in the northbound lane, made wide right turns, and sped eastward on 29th.

Must have been a helluva accident down there, thought Tim, changing his surmising of someone having a heat stroke.

He arrived at the 38th Avenue offices of the FBI, an hour late. A dentist appointment and the obligatory stop at Donut Man, combined for his tardiness.

He was walking through the front entrance when his partner, Special Agent Ron Lee, was walking out.

"Follow me, Tim!" cracked Ron.

"What's up?"

"Bank robbery."

"Where?"

"The Bank of America on Oak got hit about twenty minutes ago."

"Did anyone get hurt?" asked Tim, thinking about the ambulance careening up 17 toward the Grand Strand Hospital.

"Not that I know of."

Jumping into a black Tahoe, the two agents, with Ron driving, shot out onto 17 and headed south.

"I thought all the commotion was because of an accident," said Tim, as he took a bite of his peanut donut.

"What do you mean?" asked Ron.

Tim explained the commotion he witnessed while trying to get through the 29th and 17 intersection less than five minutes earlier.

"An ambulance?"

"Yeah. When I first saw it, I thought maybe someone had a heatstroke or something, but after seeing all the cop cars, I thought... hmm, accident."

Ron made the left onto 29th and two minutes later another right onto North Oak. Straight ahead they witnessed a cascade of flashing blue lights.

Parking on the street, the two agents made their way through the crowd of reporters and gawkers. Reaching the barricades put in place by the police, they identified themselves as FBI and passed through to the bank.

As they entered the bank, Myrtle Beach Police Chief Amy Proctor met them, saying, "Well, well, look who the FBI sent. Their two top gunslingers, Agents Lee, and Pond. How you doing, boys?"

"Not good," replied Ron. "Haven't had my morning fix as yet."

"It's 9:30 and you haven't had a damn donut yet! My, my, Agent Pond. I think you're in deep doo-doo."

"I ate mine on the way here."

"Prick," snorted Ron. "I should have let you drive."

"I think not, partner. If I had driven, you would have powdered sugar all over your suit and gobs of chocolate in each corner of your mouth. The boys outside may not have let us pass because an FBI agent, unless he was working undercover, wouldn't look like a slob."

"You guys done now?" asked Proctor.

"Yeah, what's the scoop?"

"Three men, dressed as EMTs, walk in at 9:00am, with a gurney and some AK-47s. They have the manager open the safe, they remove $265,000 and put it in a bag resembling a travel bag for golf clubs. They place it on the gurney, put a blanket over the bag and after locking the employees in the vault, walk out, locking the outside doors with a crowbar. With that, no one inside the bank could identify the getaway vehicle."

"It was an ambulance," said Tim, matter-of-factly.

"How do you know that?" asked Proctor.

"I admit it's a guess, but the gurney is a good clue. That, combined with my seeing an ambulance flying up 29th and turning toward the hospital... makes it a fair assumption."

"Descriptions?" asked Ron.

"Oh yeah, we have descriptions," responded Amy. "Let's see... one guy looked like Clark Gable, another looked like Tom Hanks, the third guy..."

"Masks," acknowledged Ron.

"Yeah, masks," nodded Amy.

"Fingerprints?" asked Tim.

"According to all the witnesses, all wore those medical type gloves."

"Were there any descriptions given? Body markings, hair color, eye color?" Ron asked, searching for the smallest of hints.

"Nay," answered Proctor.

"Nothing, Amy?" asked a frustrated Ron.

"There is one thing. But it ain't much."

"What is it?"

"It's about the guy who held the employees at bay at gunpoint."

"What about him?"

"He stuttered."

"Stuttered?"

"Yeah, it seems he had trouble saying words starting with the letters S and C."

"Well, that makes it easy then," said Tim. "We stop all men and ask them to say, 'So sorry, Charlie.'"

Ron, paying little attention to his partner's quip, asked, "What did he say that makes him a stutterer?"

"He told the employees to get down on the floor and don't do anything cc-cc-careless or I'll ss-ss-shoot you."

"Okay, well, it looks like you have things under control here, Amy. Send me a copy of your report."

"Will do, Ron. What do you plan on doing?"

"I think we'll check out Tim's ambulance theory."

It took Tim ten minutes to drive to the Grand Strand Medical Center. During that ride, Ron ate two donuts.

Tim pulled into the circular emergency entrance, where Ron asked a nearby hospital employee where they parked the ambulances.

"Back in the rear bay, sir," answered the young man.

Finding the ambulance bay, they counted five ambulances similar to the one Tim had seen earlier that morning.

"Can I help you guys?" asked a man dressed in an EMT uniform.

"We're FBI," said Ron. "Can we ask you a few questions?"

"Sure. Fire away."

"What's your name?"

"Johnny. John French."

"What time did you arrive today, John?"

"I arrived at 8 o'clock."

"Did you notice the number of ambulances on site when you arrived?"

"Yeah. Eight."

"How many left between 8:00 and 9:00?"

"I saw two pull out. One at 8:25 and another five minutes later."

"Who were the drivers?"

"Good question. Let me check the log."

They followed the man inside to a counter where they kept a logbook. He flipped it open to today's date and perused the notations.

"That's strange."

"What's that?" asked Tim.

"There's only the log out for the later ambulance. The one that left at 8:30. I know I saw one leave at 8:25."

"Can you now account for that ambulance?" asked Ron.

"Sure can. It's sitting out there right now. It's the last one in line. I saw it pull in around 9:20."

"Who was driving?"

"I can't say. I saw it pull in, but I didn't pay that much attention."

"We need to look inside that vehicle, John."

"No problem. Go right ahead."

"Okay, but where are the keys?"

"Oh, they're in the vehicle. We leave them unlocked with the keys inside. It's a normal procedure with hospitals. We can't be running around looking for a damn key when a call comes in."

Opening the rear doors, the first thing they saw was the golf club luggage bag.

"I guess you were right, Tim."

"Any thoughts as to why they left the bag, Ron?"

"I'm guessing that whatever they put the money into wasn't big enough to hold that bag."

"Seems a reasonable conclusion," nodded Tim. "Nothing on it that would indicate where it came from, and I'm sure we won't find prints."

"No, I'm sure we won't."

"And since the uniforms aren't here, I'm guessing they left the premises wearing them," added Tim.

"They planned this right down to the last detail, Tim. I'll bet that they didn't drive off in one car either. Someone might notice four men dressed in EMT uniforms getting into the same car together."

"Crafty bunch."

"Most successful bank robbers are smarter than the average Joe. This wasn't their first job. It's too clean."

"I'm thinking they are well out-of-town by now. Would you agree with that assessment, Ron?"

"Yeah, I do. Call in the lab guys to go over this ambulance with a fine-tooth comb."

"No sense in putting out a BOLO, I assume?"

"What will it say: Pull over a guy who stutters?"

"All right, so what's the plan?" asked Tim.

"Go get the security tapes for the parking lot, partner. Maybe we'll pick up the car or cars they left in. I'm betting they are rentals. I'll be in the Tahoe."

Ten minutes later Tim opened the driver's door to the Tahoe, only to see Ron, sitting in the passenger seat, munching on a chocolate-covered crème donut.

"I have the tape. We should be able to track their vehicles easily enough," surmised Tim.

"Yeah, but that seems too easy. They're way too clever not to know about the security cameras."

"Well, it's all we have. What else can we do?"

"We're going to go back to the office and do some research on recent bank robberies. You drive. I have two more donuts to eat."

CHAPTER 4

"Do you have any ss-ss-snacks, Marion?"

The four men had returned to the hotel, replaced the plates, changed into swimwear, and met their significant others on the beach. It was only 9:45.

"Yes, I did, Artie," replied his wife of four years. "There's beer in the cooler and snacks in my beach bag."

"Did you girls carry all this; chairs, coolers, towels, blankets, and food, down onto the beach?" asked Daniel.

"No," answered Marcia, his wife. "They have a shuttle that brings you down and then they have some young men to help you with your stuff."

"Where have you guys been?" asked Nick's wife, Kim.

"We went out for breakfast."

"You had breakfast?" questioned Marion. "Then why is Artie asking about snacks?"

"He's a bottomless pit," answered Aaron as his girlfriend, Ellen Carey, the youngest of the women at 22, was applying suntan lotion on his back.

"He doesn't eat like that at home," said Marion with a hurt look.

"I think it's the sa-sa-salt air, honey," said Artie, trying to assuage his spouse.

Marcia Lucas, by far the best looking of the four women, asked, "Where did you eat?"

"I don't recall the name of the place," replied her husband, Daniel. "It's down the road about a mile or so."

"North or south?" asked Marcia.

"North," answered Danial and Aaron in chorus.

"Ss-ss-south," answered Artie, simultaneously.

"Someone needs a compass," remarked Marcia.

"Artie's confused, as usual," offered Nick. "We'll take you there tomorrow for breakfast."

"Are you going to spend the day on the beach with us?" cooed Ellen.

"We decided we need something more roomy to make the drive home," answered Aaron. "We're going to the airport to upgrade to SUVs."

Flying home with what Nick hoped to be over two million dollars was not an option. His plan had them driving home with stops in Williamsburg, Washington, and Gettysburg as part of their vacation.

"Is that really something that needs doing today?" asked Marcia.

"Yeah, it does," answered her husband, Daniel. "If we wait, the new crowd coming into town tomorrow might scoop up all the best vehicles."

The four women bought his answer.

Thirty minutes later, the men left and drove their rental cars to the airport and switched them for four SUVs.

None of the women knew of the mutual hobby their men shared. Once uncovered, it would be catastrophic.

If they had been in their hotel rooms, they would have heard on television the news of the bank holdup. They also would have heard that the only lead police had was that one bandit had a noticeable stutter.

Having spent the entire day on the beach, followed by a long evening having dinner and bar-hopping, left no time for anyone in the group to catch up on the news.

But Saturday morning would be an eyeopener for one of them.

CHAPTER 5

Friday, June 28, 2019

It was going on 2:00pm when Ron and Tim finished reviewing the hospital parking lot security tapes.

At first they didn't notice the men when they arrived. It wasn't until they approached the ambulance that they could back up the tape and watch as the four of them arrived, all in nondescript Toyota Corollas. Two of them pulled into the entrance off Route 17, one from the north, the other from the south. The other two arrived through the 82nd Parkway entrance.

They watched as the four men, all wearing obvious disguises, and each carrying a black duffel bag, congregated at the ambulance that was the first in line. Three men entered through the rear door, while the fourth manned the driver's seat. No sooner had the rear doors closed, than did the ambulance drive off, exiting the hospital grounds onto Route 17 South.

"Did you see any weapons, Tim?"

"No. I'm guessing they had them in the duffel bags."

"I suppose."

Tim fast-forwarded the tape until they saw the ambulance return. They watched as the four men exited the vehicle and went to their respective cars.

Ron, drumming his fingers on the table, needed to see the vehicles leave because when the cars arrived, they could not see the rear license plates.

They watched as each car left the lot the same way they entered.

"No plates!" exclaimed Tim.

"Yeah, so I noticed."

"Did you pick up on anything, Ron?"

"Maybe."

"Are you going to share?"

"Answer me this, Tim-o-thy. How far would you drive, especially after robbing a bank and carrying a satchel full of money, with no plates on your vehicle?"

"Not too far, that's for sure," answered Tim, seeing where Ron was going.

"That hospital can't be a mile from the beach."

"That's about right, Ron."

"So, maybe our boys are staying at a hotel on the beach."

"What about the two cars that exited onto 17?"

"What are the next streets in either direction?"

Tim, bringing up a map on his computer screen, announced, "79th and 82nd."

"Let's watch the tape again where the two cars exited onto 82nd."

"What do you expect to see, Ron?" as they watched the two vehicles turn right onto 82nd Parkway.

Only 15 seconds passed before a third car, with no plates, passed by the 82nd Parkway exit.

"I bet if we could get footage of 79th, we'd see car four heading toward the beach."

"Maybe that's where they changed vehicles."

"Not likely, Tim. Why bother removing the plates of a vehicle if you planned to swap it for another? Makes no sense."

"So what's the plan?"

"Let's take a ride down to the beach and check out the parking lots for those four Toyota Corollas. If we see one, we can call the company who rented it, get the name of the customer…"

"Do you believe for one second that they would use their actual names, Ron?"

"Ahh, no, I don't, but maybe the person who rented the vehicles to them can give us a description."

"Are you aware, Ron, that most rental agencies now provide a reservation service?"

"No, I was not. How does that work?"

"It allows customers to debark their plane and go straight to the car they rented without ever seeing or talking with a rental employee."

"Hmm, that could be a problem. You're always throwing cold water on my plans, Tim."

"Just pointing out the obvious, Ron."

It wouldn't matter. They had already swapped the four Corollas for SUVs. Trying to track down the rentals would also be for naught, as they had taken precautions to rent their vehicles from multiple rental agencies.

Possessing guile and above average intelligence, this gang of thieves was not your average everyday bank robbers.

Catching them would prove difficult and dangerous.

There was, however, that one little fly in the ointment.

CHAPTER 6

Saturday, June 29, 2019

Ron had just made himself a chicken and swiss cheese sandwich with a thick slice of tomato when the phone rang.

He glanced at the stove's clock and saw it was 2:07. Ambling over to the phone, he saw the caller ID show it was his partner.

Annoyed at being called on a day off, he answered gruffly, "What the hell do you want!"

"A dollar will get you two I interrupted something important like… oh, I'm guessing at this hour, eating a sandwich?"

Smiling at his partner's clairvoyance, Ron replied, "Do you have this place bugged?"

"You know, there's something I've always meant to ask but keep forgetting to do so," said Tim.

"Oh, and what might that be?"

"Who buys your donuts for you on weekends?"

"I don't eat donuts on weekends. You might say I do a 'mini-fast.'"

"Does your wallet ever leave your back pocket, other than when you change pants?"

"Why are you calling me?" asked Ron with a tone of annoyance.

"Murder."

"Murder? Who got murdered?"

"Braddock called about ten minutes ago saying he wants us at the home of Nancy Bracken."

"I take it she's the dead one."

"Bingo!"

"What's the address?"

"She lives at 307 Ocean View Drive in the Briarcliffe Acres section of Myrtle Beach. Are you familiar with that area?"

"Yeah, I know where it is. It will take me about 30 minutes to get there. Why are we being called in?"

"She's a retired federal judge, Ron, and as you know…"

"Yeah, I know. We have jurisdiction. Got it. See you about 3:00."

"Are you going to eat your sandwich?"

"Hell, yes! That's why I won't be there until 3:00."

Ron arrived at 3:09, and Tim was waiting for him in the driveway. A yellow crime scene tape stretched across the drive and all the way across the front edge of the lawn. A black-and-white, with its blue lights flashing, also blocked the drive.

"That must have been one helluva sandwich!"

"It was. I washed it down with a… *burrrrrp*… root beer," said Ron, adding a belch for effect.

"Thanks for the sound effects," said Tim, feigning disgust.

"Have you been inside yet?"

"No. I waited for you. I asked the neighbors if they saw anyone enter or leave the house."

"And?"

"No."

"Who's inside?"

"Amy Proctor, Bill Baxter, and Robert Edge."

"Well, let's go see our dead judge, Tim-o-thy."

They entered the living room and saw the sheet-covered body of the woman. Large splotches of blood had seeped out from under the sheet.

"Why all the blood?" asked Ron.

"She had her throat slit, not once, but twice. The second cut severing the larynx was postmortem," answered Robert Edge, the Horry County Coroner. "I'm thinking he used a boxcutter."

"How so?" asked Tim.

"Because sitting on the coffee table is an empty box sliced open by what I assume was a boxcutter."

"You say the box is empty, Bob?" asked Ron.

"It is now. I can't say it was when it entered the house."

"Any markings on the box?"

"None, other than the box manufacturer's logo."

"Fingerprints?"

"Negative," answered Amy Proctor, the Myrtle Beach Chief-of-Police.

"It looks like our killer may have stepped in some blood," observed Ron, pointing to a partial footprint on the rug.

"Yeah, but we can't identify anything from it, Ron. There's little blood, and the rug is too shaggy."

"It looks like he may have been walking toward that wall," expressed Amy, nodding her head toward the shelving to the left of the fireplace.

Ron walked over and stared at three shelves.

"I'm guessing these photos on the top shelf are family pictures. There's a dozen or more books on the second shelf and knick-knacks on the third."

"Is there a Lady Justice in that mix, partner?" asked Tim.

"No, thank God."

"How long has she been dead, Bob?" asked Tim.

"I'd say 30 hours, tops."

"Got any thoughts, Ron?" asked Bill Baxter.

"Who found the body, Amy?"

"One of my officers. We got a call from her son at 1:30. He tried calling her a half-dozen times and getting no reply, called us and ask if we would check on her. We had a car in the area, so we sent it over. The officer knocked and rang the doorbell and after getting no response, tried the door. It was unlocked. He walks in and finds her where she lies."

"This box intrigues me," Ron said as he examined it. "What size would you say this box is, Tim?"

"I'd guess it was 3x3x2."

"Amy, anything in the house that fits those dimensions?"

"Sure, but most have been here awhile."

"Does it appear to you the judge kept a neat home?"

"It does," agreed Proctor.

"That being the case, do you see her letting a big box like this sit on her coffee table for any length of time?"

"I do not," agreed Proctor again.

"Neither do I. I'm guessing the killer, using the box's size as a cover, brought it into the house for her. Maybe he told her it was heavy, when in fact, it was empty, or so it seems."

"Then he uses the boxcutter to open the box for her," surmised Tim.

"That was my thinking, partner. As the judge looks into the box… he uses the boxcutter to slice open her throat."

"Are you thinking he disguised himself as a FedEx or UPS driver, Ron?"

"My head had that thought surrounded, Tim. Hell, maybe he is a Fed Ex or UPS driver."

Captain Bill Baxter, standing off to the side, halted the discussion between the two agents when he mumbled, "This is our Friday killer, Ron."

"I'm sorry. What was that you said, Bill? Our Friday killer? What does that mean?"

"Don't you read the papers or watch the news?"

"Yeah, but I have seen nothing pertaining to a Friday killer."

"Well, that's the name I have given him. This is the fourth straight Friday where someone killed a woman in her home."

"It seems like two or three people get themselves killed on weekends, Bill. What links your four victims?"

"That is the unanswered question, Ron," stated Amy. "We haven't found a link between the women. To tell you the truth, there is no similarity between the killings other than they are older women."

"Hmm, now that is strange," murmured Ron. "I assume the three previous crime scenes remain locked down."

"Tight as a drum," answered Proctor.

"I want to see them. I also want detailed photos taken of each room in this house. Did anyone notice if the judge has a calendar showing her activities?"

"I thought I saw one in the kitchen, Ron," replied Baxter.

"Go get it, Tim. Let's look at the judge's past activities, and what she had planned going forward."

"Do you guys have time to work this case, Ron?" asked Baxter.

"We were working yesterday's bank robbery. It goes without question that some real pros pulled that heist, and they have long since left the premises. So the answer to your question is, yeah, I assume we can devote all our efforts to this."

It was to be a bad assumption.

CHAPTER 7

Sunday, June 30, 2019

Ellen Corey, Aaron's oh-so-petite girlfriend, was an early riser. She didn't have an ounce of fat on her five-foot and 100 pound frame and she intended for it to remain that way through daily exercising and birth control pills.

Ellen, entering the Marriot's fitness center at 5:30am, saw that she had the center to herself. She took a few minutes to limber up before climbing onto a treadmill to do her normal three-mile jog.

The resort had mounted a dozen televisions on the fitness center walls, but at this early hour all were silent.

Ellen, using a nearby remote, turned on a television and after flicking through a half-dozen channels, found a station carrying the local news. Having spent the past two days on the beach and cavorting in nightclubs at night, she felt a need to catch up on the news.

Content with her choice, she began her warming-up exercises.

As she warmed up, she let her mind wander, but the newscaster jolted it back to the present when she reported, *"One man had a severe stuttering condition."*

Stopping her warmups, she retrieved the remote. Backtracking the broadcast, she heard: *"Police have made no headway in finding the four masked men who robbed the Oak Street branch of the Bank of America Friday morning. The armed robbers waited for the bank to open at 9:00am before three of them entered the bank wearing EMT outfits and pushing a gurney."*

Ellen turned up the sound.

"After overtaking the guard, two bank employees filled a bag, described by one employee as a golf club travel bag, with money from the vault."

She took a step closer to the screen.

"The thieves instructed bank employees to place the money-filled bag onto the gurney. Then, to make it appear as if a person was lying on the gurney, they covered the bag with a white sheet."

"Clever," remarked Ellen.

"A thief then wheeled the gurney out to a waiting ambulance, while the two others locked the bank employees in the vault. They then locked the bank's front doors from the outside with a crowbar, before making their getaway in the ambulance. It later became known that they had stolen the ambulance from the Grand Strand Medical Center."

A chill ran up her spine when the reporter added, *"In a detail defying explanation, the thieves returned the ambulance before Medical Center personnel even realized it had been missing."*

Ellen froze when she heard the reporter say, *"Other than saying all four men were Caucasian, two witnesses told police that one man had a severe stuttering condition."*

She turned off the television. Immobilized by the thoughts running through her head, Ellen stood dead still.

Her first thought was knowing the hospital was less than a mile from the hotel. She knew the four men had left that morning by 8:30 and returned by 9:45. Those things, although true, proved nothing. But she also knew that Artie had a severe stuttering problem.

She knew, in her heart, that the man she was with, the man she loved, was a bank robber.

Leaving the fitness center, Ellen rushed back to their room to confront Aaron with her suspicions. It would be a poor decision, and it would be her last.

Barging into their bedroom, she turned on the lights, which woke Aaron.

"What the hell…"

"You're a damn bank robber, aren't you?" Ellen cried.

"What? Wait a minute, Elly. What the hell are you talking about?"

"I heard it on the news this morning. Four men, all white, dressed in EMT outfits and using an ambulance from the Myrtle Beach Medical Center, robbed a bank in Myrtle Beach Friday morning."

"Okay, but why does that make me a bank robber?"

"That hospital is right up the street and you stole the ambulance when the four of you were 'quote' having breakfast!"

"We ate breakfast!" lied an emphatic Aaron.

"One man stuttered," Ellen stated with finality.

Aaron, hearing those words, felt like the last nail driven into the coffin.

"So because Artie stutters, you think we robbed the Bank of America?"

"I never said what bank it was, Aaron."

Aaron gave pause to her statement, then said, "No, you didn't, did you? Maybe I heard it on the news."

"No, you didn't hear it on the news, Aaron. We spent the day on the beach, we went out to dinner, we returned, and went to bed. We never turned on the tv."

Aaron digested her truths and then, climbing out of the bed, approached her, saying, "Okay, Elly, you're right. We robbed that bank."

"Dear God," Ellen sobbed. "Why would you do such a thing? You don't need the money!"

"It's a… hobby for us."

"A hobby! How many banks have you robbed?"

"I stopped counting last year. Maybe ten or twelve."

"What! Are you out of your mind!"

"What are you going to do, Elly?"

"Well, I'm not staying with you. I refuse to be an accessory to your crime," she said as she marched into the bathroom and began collecting her toiletries.

"You can't leave, Elly."

"No? Well, just watch me! Tell me, Aaron. Do the wives know?"

"No," replied Aaron, as he slid a bath towel off a nearby rack. "No one knows but you."

"Well, guess what, Aaron? When I leave here, everyone will know!"

"I'm really sorry you feel that way, Elly."

"Oh, I bet you are," she answered as she stuffed the last of her articles into her toiletries case.

With her back to him, he flipped the towel over her head and wrapped it around her neck. He then began twisting it like it was a tourniquet.

Ellen couldn't scream, but she could flail. Her arms and legs lashed out in all directions, but only for a few seconds. The lack of oxygen took the flailing motions to gasps of surrender, and then to death.

Aaron held on tight for another full minute before relinquishing the towel from her throat. She slumped to the floor. Her eyes were bulging, and her face was blue.

He picked her up and carried her to the bed. Tossing a blanket over her body, he closed the bedroom door. Placing a 'Do Not Disturb' sign on the outer door, he left to tell Nick that they had a problem.

Nick would know what to do. Nick always had the answers.

CHAPTER 8

Sunday, June 30, 2019 – 7:30am

"You know, Ron, it's bad enough that you insist we work on a Sunday, but is it necessary that we start at 7:30 in the friggin' morning?"

"The donuts are fresher in the early morning hours."

"What! Wait! We're going to stop for donuts!"

"I'll have my usual with a large coffee, please," answered Ron as he pulled into the Dunkin' Donut store.

"Wait just a damn minute here, partner. Are you telling me you dragged my ass out of bed at 6:45 on a Sunday morning so I could buy you coffee and donuts?"

"I hate breaking tradition, Tim-o-thy."

"Tradition? You mean the tradition where you never buy? That tradition?"

"That too."

"What about what you told me yesterday?"

"What was it I said?"

"You said, and I quote, 'I don't eat donuts on weekends. I do a mini-fast', unquote."

"I must have been delusional. My sugar was on the low-side."

"Yeah, right. Well, I have news for you."

"What's that?"

"I didn't bring my wallet."

"I know you're lying, Tim, but remember that ten-spot I borrowed from you?"

"Yes, I remember. I also remember it was seven months ago."

"Well, here you go, I'm paying you back. Now you have money for donuts. Get me two chocolate-covered creams and one cruller."

Snatching the ten-dollar bill from Ron's hand, Tim exited the door, slamming it shut, as he huffed and puffed his way into the store.

When Tim returned, Ron had slid over into the passenger seat.

"Why did you move?"

"Can't drive and eat, Tim. It's dangerous. Might spill hot coffee on my crotch, and then I'd have to sue Dunkin'. I don't need the legal hassle. You drive, I'll eat."

"Did you think if you sued them they might settle out of court for a lifetime supply of donuts and coffee?"

"Hmm, that's a very interesting thought, Tim-o-thy. I'll ponder on that as you drive."

"What about me? I'd like to eat my single donut and my small coffee. Oh, and just for your information, I got a slight shiver when the clerk gave me back a whole forty-cents in change from my ten-dollar bill."

"Well, I'm glad I borrowed ten bucks. If I had borrowed five, we would have had to cut down our order."

"Gosh, I can only imagine who would have drawn the short straw," murmured Tim as he drove off.

The first woman killed, suffocated with her own "My Pillow," was Charlene McSweeny. She lived in North Myrtle Beach in the Barefoot community.

As Tim turned onto Barefoot Resort Bridge Road, he saw the Alligator Adventure complex to his left.

"Brings back memories, doesn't it, Ron?"

"Yeah, it sure does. Bad ones. I don't think I'll ever get over the opening up of the gator and seeing all those human pieces falling out."

"They call that a necropsy, if I remember correctly."

"Yeah, it was."

Minutes later, as Tim made a left turn onto Bill Bent Lane, he said, "Well, it appears our first victim, Mrs. McSweeny, lived in a very nice neighborhood."

"She had money, that's for sure. She was also a widow. Her husband was big in construction. He passed in 2015," Ron said as he read the police report. "There's the house on your left, Tim."

Two large stone columns on either side of the driveway greeted visitors as they pulled onto the 100-yard driveway leading to the 5800 square foot stone home.

"You could burn a lot of gas money just driving up and down this driveway," remarked Tim.

"I agree, but I doubt they had concerns."

The obligatory yellow crime scene tape fronted all doors leading into the home.

Ron, having gathered keys from Bill Baxter to the homes of the three murder scenes, ducked under the tape at the side entrance and unlocked the door. The authorities had left lights on throughout the house.

Once they were inside, Ron began reading Assistant Coroner Cathy Overton's coroner's report aloud:

"Someone suffocated the victim using one of the victim's bed pillows. I calculate the time of death at 1:00am. A blade of some type, probably a boxcutter, was used to slit the victim's throat postmortem. The cut was deep enough to sever the larynx."

"Suffocating a person with a pillow isn't the easiest thing to do, Ron. The victim puts up a helluva fight."

"True," agreed Ron, "but the victim was almost 73-years of age and not in the best of health. An average-sized guy wouldn't have too much trouble. I wonder what was the point of slitting her throat?"

"Maybe he just wanted to make sure she was dead," offered Tim.

"Well, there's no doubt that would do it," concurred Ron.

"I'm guessing he must have broken in after she went to bed," Tim suggested.

"So you would think. The police report states they found no signs of a forced entry."

"Maybe she left a door unlocked."

"That would be an unlikely coincidence, don't you think? The one night Mrs. McSweeny leaves a door unlocked is the night someone kills her. I doubt it."

"Nice bedroom. I once had a house almost this big," quipped Tim. "It all starts with this big king-sized poster bed, folks," he went on as if he was announcing the prizes for the big deal on *The Price is Right*. "We have a 65-inch tv hanging on the wall, along with some very pricey paintings. Over here we have a bathroom that's bigger than my friggin' bedroom. The bedroom has an enormous walk-in closet with a separate dressing area, and all the bedroom walls have bookshelves loaded with books."

"She lived a few scales above our paygrade, Tim."

As Ron walked about the room, he stopped near a small table next to a shelf of books. The table housed a tiffany lamp, a framed photo, and a book. The book was a copy of *Catch Me if You Can*. There was a bookmark placed at chapter one.

Ron glanced over toward the bed and saw another book on the nightstand. Walking to the nightstand, he saw it was a copy of *The Three Musketeers*.

Returning to the bookshelves, he looked for the empty locations from where the two books had rested. He could only find one.

"That's strange," he said aloud.

"What's that, Ron?"

"*The Three Musketeers* was lying on the bedside nightstand…"

"The candy bar?" interrupted Tim.

"You know, Tim, one of these days, I'm going to demand to see your high school diploma."

"Sorry, but I won't turn it over. If the president doesn't have to turn his taxes over, I don't see a need for me to turn over my extensive educational background."

"Hmm, good point, partner," said Ron with a smirk. "However, I wasn't talking about a candy bar, I'm talking about the book," growled Ron. "It has a bookmark in it. I have to surmise that Mrs. McSweeny read that book."

"I'd have to agree, partner."

"Now, here, on this small table lies, *Catch Me if You Can.*"

"Okay, so what's your point?"

"I've searched the bookshelves to find the locations where these books may have been resting. I found only one opening."

"Hell, Ron, look at all those books she has. I think she ran out of room for another book."

"Maybe. Grab that book by the bed, Tim."

Picking up *Catch Me if You Can*, Ron walked over to the vacant spot and lifting the book to the open spot, found it much too thin to fit.

"There's almost room for four copies of this book. Let me have that book, Tim."

The Three Musketeers slid into the open spot perfectly.

"Hmm, I wonder where this fits," said Ron while holding the 250 page *Catch Me if You Can.*

Replacing the book on the table, Ron preceded to check out the rest of the room.

Opening a desk drawer, he found a checkbook. He flicked through the first couple of the almost unreadable copies of checks Charlene had recently written. Most were for food and clothing. He looked at a half dozen more before returning the checkbook to the drawer.

Further perusal on Ron's part, would have found a check made out to a locksmith. Answers to how the killer attained entrance into the house would have been revealed, and with it, the killer's identity. But it was not to be.

"I want the entire room photographed and taped, Tim. Check for a calendar or an appointment book too."

"I'll have the lab guys come by tomorrow, Ron. I already checked for a calendar or an appointment book but found neither."

"Where was the second killing?"

"It took place on the top floor of the Marina Inn at the Grand Dunes. The victim was Carol Holihan. Someone strangled her while she was showering."

"Well, if nothing else, Tim, we are seeing the habitats of the rich and famous while working this case. I wonder what their connection is?"

"Sound to me like it may be money."

"You always take the effortless way, partner. There's a connection, but it's not money. When we determine what it is, we'll be much closer to cracking this case."

CHAPTER 9

Sunday, June 30, 2019

Nick, a light sleeper, heard the ever so soft tapping on his hotel room's door. Glancing at the clock, he saw it was 5:55. Leaving the bed as to not disturb Kim, he made his way to the door, looked through the peephole and seeing it was Aaron, gingerly opened the door.

"What the hell do you want, Aaron, at fucking 5:55 in the morning?"

"I killed Ellen," Aaron whispered.

"You what?" gasped Nick in a shocked whisper as he grabbed Aaron by the arm and dragged him inside the foyer.

"I had to, Nick. Somehow she knew we robbed the bank. She was going to the cops. It was the only way!"

Nick digested Aaron's explanation and knew he had done what needed doing, but damn!

"What did you do with her?"

"She's in the bed, covered with a blanket."

"Doesn't she work out each morning?"

"Yeah. She's in the gym by 5:00-5:30."

"I'm sure they have cameras so we can't take her back there. What floor are you on?"

"The 11th."

"What's below you?"

"The pool area. Why?"

"Go to your room and throw her over the balcony."

"Are you fucking crazy, Nick?"

"Do it now, Aaron, before the sun gets up. Hurry!"

"Then what?"

"Get back into bed and wait."

"Wait? Wait for what?"

"The cops."

"Yeah, of course there will be cops."

"Yeah, there will be. Oh, one more thing, Aaron."

"What's that, Nick?"

"Don't, under any circumstances, mention that you're with any of us."

Aaron had many more questions he wanted to ask, but he knew the sun's rising wouldn't wait.

Following Nick's directions, Aaron returned to his room. Locking the door behind him, he made his way to the bedroom. After eyeing Ellen's still corpse, he made his way to the balcony door and slid it open. Stepping out, he made his way to the railing. Peering over the edge, he searched for activity but saw none. He glanced around at all the nearby balconies. Seeing that no one was enjoying the early morning air, he breathed a sigh of relief.

Rushing back into the room, he gathered Ellen's body and carried it to the balcony's threshold. Peering out the sliding door, he took another cautionary glance at all the nearby balconies. Seeing no activity, he made his way to the edge of the glass railing.

It was only slightly past 6:00am, but already the early morning air was hot and sticky. He was sweating profusely, but the weather was not to blame. Fear was the culprit. Fear and guilt.

The situation required another glance downward to ensure there was no one below. All was quiet.

Raising Ellen's body up and over the edge of the railing, he let her slip from his arms. He didn't follow her fall, but instead rushed back toward the bedroom. He was two steps from the sliding door's threshold when he heard the thud of her body hitting the macadam that surrounded the pool area.

Hearing Nick's instructions in his head, he undressed and crawled into the bed where Ellen's body had been lying just moments earlier.

Waves of nausea swept through his body as he felt the warmth of Ellen's escaping body heat in the bedsheets. He laid there, soaking the bedding with sweat before the fear finally overtook him. He left the bed as if it were on fire. Seconds later, he stood in the shower, letting cold water wash over his body.

The shower was brief, but the cold water seemingly did its job. Sitting naked on the edge of the bed, Aaron thought he had regained his composure, but when the phone rang, he almost jumped out of his skin.

It shrilled three more times before he answered.

"Ring!"

"Ring!"

"Ring!"

He answered with a groggy tone that made it sound as if the caller had woken him from a deep sleep. It was 6:29.

"Mr. Aaron Morris?"

"Yes," replied Aaron with the phony sleepy growl.

"Sir, this is Emma Langford. I'm the hotel's morning manager. There are people here in my office needing to speak with you."

"What! At 6:30 in the morning? Whatever for and by whom?"

"It's the Myrtle Beach police, sir."

"The police! Why? What's happened?"

"I'm not at liberty to say, sir."

"Very well, miss. I'll be there as soon as I get dressed."

Five minutes later, Aaron, dressed in a t-shirt, shorts, and sandals was standing in the hotel manager's office answering the questions being asked by two Myrtle Beach uniformed officers.

Gazing out the office window, he could see an EMT unit parked at the front lobby entrance.

Too little, too late, he thought.

"Mr. Morris…"

"Please call me Aaron, Officer."

"Sir, you arrived at the hotel with Miss Ellen Carey. Is that correct?"

"Yes. We are here on vacation. We were planning to be engaged…"

"Were, sir?"

"What?"

"You said you were planning to get engaged. Did something change?"

"Yes, I guess you might say that. I told her I was having second thoughts. Why do you ask?"

"Do you know her whereabouts, sir?"

Aaron glanced at his watch and seeing it read 6:44, replied, "I imagine she is in the spa's steam room about now. That's where she goes after working out for an hour in the fitness center."

"Have you seen or talked with her this morning, sir?"

"Hell, no! She gets up way too early for my taste!"

"What's her routine after the spa, sir?"

"She returns to the room, makes some coffee and sits out on the balcony. Then she showers and gets ready for whatever activity the girls have planned for the day. Hey, what's this all about, anyway?"

"So, you didn't see her out on the balcony this morning."

"Ah, no, I didn't. I suppose I could have passed her in the elevator on my way down. You haven't answered my question, Officer. What's this all about? Has Ellen done something wrong? Is she all right?"

Aaron watched as the two officers glanced at one another. He saw the elder of the two giving an almost imperceptible nod to the younger.

"Mr. Morris, I'm sorry, but a hotel employee found Ellen Carey dead in the swimming pool area this morning. It appears as if she fell from a height."

"What!" screamed Aaron, feigning disbelief. "There is no way! You're wrong!"

His act was impeccable and worthy of an Academy Award.

"The victim's key was on her person, sir. It matches your room number."

"Maybe she put it down and someone…"

"No, sir. The victim is your roommate, Ellen Carey. Because you and the victim shared the same hotel room, we need to make you aware that two detectives are canvassing your room as we speak. When they have completed their investigation of your room, they will need to speak with you. They ask that you remain here."

"Am I under suspicion?"

"For now, it is just standard procedure, sir."

Ten minutes later two suited detectives, who after speaking with the uniformed officers, approached Aaron, who had taken a seat in front of the hotel's fireplace.

"Mr. Morris, I'm Lieutenant Miller and this is my partner, Detective Calley. We are sorry for your loss, sir."

"Thank you, lieutenant."

"We have a few questions that need asking, sir."

"Yes, of course. I understand."

"What was Miss Carey's state of mind when you last spoke to her?"

"Well, to tell you the truth," Aaron lied, "she was quite upset."

"Why was that?"

"I told her in so many words that I was getting cold feet about getting engaged."

"Why the cold feet?" asked Detective Calley.

"I've been having it good, detective. I have a thriving business, plenty of money, had plenty of lady friends, and I just thought about losing my freedom and having to give up all of that. It sounds selfish, and it is, but…"

"So she didn't take it well."

"I don't think she slept in the bed last night."

"We did some checking on the comings and goings for your room since 10:00pm last night," stated Miller.

"Oh? We returned from dinner about that time. We had our talk… and she, not taking it well, which is understandable, stepped out onto the main balcony. When she's pissed, there is no reasoning with her, so I went to bed."

"What time was that?"

"I think it was close to 11:00."

"And she didn't come to bed?" asked Calley.

"I sleep like the dead… oh, shit, that was a terrible choice of words. Sorry. Anyway, I'm pretty sure she didn't."

"According to the key log, your room key logged into the fitness center at 5:28. The security cameras show it to be Miss Carey."

"Yeah, well, that's her normal time."

"The cameras show her doing stretching exercises, but she never used the equipment."

"Hmm, that's not Ellen's normal routine. I know that she spends time on the treadmill, the elliptical, and the bike, before heading to the spa for a steam and a shower."

"Now here is the strange part, Mr. Morris," said Lieutenant Miller. "Someone entered the room at 5:39 and again at 6:02am."

"Are you saying she came back, left a second time, and then returned, Lieutenant?"

"We don't know. Did she? It wasn't you?"

"Hell, no. I was asleep until the girl at the front desk called."

"Did you shower before you came down here, Mr. Morris?"

"No. I dressed and rushed down here."

"That's right. The officers said you were here within five minutes of receiving the call."

"That sounds about right."

"Hmm, strange."

"What's strange, lieutenant?"

"Well, you said you didn't shower, yet we found a wet towel in the bathroom."

"Maybe Ellen showered," offered Aaron.

"She wouldn't shower before working out and then shower again. Would she?"

"I wouldn't think so," answered Aaron, now feeling uncomfortable.

"No, neither would I," agreed Lieutenant Miller. "It's strange that the towel she carried downstairs, the one from your suite, was lying on your suite's couch. She must have dropped it there when she returned from the fitness center."

"Well, you did say that she didn't exercise while in the fitness center."

"That we did, sir," replied Lieutenant Miller. "But I have this question lingering in my mind. Why would a woman bother to take a shower just minutes before throwing herself over a railing to her death? Doesn't seem to make sense to me, Mr. Morris. Does it to you?"

"Who knows the state of one's mind, detective."

"That is so true, sir."

"A hotel employee discovered her body at 6:14," interjected Detective Calley. "That means she fell somewhere between 6:02 and 6:14."

"There are some holes that need filling," voiced Lieutenant Miller. "If you look at the timeline, we have a 23 minute hole to fill."

"Timeline?"

"Yes, Mr. Morris. She checks into the fitness center at 5:28. She leaves five or six minutes later and returns to your room at 5:39. How long she stays, we don't know, but she leaves and returns at 6:02. Then between 6:02 and 6:14 she plunged 11 floors to her death. Makes you wonder where she went and what she did between 5:39 and 6:02."

"It does that, lieutenant, but I don't have a clue."

"I have to confess, neither do I, Mr. Morris."

"No one is this entire hotel saw anything?" asked Aaron.

"No one has stepped forward, but that may be because of when she fell."

"What are you saying, lieutenant?"

"I'm guessing when she went over that railing it was closer to 6:02."

"Why is that lieutenant?"

"The sun."

"What about it?"

"It didn't rise until 6:08 this morning."

"So?"

Lieutenant Miller didn't answer the curt question. He did, however, let his eyes say unpleasant things.

Aaron recounted himself as he showed remorse, sometimes even shedding a tear.

He did, however, make one minor mistake that the two uniformed officers didn't catch. He mentioned that Ellen would join the *girls* in planned activities. Realizing his mistake the moment it left his mouth, he made sure not to repeat it to the detectives.

If the slip had been caught, none of what was to come, would have happened.

CHAPTER 10

As Tim drove to the Grand Dunes Marina Inn, Ron read aloud from the police report on the murder of Carol Holihan.

"Mrs. Holihan was a 78-year-old widow of ten years…"

"Holihan!" yelled out Tim with an enormous grin. "I remember her! She played that nurse in Mash who was sleeping with that asshole doctor… ahhhhh…"

"Frank."

"Yeah, that weasel, Frank. Her name was…"

"Margaret Holihan."

"Right again, partner!"

"Our victim's name is Carol Holihan. She was married to a Peter."

"Are you trying to sugarcoat that she married a dick," said Tim with a wide grin, "or is Peter his actual name?"

"You're an asshole, Tim," said Ron, grinning like a Cheshire cat at Tim's play on words.

"Gee, I think I'd rather be a peter, if you don't mind."

"Peter was a banker. He died in a boating accident back in 2010."

"Where and how?" asked a curious Tim.

"On the Waccamaw River down near Georgetown. It seems his boat ran into a piling, flipping it over and tossing him and the missus into the river. It says Peter couldn't swim, but his wife swam to shore."

"Hmm, that's fast moving water in that area. That's strong swimming for a 68-year-old woman. I'm guessing that Peter must have 'petered-out' before he went down for the count."

"Well, he was 74. It must have been hard for the old Peter to keep the head above water," said Ron, joining in on Tim's play on words.

"I doubt there's many 74-year-old Peter's who can stay up for an appreciable length of time."

"Or even an appreciated length of time," added Ron with a belly laugh.

"Down goes Peter!" shouted Tim, imitating Howard Cosell's legendary call of "Down goes Frasier!"

They both were still laughing when they pulled into the Marina Inn's parking lot.

"What floor, Ron?"

"Penthouse."

"A penthouse normally requires an access code for entry. I suppose she could have invited him up, but who invites someone in while they are taking a shower?"

"That's a good question, Tim-o-thy. If we come up with an answer, maybe it will take us a step closer to solving this case."

Entering the hotel, they approached the front desk and flashing their badges, asked to speak with the manager.

"That would be Neil Tanner," replied the front desk receptionist. "I'll page him for you."

While they waited, Ron scrutinized the coroner's report about the cause of death.

Robert Edge had performed the autopsy.

The victim died of head trauma caused by numerous blows against the ceramic threshold of the shower. There was also a postmortem wound of a slit throat that was deep enough to slice the larynx. This wound was most likely inflicted by a boxcutter's blade.

Hmm, another post-mortem wound with a boxcutter, thought Ron. *It's gotta mean something.*

After a five-minute wait, a distinguished-looking black man, standing well over six feet, approached the two agents, saying, "Gentlemen, I'm Neil Tanner. I am the Marina Inn's manager. I understand you need to speak with me?"

Ron, as he always does, silently profiled the man.

I'd say he is in his early forties, very athletic, six-foot three and 190. College graduate, most likely in Liberal Arts. Perfectionist. Probably irons and folds his underwear.

"Mr. Tanner, I'm FBI Special Agent Ron Lee and this is my partner, Agent Tim Pond. We're here to investigate the murder of Mrs. Carol Holihan."

"An unfortunate and tragic situation," said Tanner. "We will all miss the lady."

"We need to get into her apartment."

"Suite, sir."

"I beg your pardon, Mr. Tanner?" Ron said with a quizzical look.

"We refer to them as suites, sir, not apartments."

"Oh, well then, my sincerest apologies, Mr. Tanner. I trust you won't report me to the Uppity Club's board of asshole directors," Ron replied with wry sarcasm.

Flustered by Ron's retort, Tanner, now humbled, replied, "Follow me, gentlemen."

They walked across the lobby to a bank of four elevator doors. Bypassing the first three, Tanner entered a three-digit code into a keypad that occupied the space where a call button would normally be.

"A code just to call the elevator?" said Tim in mild surprise.

"Yes. It ensures that no one but the resident can access this elevator."

"We understand that a resident needs an access code to gain entrance to the penthouse floor. True?"

"That is correct, Agent Lee," replied Tanner.

"Is the code supplied by the hotel..."

"This is an inn, sir, not a hotel," interrupted Tanner.

"Gee, I must apologize again. How many strikes do I get before I'm taken out behind the woodshed, Mr. Tanner?"

Tanner ignored Ron's snotty response, but not without a look that spoke volumes. Then, looking the FBI Agent straight in the eye, he said, "To answer your original question, sir, the inn does not supply the code. The resident selects the code."

The elevator door opened, and the three men stepped inside to an elegant interior.

Ron noticed that opposite their door was another.

"Two elevator doors?"

"There are two 5000 square foot suites on the penthouse floor," replied Tanner.

"Is the other... suite... occupied?" asked Ron.

"It is."

"By whom?"

"A couple by the name of Leftwich. They were vacationing in Europe when the murder occurred."

"Are they here now?"

"Yes, I believe they are."

"Good. I will need to speak with them."

"Very well. While you are investigating Mrs. Holihan's suite, I'll contact the other residents. Should I have them come over?"

"Please give us about twenty minutes and then bring them in."

The elevator walls were padded velvet, and the floor covered in a lush carpet.

"Nice decorations," said Tim, knowing the comment would bring a response from the manager.

There was no verbal response, but Tim received a stare of indignation from the inn's manager.

After sufficiently staring down the undersized agent, Tanner, seeing the elevator door had closed, pressed a single button, and the elevator ventured upward.

"I don't think Mr. Tanner appreciated your comment, partner," said Ron with a sly grin.

Tim, beaming, asked, "Mr. Tanner, would I be correct in saying that this elevator services just the penthouse?"

"That would be correct, Agent Pond, although I doubt you could reach high enough to press the up button."

Ron almost fell out with laughter.

Tim, biting his lip, gave Tanner a nodding smile, saying, "Touché, Mr. Tanner."

The elevator stopped, but the doors didn't part.

"Here is where the resident would key in their code," explained Tanner, pointing at a numerical keypad.

Reaching into his inside jacket pocket, Tanner extracted a key card and inserted it into a slot in the elevator's control panel.

The doors parted to reveal the suite's foyer.

"So you step right off the elevator into the residence," observed Ron.

"That is correct, sir."

"Does the elevator remain here?"

"It does, unless called to the lobby."

"So we had to wait because the elevator had dropped off the Leftwich couple?"

"That is correct, Agent Pond."

"Who discovered Mrs. Holihan's body, Mr. Tanner?" asked Ron.

"I did, sir."

"Under what pretext?"

"Mrs. Holihan subscribed to the Wall Street Journal. I would bring it up to her each morning at 8:30am. She would stand at the elevator doors to greet me every morning, without fail, for the past three years."

"And?"

"On that morning when the doors opened, she wasn't standing there. I knew something was wrong. I entered the apartment and after checking the primary rooms and the balconies, I went to the master bedroom. The door to the master bath was half-way open and I could hear the shower running."

"Knowing what I know of you so far, I'm sure you acted as would a gentleman."

"But of course. I called out to her three times. She didn't answer for what now are obvious reasons."

"Then what?"

"It was then that I saw, in the vanity mirror, her body lying across the shower's threshold."

"Tell me what you did, Mr. Tanner."

"What anyone would do, I guess. I rushed in thinking she had slipped and cracked her head or something."

"What part of her body was lying inside the shower, sir?" asked Tim.

"Her upper body was inside."

"Please, don't misunderstand what I'm about to ask you. I know you were acting in Mrs. Holihan's best interest, but did you touch any part of her body that was not inside the shower?"

"She was lying on her side. I turned her over. I believe I pushed her over, touching her just above the knee."

"Do you recall if her leg was wet?" asked Ron.

Tanner, tearing up by the memory of the moment, searched his recall, then announced, "Her leg was dry."

"Was the shower running, Mr. Tanner?"

"Yes. I turned it off and then I called the police."

"Was the water hot or cold, sir?"

They watched as Tanner's eyes searched his memory.

A moment later, he replied, "Hot."

"Any idea how long the shower could run with the water remaining hot?"

"I'd have to ask the maintenance people, but I'm guessing it would be for quite some time."

"Why is that?"

"This is a hotel and when called upon, the hot water needs of every unit, must always be available at all times," answered Tanner.

Ron grinned at the manager, saying, "Tsk, tsk, Mr. Tanner. Have you forgotten that this is an inn, not a hotel, and it has suites, not units?"

Tanner took on a look of embarrassment.

"Don't worry, sir. We won't report you… this time!" said Ron with a devilish grin.

"Why the questions about the water, Ron?"

"The coroner's report set time of death between 6:00am and 8:00am. I was thinking if the hot water ran cool within thirty minutes then we could narrow the timeframe."

"Hmm, good try."

"Hey, Tim, do us a favor. Get in the elevator, go to the main floor and tell me how much time passes between the doors opening and closing."

A few minutes later, Tim returned.

"Well?"

"Ten seconds."

"Okay. So it's possible our killer waited for someone to come off the elevator and slipped in before the doors closed."

"Bad thinking, Ron."

"Is that so? Well, please reveal why that might be the case, partner."

"Who, other than Mr. Tanner, has access to the elevator? Don't answer! It was a rhetorical question. The answer being, our murder victim, and..."

"The Leftwich couple and they were in Europe," mumbled Ron, completing Tim's statement.

"Correct."

"So how in the hell." roared a frustrated Ron, "did our killer get in and out of that suite?"

"There's that $64,000 question again. I'm sure we'll figure it out, eventually. C'mon, let's check out the apartment... I mean, suite."

The penthouse suite, appointed with only the finest of furnishings, was breathtaking.

Crafted reproductions of various well-known masterpieces, each looking like the originals, hung on walls throughout the suite of rooms.

An elegant French door separated the living room from a modest-sized reading room where, but for a shuttered window overlooking the waterway, fully stocked bookshelves occupied the remaining wall space.

Sitting in the middle of the room were a pair of comfortable looking lounge chairs. They were each accompanied by a small table, set with wine glasses and a vase with a red rose. Against the inside wall sat a rolltop desk and matching chair, made of mahogany. The rolltop was in the down position.

The kitchen looked almost unused.

Its highly polished stainless-steel appliances showed little sign of use, but for the refrigerator's numerous fingerprint smudges.

Inside the fridge were 24 bottles of water, 2 bottles of champagne, jars of olives, an avocado, and cheeses of various descriptions.

"It appears as though Mrs. Holihan did no cooking, Ron. The pantry is almost bare but for some boxes of crackers and... get this, gummy bears!"

"I like gummy bears," replied a stoic Ron.

"Why didn't I see that coming," replied Tim.

"Does the police report say if those French doors were open or closed, Tim?"

"Let's have a look." A minute or two passed before Tim replied, "Open. Why do you ask?"

"It may be nothing, considering the lifestyles of the victims, but each has a vast collection of books."

Tim nodded his agreement with Ron's assessment before adding, "They all have large bank accounts too."

"True, partner. True."

"Have you found an appointment book or a calendar, Ron?"

"To tell you the truth, Tim, I haven't been looking for one."

"I'll look around."

Ron remained in the kitchen. As he circled the 3x6 island on wheels, he noticed a faint impression on its marble top. Bending down to eye level with the top, he scrutinized the smudge with curiosity.

Is that a shoe print?

"Hey, Tim. Come into the kitchen for a minute."

A moment later, Tim appeared holding a leather-bound booklet.

"I found her appointment book. Haven't perused it yet. What's up?"

"Tim, take a gander at this smudge. Tell me what you think."

At first Tim had difficulty seeing what Ron was talking about, but after leaning lower, he saw it. He spent thirty seconds examining it from all angles before he pronounced, "It looks like the sole of a sneaker or something akin to it."

"Akin, you say? Not similar, but akin?"

"Yeah, akin. Do you have a problem with akin?"

"I didn't get the memo. Is that the word for the day?"

"Would you prefer affiliated?"

Ignoring Tim's retort, Ron stated, "I doubt Mrs. Holihan was standing on this island."

"I'll assume that's a good assumption."

"You know, Tim, you're becoming a bigger asshole every day. If you keep it up, I believe I'll see your name in the Guinness Book of World, as the biggest ever!"

"I suppose I must agree with your supposition. But, putting that aside for a moment, let me ask a question. Have you looked up?"

"Looked up what?"

"Up! Up!" said Tim, nodding his head toward the ceiling.

Ron, his eyes peering upward, saw the drop-down door.

"Hot damn! Go get Tanner!"

Two minutes later, Tim, Tanner, and an older couple walked into the kitchen.

"Agent Lee, this is Mr. and Mrs. Leftwich," announced Neil Tanner. "They are the couple owning the other suite. You said you wanted to speak with them."

"Hi, folks. Nice to meet you," said Ron with a half-smile. "You can return to your suite now. Thank you. Mr. Tanner, please stay."

They watched the bewildered Leftwich's return to their suite before Ron, directing his question at Tanner, asked, "What's up there?"

"The air-handler for this suite."

"When was it last serviced?"

"Last November. We have it check every year on the first Monday in November."

"What is it like up there?"

"I have no idea, sir."

"Well, why don't you hop on up this island, open the drop-down, stick your head up there and tell us what you see."

"It will be dark."

"Use your phone's flashlight."

"Very well, Agent Lee."

A moment later, Tanner was atop the island and pulling the drop-down open. A closed up flight of stairs exposed itself. Tanner pulled them downward until the top of the island halted their full extension. Realizing that the stairs would reach the floor, Ron wheeled the island aside, allowing the ladder's steps to extend to the floor.

"Agent Pond will take over now, Mr. Tanner. I should have known about the ladder. Sorry to have troubled you."

"Not a problem, Agent Lee. Glad I could be of service."

As the two men talked, Tim climbed the ladder to its top step.

"See anything, Tim?"

"I can tell you that there is no lack of floor insulation. Neither heat nor cold will seep into the suites. It also provides a nice barrier against the noise."

"What noise are you talking about, partner?"

"The noise from the elevators. I can see the cables from here."

"So that's how he did it," whispered Ron. Turning to Tanner, he asked, "Do you recall if you had to wait for the elevator that morning, Mr. Tanner?"

Hearing Ron's question, Tanner's eyes blinked, as if he had a flash of a vision. "I'm sorry, Agent Lee, but I forgot to mention an important detail."

"Oh? What might that detail be, Mr. Tanner?" Ron growled, as his eyes glared at the inn's manager for overlooking the upcoming revelation.

"The housecleaning service."

"What about them?"

"They clean the elevator interior each morning."

"What time each morning?"

"Between 5:00 and 6:00."

"How do they summon the elevator?"

"If the elevator is at the top, as it normally is, the night manager brings it down for them to clean."

"And it would remain at the lobby level until needed?"

"Yes, and under normal circumstances, that would be my taking Mrs. Holihan's paper up to her."

Tim, having climbed down the stairs, asked, "Got it figured out, Ron?"

"Yeah, I think I do. Our killer comes into the inn early in the morning and walks into an adjacent elevator. He climbs on top of the elevator, steps over onto the penthouse elevator and once the cleaning crew has finished, climbs down into the elevator and pushes the up button."

"I got it from there, Ron," stated Tim. "Once it reaches the top floor, he climbs on top, makes his way across our ceiling, and using the drop-down, climbs down onto the island."

"That's about it, Tim."

Overhearing the entire scenario explained, Tanner asks, "Excuse me, gentlemen, but how does he get out?"

"The same way he got in, Mr. Tanner," answered Ron.

"Explain," said Tim.

"He kills Mrs. Holihan as she's stepping into the shower. He then climbs the drop-down, makes his way to the top of the elevator and waits until it gets called."

"I called it at 8:30!"

"That you did, Mr. Tanner. When it reaches the lobby, he steps across to the adjacent elevator. Once it is safe to do so, he drops into it, opens the doors, steps out, and goes home. Job well done."

"So what does all that tell us, Ron?" inquired Tim.

"If nothing else, it tells us our guy is very athletic. It is no easy feat jumping up to the ceiling hatch and climbing out on the top of the cabin. I'm guessing our guy is near six-foot and in excellent shape. He's also oh, so clever."

"It sounds like catching him won't be easy," expressed Tanner.

"If it were easy, Mr. Tanner, anyone could catch him," voiced Tim.

"He has left behind clues, Tim. We just need to recognize them."

"Maybe I found a clue, Ron."

"What? Where?"

Before Tim could answer, Ron's phone rang. It was Jim Braddock.

Ron stepped away for a moment, then returned, saying Braddock wanted them to return to the office.

"Now what is this supposed clue you found,?"

"I found an open book in the rolltop."

"What book?"

"*Catch Me If You Can.*"

"Oh?" Anything else?

"Yeah, and it had a bookmark at the beginning of chapter two."

"Coincidence? I think not," murmured Ron.

CHAPTER 11

Sunday, June 30, 2019

They were huddled in the Jonas' hotel suite. Nick had summoned them to meet at 11:00.

"Where's Aaron and Ellen, Nick?" asked his wife, Kim.

Ignoring his wife's question, Nick, with a solemn-filled voice, said, "I want you all to sit down, please. I need to tell you something."

"Aren't you going to wait for Aaron and Ellen?" asked Marion Silverman.

"What's going on, Nick?" asked Kim.

"I ss-ss-saw police and an ambulance outside my window, Nick," voiced Artie.

Nick nodded and said, "Yeah, Artie, I saw them too."

"Let's hear it, Nick," said Daniel Lucas. "There's little doubt, based on your body language and the tone of your voice, that unpleasant news is coming. Just how unpleasant is it?"

"Yeah, you're right Dan, the news isn't good." Then, with the same breath, he stunned them all as he blurted, "It appears as if Ellen jumped to her death from their balcony sometime early this morning."

"Omigod!" screamed Marcia. "Oh, that poor girl. How can that be? They were about to get engaged."

"She was only 22, with her entire life in front of her." remarked Marion Silverman, herself only 28-years of age. "Why would she do that?"

"We were all together all day on the beach yesterday," Kim stated. "Her eyes, filled with happiness, showed no signs of depression. Something isn't right, Nick."

"I don't have any answers, Kim."

"How do know about this, Nick?" asked Artie.

"I went downstairs around 7:00 to get some coffee and pick up a paper. The lobby was buzzing with police and EMT people. I asked, why all the commotion? A passing employee told me they had found a woman dead by the pool."

"It could be someone other than Ellen," cried out Marcia.

"No, Marcia. I saw Aaron sitting in the lobby being questioned by a couple of detectives. I saw slumped shoulders and his hands covering his eyes. When I saw his face overcome with sorrow, I knew it had to be Ellen."

"Where's Aaron now, Nick?" asked a concerned Daniel.

"I don't know, but I imagine he's still with the police. I'm guessing he has a lot of questions to answer."

"Do they think he…"

"I don't know what their thinking is, Dan. If their thinking is she didn't jump by her own accord, then I'm guessing he's their prime suspect."

"What should we do, Nick?" asked Kim. "Should we go home?"

"I would suggest that you girls pack up and leave. Meanwhile, Dan, Artie, and I will stay here and provide support for Aaron. We'll be home later in the week."

"I wonder why we haven't heard from the police?" asked Marion. "Surely Aaron would seek help from his friends."

"I'm sure that will come, Marion," answered Nick. "Now you girls should go pack your things. I'll call and get you flight reservations. There's a 2:00 flight to Charlotte with connections to get you home by early evening."

"What do you want Artie and me to do, Nick?"

"We'll talk about that after we get the girls on that 2:00 flight."

Nick held the door open as the two couples left. After closing the door, he turned to see Kim staring at him.

"What's the actual story, Nick?"

"What do you mean?"

"I heard you get out of bed this morning. I looked over at the clock. It was 5:55. Then I heard voices. You and Aaron were talking, but I couldn't hear what it was you were saying. What were you talking about?"

Cornered, Nick knew he wasn't about to fool his wife. Thinking fast on his feet, he told her a half-lie.

"Okay, you're right. It was Aaron. He told me that he had told Ellen that he didn't want to go ahead with the engagement. He said she was beside herself, and that she woke him sometime early this morning to tell him she would kill herself. Thinking she was just being over-dramatic, he said, go ahead. Then she went ballistic and before he could stop her, she ran out onto the balcony and threw herself over the side."

"Omigod!"

"Yeah, I agree. Anyway, he said he didn't know what to do. He was beside himself with grief. He's afraid they will charge him with her death."

"What did you advise him to do, Nick?"

"My thinking wasn't clear. I told him to go back to bed and wait until they contacted him."

"What! Why in God's name would you tell him to do that, Nick! Why wouldn't you tell him to call the police?"

"I don't know. But either way, it's the same story."

"What if they charge him with murder?"

"If it happened, as Aaron said, they have no proof to bring murder charges."

"And if it didn't?"

Nick didn't answer, but he knew what needed doing. He couldn't let Aaron crack under the pressure. Aaron needed to go away.

CHAPTER 12

Sunday, June 30, 2019

They had spent the last two hours meeting with their immediate superior, Captain Jim Braddock, the regional FBI Director.

Braddock had a shit list, and Ron and Tim sat at the top. He objected to the reckless manner in which they took down The Mamba. He called them irresponsible cowboys.

It was after 2:00 and they had spent valuable lost time reviewing the progress of their two cases.

"What are your thoughts on the bank robbery, Ron?"

"They are professional bank robbers, Captain, of that there is no doubt."

"What makes you so sure?"

"Their modus operandi is well-planned, well-rehearsed, and well-executed."

"These aren't your two-bit hoodlums that get themselves a wild-ass brain fart, Captain," added Tim. "These guys can chew gum and walk at the same time."

"It is my opinion this crew left town on Saturday with all the other tourists," said Ron. "We will need a small army to get these guys. Is Washington willing to give us an army?"

"No, I doubt they will. Make sure you have done all you can and then get back to catching this serial-killer we have in our midst."

"I don't think he's a serial-killer, Captain," announced Ron, to Tim's surprise.

"Huh!" said Braddock.

"This is new to me too, Captain. Where did this come from, partner?"

"I may change my mind, fellas, but after seeing two of the crime scenes, they just don't ring true as a serial killer's MO."

"We're heading to crime scenes two and three today, Captain," offered Tim. "I'm sure we'll have a good grasp of the situation by the end of the day."

"If it's not a serial killer, Ron, then what is it?" asked Braddock.

"Not sure, Captain. It could be about revenge."

"If it's about revenge, it shouldn't be difficult to catch the son-of-a-bitch."

"It won't be easy until we determine what the link is between the victims, and even then, I'm not so sure."

"Well, what the hell are you doing hanging around here? Get your asses out there!"

As they were rising from their seats, Braddock's intercom announced he had a call from Chief Amy Proctor.

Picking up his phone, Braddock greeted the Myrtle Beach top cop with a cheerful, "Afternoon, Chief Proctor. What can I do for you?"

As Ron and Tim made their way toward the door, Braddock sat quietly, listening to what the chief was saying. Then he spoke, "Hold up a minute, fellas."

Turning back to Braddock, they heard him say, "I'll send them over, Chief."

As Braddock hung up, Ron, sensing a detour from their intended destination was in the wind, inquired, "What was that all about?"

"That was Chief Proctor. She's at the Marriot Resort and Spa hotel."

"We were just there on Friday," voiced Tim.

"She thinks you two should stop by."

"May I ask why?" inquired Ron.

"A woman took a header from the 11th floor onto the pool deck. It seems the last foot or so was fatal."

"That's too bad, Captain, but tell me, what's our involvement?"

"Do you believe in a woman's intuition, Ron?"

"Yeah, I do. My wife, for no reason at all, would always disappear whenever I would even think about wanting to get frisky."

"Damn!" yelped Tim. "Wilma has that same knack. She disappears like the wind, only I don't feel a breeze."

While grinning at the responses of his two agents, Braddock continued, "Good. Proctor thinks this fallen angel has something to do with the bank robbery."

"What makes her think that?"

"The boyfriend's story is shaky, and shortly before the woman flew like a rock, she was watching tv in the fitness center."

"So far, Jim, nothing you're saying is making much sense."

"Proctor figured out what she was watching."

"Which was?"

"The local morning news."

"Okay, Captain, how about dropping the shoe before I become eligible for retirement?"

Frowning, Braddock continued, saying, "They calculated the exact time of her viewing. Then they called all the local stations to ask what was airing at that time. Two were broadcasting infomercials, the third was broadcasting the local news. During the brief time she watched, the station was reporting on the bank robbery. Almost as soon as it was over, she returned to her room. Twenty minutes later she was a wingless bird trying to fly."

"You said 'almost as soon.' Why?"

"They said the tape shows her standing almost comatose for a minute or two, before she fled the room. She appeared, after hearing and seeing the broadcast, to be in shock."

"If Proctor's right, do you realize what it means, Ron?" asked Tim.

"Yeah. It means our bank robbers are still in town, and they are staying at the Marriot Resort."

Ron was half right. The bank robbers were still in town, but they were no longer staying at the Marriot.

****

The three of them, looking skyward, stood in the parking lot of the Myrtle Beach International Airport. They watched the 2:00 flight to Charlotte, carrying their wives, lift off the ground, head out over the ocean, and then bank westward. Two minutes later, it was nothing but a speck in the sky before disappearing completely.

No sooner were its wheels up, did Nick pull out his phone to call Aaron.

Three rings and Aaron answered.

"Are you alone?"

"Yeah, the cops let me go about thirty minutes ago. Where are you?"

"Never mind about that. Did they take your cell phone?"

"Yeah, but they gave it back to me just before they let me go."

"Aaron, get out of that hotel – now! Don't be seen. Don't go to your car. Take the chip out of your phone and flush it down the toilet. Take only what you can carry in your pockets. We will meet you where we had our last meal."

"You mean the…"

"Don't say it, Aaron! Just be there in an hour."

"What's going on? They bought my story."

"Maybe they did, Aaron, but don't bet on it. Get out of there! We'll be there in one hour."

Nick hung up and put his phone away. Artie and Daniel, standing nearby and overhearing Nick's part of the conversation, asked, "What was that all about, Nick?"

"Okay, guys, it's time to be square with you. Somehow Ellen figured out that we robbed that bank on Friday. She confronted Aaron and threatened to turn us in to the police. Aaron panicked and strangled her. Then, wanting to make it look like an accident or a suicide, he tossed her body over the balcony railing."

"What the hell are you saying, Nick!" exploded Daniel. "That's crazy talk. Aaron wouldn't hurt that girl!"

"Under normal conditions, I would agree with you a hundred percent, Dan, but this wasn't normal."

"What are we going to do, Nick?"

"We're going back to the hotel to check out and grab our stash. Then we'll meet up with Aaron."

"So we're leaving town?" asked Dan.

Nick paused before saying, "No, not yet. We'll leave after we get what we came for."

"Are you sa-sa saying we're ss -ss-still going to rob that bank on Wednesday?" asked an astonished Artie.

"We will rob a bank of sorts, Artie, but it's not your everyday conventional bank."

"Any other surprises you have for us, Nick?" asked Dan.

"Just one. Aaron, I'm afraid, needs killing."

CHAPTER 13

Sunday, June 30, 2019

Her name was Judi Kiernan, and her husband was Bob. They'd been married 54 plus years. They were both in their mid-70s, with Bob holding a two-year advantage.

When they lived in Connecticut, Bob made his living as a firefighter, while Judi was a school instructor. Bob now worked as a plumber and Judi played the homemaker. They weren't rich by any means, but they weren't hovering around the poverty line either.

They had two things in common: they liked shag dancing, and both were avid readers.

But neither was no longer enthralled with the other.

Bob, a hard-working man who insisted on having all his ducks in a row before delving into any task, had built his reputation on careful planning and preparedness. Both qualities had served him well. His motto? "No mistakes."

But for Judi, Bob lacked the two redundant qualities Judi desired in a man: lots of money and big bank accounts. He no longer was the apple of her eye. In fact, she resented him. She knew in her heart she could have done better. After all, she was the runner-up to the queen of her junior prom in high school.

Bob had become disappointed over the past twenty years with the intimate side of their marriage. Somewhere along the trail, Judi had decided she would take total control of the sex purse strings. She doled it out as if they were crossing the Sahara, and she controlled the last canteen of water on earth. It was unfortunate, seeing that Bob still had a thirst.

All this unhappiness, however, was soon to end. One of them would die on Friday, of unnatural causes.

CHAPTER 14

Sunday, June 30, 2019

It was 2:53 when Ron and Tim appeared at the Marriot Resort.

Chief Amy Proctor was there to greet them, as was Captain Bill Baxter of the South Carolina State Police.

"Well, well, it appears the entire gang is here," shouted Tim.

"Ahh, the top guns of the F-B-I have arrived," chided Baxter. "This must be top priority, Chief Proctor."

"I'd say that it's right up there, Captain Baxter."

"Let's get down to business, Amy. Braddock told us how you figured out what she was watching on the tv in the fitness center. That was exemplary police work, Chief."

"Thank you, Ron."

"Now what makes you think this guy is part of the crew that robbed the Bank of America?"

"I'm saying that based on her reaction to what she saw on the news."

"So based on her reaction, you think her roommate is a bank robber."

"Yes, I do."

"Might it be possible the news account jogged her memory about something she witnessed in the past day or so and she wanted to share that news with her roommate?"

"And was so excited she decided she would try to fly?" replied Proctor with an annoyed scowl.

"Okay, I see how you could put this together, Amy. So let's visualize what may have happened."

"Sounds good, Ron. You start."

"Okay, so the girl hears the story on tv and something in the story catches her attention. Any idea what that might be?"

"Not a clue."

"There has to be something. Otherwise, it's just a story about four guys robbing a bank. She saw or heard something specific that caught her attention. Let's see the tape."

"We have it all set up in the 2nd floor conference room."

Minutes later, they were staring at two monitors sitting side-by-side on a long table that could accommodate 20 people. Seated in front of the two monitors was a youthful man dressed in a cop uniform.

"This is Corporal Dave Price from our Communications Department," said Proctor.

"Afternoon, sirs," replied the young corporal with a polite nod.

"Dave will run the tapes for us. The monitor on the left is the television feed," Proctor pointed out. "The one on the right is the hotel's tape of the fitness center."

"Let's see it," voiced Ron.

"Ellen, that's the victim's name, enters the fitness center at 5:31:16. The newscast begins at 5:30 so we need it to run until it matches with the hotel tape. Go ahead Dave, start it up," instructed Proctor.

The newscast had a digital timer in the righthand corner of the screen, and when it reached 5:31:16, Dave started the hotel's tape.

They watched as Ellen entered the center and began warming up exercises. After two minutes, she stopped, and finding a remote, turned on a tv and surfed through the channels. They saw her put down the remote and continue her warmups. At the 5:36:23 mark, she stopped and looked up at the tv.

"Stop them both!" shouted Ron. "Reverse the tv feed about 20 seconds, corporal."

Dave rolled the tv feed back to the 5:35:00 mark.

"Let's hear it," said Ron.

Dave turned up the volume and pressed the play button.

They all stood staring at the monitor, hanging on every word the reporter uttered.

The tape started with the reporter saying:

Later, it became known that they had stolen the ambulance from the Grand Strand Medical Center.

In a detail defying explanation, the thieves returned the ambulance before Medical Center personnel even realized it had been missing.

Other than saying all four men were Caucasian, two witnesses told police that one man had a severe stuttering condition.

Seeing the time in the corner read 5:35:22, Ron said, "It was the reference to the stuttering man that caught her attention. Does her boyfriend stutter, Amy?"

"No, not at all."

"Are they here with friends?"

"No. He says it's just the two of them. They came down for a brief vacation. He mentioned no friends."

"When did they check in?"

"He said they checked in on Thursday around 2:00."

"Amy, have the manager and the front desk clerk come up here."

Proctor turned her head to speak into the mic attached to her uniform. "Lieutenant Miller, bring the hotel manager and the desk clerk up to the conference room, please."

"Do you have a photo of them, Amy?"

"Yeah, but hers isn't one you'd want to frame."

"Let me see them."

As Ron shuffled through the photos, he took an extended look at the pictures of the victim.

"She didn't land on her head, did she?"

"It doesn't appear that way to me, Ron," replied Amy. "You can see the head carnage, but not what you'd expect if she had done a header."

"How about her legs? Were they driven up into the body?"

"No, although both were broke and mangled," answered Proctor.

"If she jumped feet first, the impact would have driven her legs upward into her body," stated Ron, "and if she dove headfirst, the fall would have crushed her head. It looks to me like she rolled off or someone dropped her. Is Robert Edge still here?"

"No, he left hours ago."

At that moment, Lieutenant Miller entered the room with the hotel manager and the front desk clerk.

Miller introduced them to the room's occupants, saying, "This is Mr. Simon Cox, the hotel's manager, and this young lady is Katy Oswald, the front desk manager."

Ron introduced himself, and then showing the two hotel employees Aaron's picture, asked, "Do you recognize this man?"

They both nodded in the affirmative, with the manager saying, "The police had him in the lobby most of the morning."

"That's true, sir," said Amy, "but do you recognize him otherwise?"

"I do," said Katy Oswald, the desk clerk. "I was on duty when they checked in last week."

"Do you recall the day and time?"

"It was Thursday. I believe it was about an hour before our regular check-in time of 3:00."

"Can you recall if they were alone?" asked Ron. "Did anyone else check-in before or after them?"

"Yes, there were three other couples. One checked in ahead of them, the other two just minutes after them."

"Do you remember what rooms those three couples are in?"

"I don't off the top of my head, sir, but given a few minutes, I'll be able to determine their room numbers."

"Please find those room numbers for us, Miss Oswald. My partner, Agent Pond, will accompany you. Give him the room numbers as soon as you have them."

"Oh, I have one other question, miss."

"Yes?"

"Did either of those three men stutter?"

"I recall that one of them did. I remember because he found it difficult saying, 'suite.'"

Ron's eyes lit up.

"When did you last see these men?"

"I saw them leave with their wives, who had suitcases, about three hours ago, but I saw the three men return about 30 minutes ago."

"Quick, Tim! Go get those room numbers."

"What do you think is happening, Ron?" asked Proctor.

"I think our crew sent their wives home. Why they didn't leave with them, is a mystery that I'm sure will reveal itself sooner rather than later."

"Send someone to get Mr. Morris. I want to speak with him."

Five minutes later, Ron's phone rang. It was Tim.

"What do you have?" Ron said anxiously.

"Their room numbers are 546, 717, and 920."

"Okay, Tim, take three men to 920. I'll get 717, and Amy will cover 546. Once you have your man secured, bring him to the conference room."

The hotel had a bank of eight elevators, four to a side. As Ron, Amy, and Tim, along with a small army of police officers, were climbing to their respective floors, three other elevator cabins were making their way to the lobby.

Nick, who occupied room 920, had his elevator stop on the 5th floor to pick up an older female passenger. While waiting for the doors to close, he saw Amy Proctor and three officers exit the elevator across the way. As the lawmen made their way toward the hallway, he saw them draw weapons.

Artie's room is 546, he thought. *I hope he's long gone.*

He had no worries. Artie had left ten minutes earlier. He had walked within ten feet of Tim as the FBI agent waited for Katy to locate the room numbers.

Wearing a pair of slacks, a golf shirt and a light blazer, Nick unbuttoned the blazer so he would have access to his Glock.

When the doors opened, Nick let the older woman exit first. As he stepped from the elevator, the elevator next to his opened and Dan stepped out into the lobby.

Both men carried a suitcase and a garment bag.

As Nick passed by Dan, he whispered, "Cops are on their way to our rooms. Be prepared."

Dan, dressed much like Nick, stopped, placed the suitcase that contained his share of the stolen cash on the floor, and unbuttoned his jacket before proceeding.

Neither bothered to check out. As they walked past the registration desk, Katy, who had returned to duty, saw them pass by.

Rushing into the manager's office, she told Simon that two of the men who the FBI were seeking, were walking out the front door with their luggage in hand.

Cox, attempting to delay them, ran from his office, and chased after the men, yelling, "Wait!"

Nick, hearing the yelled command, pulled his gun from its holster and turned around to see it was just the hotel manager. Pointing his gun at the man's head, he smiled while saying in a calm voice, "Sir, if I were you I'd turn around and run back into the hotel."

Simon Cox took Nick's suggestion, verbatim.

Nick, smirking as he watched the manager high-tailing it back inside the hotel, holstered his weapon, made his way to his car, and drove off toward Route 17.

His journey would be short. He would make a right turn onto 17, then travel a half mile, before turning right into a small strip mall. The strip housed about 10 businesses, including an Italian restaurant called Ducatis Pizzeria and Trattoria.

Inside, waiting for Nick, sat three men, each nervously nursing a drink they had ordered.

CHAPTER 15

Sunday, June 30, 2019

Just about the time the FBI was busting into four empty rooms at the Marriot Resort, the Dispatcher, as he preferred to call himself, was planning his next revenge.

He had long-ago selected his next two victims. Entry to victim five's home, which he had detailed a dozen times over the past year, would be no problem. He had scrutinized the victim's redundant routines to where the Dispatcher could do them in his sleep.

Determining the means of dispatch was all that remained.

He preferred the term 'dispatch or dispatching' over 'kill and killing.'" The latter resonated violence, whereas the former was more like sending someone on their way.

His killing techniques had already included suffocation, strangulation, stabbing, and clubbing.

Now he sought something new, something original.

He gave thought to using a firearm, but it would be too noisy for his taste. Besides, he didn't possess a gun.

"Fire!" he whispered to himself. "I'll give that old bitch a taste of hell before she even gets there."

Satisfied with his selection of dispatch for victim five, he turned his thoughts to how he would eradicate victim six.

Victim six would be a whole new ballgame. The previous dispatches were of old and weak women. Target six was younger, and much stronger. This meant that the dispatch method he chose had to give him complete control.

He had narrowed his choices down to two selections. One was dirty, the other clean. The first required a strong back, the other required guile.

Not a fan of hard work, he chose guile, and knowing the victim's propensities, he knew how he would dispatch victim six.

His goal was to dispatch ten of the hecklers, but that could change depending on how they treated him at future meetings. If the heckling continued, he might not stop at ten.

Having no fear of being caught, he could only imagine what a superb story he was writing. A story that would enthrall all who would read it. Once read, he knew the heckling would stop.

There was no hurry. Writing one chapter a week would suffice. He wanted quality, not quantity.

He could hardly wait for Friday morning to write the next chapter.

Turns out, he wouldn't have to wait.

CHAPTER 16

Sunday, June 30, 2019

After all four men escaped the authorities at the Marriot, they met, as planned, at the Ducatis Pizzeria and Trattoria.

Since it was just past four o'clock, it was much too late for lunch and way too early for dinner. They sat drinking a beverage of choice while snacking on complimentary garlic bread and olives.

As they huddled around the table, Nick spoke in whispers.

"When we leave here, we'll take just one car. I made reservations at the Marina Inn, just a quarter mile away. Aaron and I will check in first. I'll use the name of Thomas Bidwell. Artie, wait about 20 minutes before Dan and you check in. Your reservation is under the name of Norm Sedgefield. Here is your credit card."

"Who ss-ss-should ch-ch-check in, Nick? Dan or me?"

"Let Dan do the check in, Artie."

"Good cc-cc-choice, Nick," stammered a relieved Artie.

Nick, smiling at Art's obvious relief, gave an agreeing nod. Then, he addressed the three men, saying, "Tomorrow morning we'll meet at the Anchor Café, down at the end of the pier. It's a two-minute walk from the hotel's entrance. We'll go over what tasks we will need to complete before commencing with Wednesday's activities."

"I don't think the Anchor Cafe serves breakfast, Nick," said Aaron.

"Who said anything about eating?"

"Okay, Nick, so what's the target?" asked Dan. "I thought we were hitting the Wells Fargo down on Oak."

"There are bigger fish to fry, Dan, and they are much closer. I'm guessing the FBI is also thinking we stuck around to hit another bank, and that's where their resources will be. We won't disappoint them though."

"What the hell does that mean, Nick?" asked a confused Aaron.

"I'll explain in the morning, fellas. Tonight, I have a few loose strings to tie up. Pay the bill, Aaron, and don't forget to give the waitress a nice tip. We'll wait for you in the car I drove."

While waiting for Aaron to emerge from the restaurant, Dan asked, "What about that dirty business you spoke of, Nick?"

"I'll take care of that."

"How?"

"Don't let it worry you, Dan."

"I'm not worried, Nick. Just inquisitive."

"Oh, did I fail to ask how you might feel about two million dollars?"

"Two million? I thought we were talking a quarter million."

"Yeah, well, I've been down here four times in the past few months, Dan, and I discovered a gold mine."

"A gold mine! What gold mine, Nick?" asked an anxious Artie.

"Tomorrow morning all will become clear, fellas. Here comes Aaron. Say nothing about this to him."

A moment later Aaron, seeing the driver's seat empty, and assuming Nick wanted him to drive, climbed in behind the wheel.

"Aaron, after dinner tomorrow night, you and I need to find new transportation. I'd like a big SUV. Any ideas?"

"I guess a Chevy or GMC dealer would be our best choice. They sell the Tahoe and Yukon. They may not notice one is missing for some time, whereas an individual would know it almost immediately and report it to the law. Stealing a vehicle from a dealer is the better choice."

"Good thinking, Aaron. I'll leave it to you to pick the right dealership. You'll have all day tomorrow to do your homework."

"Sounds good, Nick," said Aaron as he headed toward the Marina Inn.

Five minutes later Nick and Aaron were standing at the front desk, checking in.

"Reservation for Bidwell. Thomas Bidwell," said Nick with a smile to the desk clerk.

"Yes, sir, we have you in room 601. Enjoy your stay."

"Thank you," replied Nick as the two men, carrying their satchels of stolen money, headed toward the bank of elevators.

When they arrived at the elevators, they saw a man assisting an older woman with her packages as she entered an elevator car.

They watched as the man placed the packages inside and then said, "I'll call your husband and tell him you're on your way up, Mrs. Leftwich."

"Maybe we can ride up with her and help her with her packages, sir," offered Aaron.

"Oh, no, sir, that won't be necessary," answered Neil Tanner. "Besides, this is a private elevator. It only accesses the penthouse floor."

"Just trying to help," said Aaron.

"Well thank you, sir. It was a gracious gesture on your part. I'm Neil Tanner, the Inn's manager. If you need anything during your stay with us, just let me know."

Nick, having stood aside as Aaron and the Inn's manager talked, asked, "What would keep two guys like ourselves from using that elevator, Mr. Tanner?"

"Oh, you would need a key card to open the elevator doors, sir. When you reached the top floor, a code is required to enter one of the two penthouses. It's very secure," replied Tanner, knowing it wasn't as secure as anyone had thought.

"Two penthouses, you say," exclaimed Nick. "Is the other one occupied also?"

"Not any longer, sir. The previous owner… died."

"Well, damn! I'm sorry to hear that. Is it available to rent now?"

"Ahh, not exactly, sir."

"Oh? Why not?"

"It's a crime scene, sir," admitted an embarrassed Tanner.

"A crime scene? What kind of crime?"

"Someone murdered the previous tenant."

"Damn! How did that happen?"

"The FBI is investigating it, sir."

"The FBI?"

"Yes, sir. It seems there has been a series of murders with one victim being a federal judge."

"I see. Since it was federal, the FBI has jurisdiction."

"That's correct, sir."

"Have they determined how the killer got into the penthouse?"

"They have."

"How?"

"I'm afraid I'm not at liberty to comment on that, sir."

"I see," said Nick just as their elevator arrived.

"Enjoy your stay, gentlemen," voiced Tanner as the two men entered the elevator and the doors closed.

Fifteen minutes later, as Tanner was passing through the lobby, he saw Dan and Artie checking in.

"Welcome, gentlemen!" announced Tanner. "Enjoy your stay with us."

"Thank you, ss-ss-sir," answered Artie.

Artie's politeness didn't register with Tanner at that moment. But later, when it did, it would cost him… dearly.

CHAPTER 17

It was only 8:30am, but representatives of every law enforcement agency, within 100 miles of Myrtle Beach, sat in the FBI's conference room.

Captain Jim Braddock was chairing the meeting.

The previous day's fiasco at the Marriot Resort and Spa was a black eye for all those involved.

The list of embarrassments started when a suspected killer and bank robber walked, unseen by dozens of lingering law enforcement officials, out of the hotel.

Further indignities followed as three other suspected bank robbers waltzed right past, not only the police flooding the hotel's lobby but also the local FBI's top agents.

The situation then became even more embarrassing when the press revealed that the only resistance to their escape came from a meek and unarmed hotel manager.

"What do we have, Ron?" probed Braddock.

"Not much, I'm afraid. All four men used an alias when they checked in. They rented vehicles at four different rental agencies, using yet another alias."

"What about the wives?"

"We think they sent them packing on a flight out of Myrtle Beach. There were 12 flights before 3:00. Their wives may have been on any of them. We're checking the airport surveillance tapes. If the men didn't accompany their wives inside, which I doubt they were dumb enough to do, we have no chance of identifying them."

"What about the rooms? Anything turn up? Fingerprints?"

"Wiped clean. All except that of the Morris guy. We have Morris's fingerprints because of the death of the girl. Chief Proctor ran them and they turned up clean."

"Did they leave anything behind?"

"Only in Morris's room. We found his cell phone minus the chip, clothes, and $10,000. He scooted, taking only what he could carry in his pockets. We figure his buddies called him and told him to get out as fast as he could."

"Being a murder suspect, wasn't he being watched?" asked Braddock.

"In a manner of speaking, he was."

"What the hell does that mean, Ron?"

"They had him confined to his room. There were officers posted at the elevators in the lobby to stop him if he tried to leave the building."

"Well, it's apparent Mr. Morris left the building. Please explain how in the hell that happened!"

"Yeah, well," Ron said, not wanting to tell the story, "let's just say he embarrassed a law enforcement officer."

Pursing his lips, Ron told how he sent Lieutenant Miller to collect Morris on Ron's behalf, and bring him to the hotel's conference room for questioning.

"When the elevator reached the 11th floor, and the doors opened, Morris was standing there waiting to get on. In seconds, Morris overwhelmed Miller and disarmed him. Then, using the detective's weapon, Morris forced Miller to walk him out the door, unscathed."

"The lieutenant lost his gun to an alleged killer?" questioned Braddock, his voice filled with disdain.

"It happens, Jim," said Ron, trying to defend the city detective.

"It shouldn't happen," responded Braddock.

"Well, it did!" shouted Chief Proctor, defending her man.

"If you say so, Chief," commented Braddock. "Finish the story, Ron."

"Miller, at gunpoint, walked Morris out the door, and once outside, Morris handcuffed the detective to a lamppost, gagged him, and walked off."

"He walked off. He didn't take a car?"

"Yes, sir, or maybe the answer is, no, sir." answered Ron.

"Your answer sounds like scrambled eggs look, Ron."

"That was a good analogy, Jim. Let me rephrase. Yes, he walked off. No, he didn't take a car."

"If he walked, then he was meeting them somewhere close by, I would think."

"I'm thinking he was going somewhere they all knew, Jim, since he was the first to leave. The others left as our teams were raiding their rooms. We missed them by minutes."

"So where do we go from here?"

"Most think they are long gone, Captain."

"Hmm, most, but not you. Is that correct?"

"That's right."

"Let's hear your version."

"If I were them, I'd find a place, not too obvious, and reshuffle the plans. We now know where they rented their vehicles, so they can't take them back and get something else. The three cars they now possess are unusable. They'll be seeking transportation to finish what they came for."

"Which is?"

"I believe they plan on hitting another bank on Wednesday."

"Hit another bank! What makes you think so?"

"What else would be a big enough payoff for them to risk sticking around? Anybody care to venture a guess?" Ron asked, glancing around at the audience.

Ron heard nothing but murmurs.

"Okay, Ron. Tell me. Why a bank?"

"Multiple reasons, Jim."

"Well, let me hear the first multiple reason."

Grinning at Braddock's sarcasm, Ron said, "They just scored a big hit at Bank of America, in what we must all agree was genius in its execution. So why stick around? You have your money, no one saw your faces, so you're free to go. You have a quarter-million dollars. Why not get out of town? What's keeping you here?"

"So you're saying they are sticking around for something even bigger," stated Braddock.

"I believe they are, Captain."

"Sorry, but I'm not convinced. Could we hear another of your 'multiple reasons?'"

"They need to get rid of one of their partners. Mr. Morris is a ticking time bomb. They know he killed the girl, and they know that we know. When we get our hands on Morris, we'll put him in the box, where he'll burst like an over-ripe tomato. We know it, and they know it. I hate to use an over-used cliché, but he's a dead-man walking."

"That makes perfect sense, Ron," commented Amy Proctor. "Any more multiples?" she asked with a smile.

"One more. They sent their wives packing, but they stayed behind. Why? It isn't because they came here to play a round of golf or two. Whatever they have planned is worth the risk of sticking around. It must be big. Real big."

"What makes you think it's a bank, Ron?" asked Tim. "They could plan to hit something else."

"Because their checkout date is Wednesday."

"So?"

"The banks are closed Thursday and Friday for the July fourth holiday."

"That still doesn't mean they are hitting a bank," quipped Amy.

"Do you know," Ron asked, "of anything else around Horry County that could cough up a half-million or more?"

Everyone's mind went into third gear trying to come up with a legitimate answer, but no one could.

"It will be a bank. The question now is, which one?"

"How many banks are in the county?" asked Braddock.

"Just a couple hundred," snickered Tim.

"These guys are big time hitters. They won't mess with some small satellite bank. We only need to concern ourselves with the major branches," Ron announced.

"In that case, we're talking about a half-dozen," offered Bill Baxter.

"Then that's where we concentrate our forces," said Ron. "We only have 48 hours before they strike. Let's get a list put together of potential targets, get some intel on the locations, and plan how we're going to set-up our teams."

Unbeknownst to the gathering of lawmen, there is another business in town, which, on the first Wednesday of the month, moved more money than any bank on the Grand Strand.

It was ripe for the plucking, and there would be no law enforcement team assigned to watch it.

CHAPTER 18

Monday, July 1, 2019

"Okay, partner, what's the plan?"

"What do you mean?" asked Ron.

"Do we spend all of our time on these bank robbers, or do we try to catch the killer of the women?"

Ron glanced at his watch and saw that it was almost noon.

"We have one more murder scene to visit. Is that correct?"

"That's a bingo!"

"Who and where?"

"Let me look at the file. It's on my desk."

"You do that. I'll google a map."

"A map of what?"

"The area around the Marriot. If they were meeting Morris, or whatever the hell his name is, and he was walking, they wouldn't expect him to walk too far."

"Makes sense to me, Ron."

"Where would you expect them to meet him?"

"Someplace they all know."

"Yeah, that's my thinking too. And what someplace might that be?"

"I'm thinking a restaurant."

"That's also my first thought, Tim-o-thy."

"You might give Robert Edge a call."

"Why?"

"See if he's done an autopsy on the flying nun. Maybe he can tell you what she last ate. It might lead us to the right restaurant."

"You had better be careful, Tim. You keep coming up with these brilliant ideas, and you just might be mistaken for a detective."

"Up yours, Colonel!"

"Ahh, there is that standard retort. Simple, but specific."

"Yeah, well, I can tell you about someone who is simple, but specific, with the onus on simple."

"Touchy, are we?"

Ignoring Ron's question, Tim said, "I'm going to the office to determine the 'who and where.' When I've done that, where might I find you?"

"I'll meet you in the lobby."

"10-4, partner," answered Tim as he headed for his office.

Ron, using the computer in the conference room, printed off a google map of the area within two miles of the Marriot. He didn't know it, but a one-mile radius would have sufficed.

He waited for Tim in the lobby, talking with Pam O'Dell, at the receptionist's desk.

"Do you have plans the 4th of July weekend, Pam?"

"Well, I'm spending the 4th on the beach with my two grandchildren. Friday I go to my book club get-together. And for the weekend, I'm going out with my gentleman friend on Saturday, and doing nothing on Sunday. How about you? Got plans with Heather?"

"We had plans, but they are on shaky ground right now. Tim and I have two cases going…"

"Nothing unusual about that," stated Pam.

"Yeah, that's a fact. Anyway, we have this bank robbing gang to deal with, and we also need to work on a series of killings."

"Police found an acquaintance of mine dead in her home two weeks ago," Pam said with a faraway look in her eyes. "Annie Pott was her name. Likeable woman. She was in my book club."

"How did she die?" asked Ron, curious that the police found her.

"The police said she tripped and hit her head against a bookshelf. She was old. I believe someone said she was nearing 78."

"Sorry to hear that, Pam. Oh, look, here comes Tim. If I don't see you, have an enjoyable weekend."

"You too, Colonel."

As Tim approached, Ron asked, "Did you get us a car?"

"Yeah," replied Tim. "Dark blue Buick Lacrosse. Here are the keys. You can drive."

Ron, while turning out of the parking lot onto 38th Avenue, turned to Tim and asked, "Well, what do you have?"

"The victim lived on 71st street. They found her on Friday, June 19th, in her living room. She had multiple head wounds."

"She's the third of the four he's killed," commented Ron.

"The four that we know about," Tim pointed out.

Ron, nodding his head in agreement, asked, "She has a name?"

"Yeah. The name is… Annie Pott."

Ron slammed on the brakes so violently that Tim lost the contents of the folder he was holding. They flew up onto the dashboard before sliding to the floor.

"What the hell!" screamed Tim. "You flunked Driver's Ed, didn't you?"

Ron turned toward his partner, asking, "Tell me that name again!"

"Pott. Annie Pott. Why?"

"Pam just told me she was an acquaintance of an Annie Pott. She said the woman tripped and hit her head on a bookcase."

"Yeah, well, she must have gotten up and fell again about a dozen times, because that's how many times her head hit the bookshelf. Word is her face looked like a half-eaten bowl of spaghetti."

"Where did Pam get her story?"

"I'm guessing," replied Tim, "she, like most people, reads the newspaper or watches television."

"It seems strange that they didn't report it as a homicide."

"Maybe the locals didn't want it getting out that someone killed another woman on a Friday."

"Yeah, maybe."

"What about you? Did you find a map?"

"Yes, I did. I also called..."

Ron's cell phone interrupted whatever he was about to say.

"Yeah, Robert. Talk to me."

Tim sat and watched the conversation, hearing only Ron saying, "Ah ha" and "Okay" and "I see."

Ron hung up, turned to Tim, saying, "That was Robert Edge."

"I gathered that. What did he say?"

"He said the girl's last meal was fettuccini with shrimp."

"Italian restaurant?"

"That would be my first choice," agreed Ron.

"What's on the map that's close?"

Ron surveyed the map and saw that Ducatis Pizzeria and Trattoria was 1.3 miles from the Marriot.

"Morris could have walked there in less than 15 minutes, Ron."

"Let's go there first, then we'll drive to the home of Annie Pott."

"Sounds like a plan, partner."

Twenty minutes later, the two FBI agents entered Ducatis Pizzeria. As they stood next to a podium at the entrance, a young lady approached. She took two menus from the podium, saying, "Would you prefer a table or booth, gentlemen?"

"We're not here to eat," replied Ron, flashing his credentials. "May I have your name?"

"My name is Billie. Billie Paterson."

Taking a photo from his pocket, he showed the girl the picture of Aaron, asking, "Has this man been in here, Billie?"

The young girl took a quick glance at the photo, then nodding her head in the affirmative, replied, "Yes, he was here Saturday night with a group of people."

"How many other people?"

"I believe it was eight but let me check."

They watched as she opened the reservations book and turned the pages back to Saturday. She ran her finger through a half-page of names before stopping.

"Ahh, here it is," she announced. "There were eight of them."

"What name did they use for the reservation?"

"Smith, party of eight," she read from the reservation book. "Samantha Higgins was their server. Would you like to talk to her?"

"She's here? Now?"

"Yes. She works from 11 to 2 and then returns at 5 for the dinner hour. There she is now. I'll get her for you."

As Billie rushed across the floor, they heard her say, "Sam, those men, standing up front, would like to speak with you."

She was tall, dark, and beautiful. She had brown eyes that looked like melted chocolate, beautiful full lips, dark black hair hanging down to her shoulders, and a smile to die for.

"Yes, can I help you?" she asked as she joined them.

"You know this man?" questioned Ron, thrusting the photo in front of her face.

"Know him? No, I don't know him, but I waited on him twice."

"Twice?" asked Tim.

"Yes. He and three others, along with whom I assumed to be spouses, were here on Saturday night. They sat over there at that table," she said, pointing at some obscure table across the room. "They spent hours here drinking wine and whisky."

"How did they pay?"

"All of them paid in cash. They were very generous. I collected a fifty-dollar tip from each of them."

"Could you describe each man?"

"Yes, I think so."

"Tim, let's get sketch artist sent over to sit with these two young ladies."

Turning his attention back to the waitress, Ron asked, "When else was this man here?"

"He met three other gentlemen here yesterday afternoon around 3:30. They bought drinks, but no food. They ate garlic bread and olives that we offer to our customers."

"Did they talk to where you could hear them?"

"One of them did most of the talking, the others just listened. But to answer your question, no, I couldn't hear anything."

"So you didn't talk with any of them."

"I talked to that man," she said, pointing at the photo. "He paid the bill while the others sat outside in a car."

"What kind of car was it, Samantha?" asked Tim.

Giggling, she replied, "Black. I don't know one car from another. Sorry."

"You said you talked with this man," Ron stated while holding out the photo. "What did you talk about?"

"I asked if they were enjoying themselves, where they were staying, and how long they would be in town."

"And he answered how?"

"He said they were here on business, and they would leave sometime Wednesday morning."

"What about where they were staying?"

"He said something about it being close. He didn't say where."

"Anything else?"

"That's about it. He left me another big tip, though. I hope he comes back in again."

"I wouldn't hold my breath," snapped Ron.

CHAPTER 19

Tuesday, July 2, 2019

Her name was Lillian Black. She was 92 years of age and fit as a fiddle. She cleaned her own house, made her own meals, and drove her own car. Lillian Black was an independent, feisty, and busy woman. She belonged to several organizations and attended multiple functions and events.

Because of her years of socializing, she knew many people, including the murdered Charlene McSweeny and Carol Holihan.

Lillian Black thought she knew why someone would kill those women, and she also had strong thoughts about who was doing the killing.

An early riser, Lillian, dressed and ready to talk to the FBI, had to wait. It was only 6:15 and nothing, including the FBI, was open at this hour. She would wait until 8:00 before leaving.

She was coming back into the house after taking a bag of garbage out to the trash can, when the phone rang. Glancing up at the clock and seeing it was only 7:05, she muttered, "Who would call me at this early hour?"

"Hello," she answered.

"Lillian?"

"Yes, this is she."

"I'm coming for you, Lillian."

"You are, eh? Well, when you get here, expect to get your balls chopped off and fed to my daughter's dog. I know who you are, you pathetic loser! I'm on my way to the FBI. If I were you, sonny, I'd bend over and kiss my sorry-ass goodbye."

Click.

Hearing the click, Lillian squeezed the phone with a combination of fear and rage.

He's coming for me, she thought. *Well, let the bastard come. I'll kill that mother....* She didn't allow herself to complete the thought. *Not ladylike,* she told herself.

She went to a kitchen drawer where she kept her knives. Drawing out a nine-inch serrated carving knife, she held it up in front of her eyes.

Whispering to herself, she said, *First I'll take his eyes out and then I'll cut off his balls, and what I'm guessing is a miniature dick. I mix those in with Bull's dinner tonight. Then I'll plunge this knife into that prick's heart a half-dozen times.*

Lillian meant what she said and no doubt would try to do exactly that. However, Bull, her daughter's huge Rottweiler, wouldn't get the meal Lillian had planned for him.

✷✷✷✷✷✷✷✷✷✷✷✷

She knows who I am, thought The Dispatcher. *How could she know? She wasn't there that day when they first humiliated me.*

He had to kill her now, before she went to the FBI.

Leaving his house, he made his way to his car.

"Bitch!" he mumbled as he pulled out of the driveway.

Lillian would have a visitor much sooner than she expected. The Dispatcher lived just blocks away.

CHAPTER 20

Tuesday, July 2, 2019 – 7:30am

He was so enraged and left in such a rush that he failed to take with him the can of gasoline he planned on using to dispatch her. As he drove past her house, and parked just a few houses down the street, he realized that it would necessitate a spur-of-the-moment dispatch.

Spur-of-the-moment actions were not his forte. Everything he did in life had structure and purpose, right down to the tiniest detail. What he was about to attempt was foreign territory for him.

He didn't know it, but his off-the-cuff reaction, along with what would happen on Friday, would throw a huge monkey-wrench into the solving of these multiple murders.

The puzzle was about to have pieces introduced that didn't fit.

It was moving on 7:25am when he left his car, went to the trunk, and removed a tire iron. He marched down the street, wielding the tire iron in his hand, as if he were the invisible man and no one could see him. He was irrational, but he was also lucky because there wasn't a soul around who could bear witness to his presence.

Using stealth, he moved along the right side of Lillian's home. Hoping to glimpse the woman, he stopped at the two side windows and peered inside. It was at the second window that he saw her standing in the kitchen. She had a very large knife in her hand. She looked scared.

Rightfully so, he thought.

Smiling a wicked grin, he moved around to the back of the house. Three brick steps had him standing at a screen door that fronted a back door that had three windowpanes built into it.

Standing to the side of the rightmost windowpane, he turned his head to peer inside. He could see a washer and dryer, and a standing ironing board with an iron resting on it.

The laundry room, he thought.

A door at the far end of the room had him guessing that it opened into the kitchen.

Grabbing the screen door handle, he gave it a twist. It was unlocked.

He opened it wide and stepped into the space between the screen door and the back door. As his back held the screen door open, he reached for the back door's doorknob. Turning it, he found the door to be unlocked.

Lillian, in her rush to answer the ringing phone, had failed to lock the door behind her after taking out the trash.

Luck continued to be on his side.

I must live at the foot of the cross, he told himself.

The smell of bleach and detergent filled his nose as he entered the laundry room and closed the door behind him. He crept toward the door leading to the kitchen and pressed his ear against it.

He could hear the woman talking – no, not talking – it was more like yelling!

"I'll cut his balls off if he gets anywhere near me!" he heard her rant.

As he thought about how he would enter, he unconsciously pounded the tire iron he held in his right hand into the palm of his left.

But before he could gather his thoughts, the door flew open and there stood Lillian, with the carving knife held high over her head.

"I saw you at the window, you stupid son-of-a-bitch!"

The knife was a blur as it came slicing through the air, missing the Dispatcher's chest by an inch.

Before he could react, he saw the knife, raised high again, being brought downward. Seeing the glint of the blade in the light from the kitchen, he stepped back, and the knife missed by more than a foot.

He smiled.

"Go ahead, smile, asshole! When I cut your miserable balls off, let's see you smile then!" screamed Lillian.

Quarters were tight in the now crowded laundry room. While backpedaling to avoid the slashing knife, the Dispatcher kicked the ironing board, knocking it over and sending the sitting iron crashing to the floor. Her flailing hand struck a box of detergent that had been sitting on the washer, spilling its contents onto the floor. The powder turned the floor into a miniature ice rink.

The speed and agility of the old woman had set him back on his heels. His backward retreat ended as his body slammed against the back door. He had nowhere to go. Again she raised the knife and swung it down towards him. He could back up no further. The knife would find its mark.

He reacted.

Holding the tire iron in his right hand, he took a wild swing at the descending arm, striking it solid.

The radius and the ulna in the 92-year-old woman's forearm cracked and splintered like two dried twigs. The knife flew from her hand and struck the backdoor, just missing his left ear. Lillian looked down to see her forearm dangling at a right angle. She screamed.

The scream intensified when a downward swing of the tire iron struck her left shoulder and cracked the clavicle in half. It would, however, be her last utterance.

The third blow was to her head, crushing her skull. She was dead before she hit the floor.

Five additional blows to the head ensured what already was: death.

The Dispatcher kicked the woman one time, and seeing she was lifeless, opened the back door and returned to his car.

No one saw or heard a thing.

The Dispatcher returned home, showered, put on his coat and tie, and went to work. He wasn't happy. Lillian had messed up his planned routine.

What bothered him most was his inability to leave his calling card. That omission would prove to be, at least temporarily, very beneficial.

CHAPTER 21

Ron had been at his desk since 7:15 when Tim came waltzing in with the usual half-dozen donuts at 8:28.

"Wow, two minutes early. What, you couldn't sleep?"

"Yeah, I was tossing and turning for almost 30 seconds wondering what donuts would satisfy your insatiable appetite this morning."

"A few chocolate éclairs might do."

"Boy, did I ever luck out. I got you three and two Boston cremes. Those five donuts should move the prong on your belt to the left a notch or two. Assuming that is, there are notches remaining."

"How about a coffee?"

"Damn, Ron, you sure are a grateful son-of-a-bitch. I spend seven bucks on your damn carbs and calories and you want me to spring for a two-dollar cup of joe too. You're sure one helluva guy, partner."

"Why, thank you, Tim. I'll put that in your record as showing respect toward your superiors. Now, let me ask you once again. Did you get me a coffee?"

"Yeah, I got you a damn coffee."

"Ahh, now that's too bad. That nice notation I was about to put in your file just went *poof*!"

"Ahh, gee, does that mean I don't get a raise… again this year?"

Ron, ignoring Tim's sarcasm, stuck out his hand, saying, "Let me have it before it gets cold. I hate to wash down a nice éclair with lukewarm coffee."

"Oh, yeah, I can see where that would be one of life's setbacks."

"Our plate is overflowing, Tim-o-thy."

"Maybe yours is, but I just have this single peanut donut, whereas you..."

"Yeah, I know. Enough of the donut talk. We have some serious business to tackle. I want to get to that third victim's house this morning. Have you examined any of the things we found in the other victim's homes?"

"I have. I don't know if they connect, but on almost every Friday on Judge Bracken's calendar, all the way back to January, was a notation written in small letters."

"What was the notation?"

"The letters 'mf.'"

"MF? Might it be a doctor she saw?"

"How many people visit their doctor on a weekly basis?"

"Excellent point. How about a family member that she called, or they called her on Fridays?"

"Possible, I guess. She has a daughter named Mary whose last name is Funkhauser."

"That's it, Tim. Mystery solved!"

"It would if it weren't for what I found in Carol Holihan's appointment book."

"Oh, and what was that?"

"She had 11:00am checked on almost every Friday, dating back to January."

"Just a check mark. Nothing saying what it was?"

"Nope."

"Coincidence?"

"I think not, Ron."

"Yeah, neither do I. You said almost every Friday. Tell me the dates of the open Fridays."

"They would be April 19, May 12 and 24, June 14, July 5, August 31, November 29, and December 27 for both women. The judge also had July 12 and 19 open, while Holihan had June 21 and 28 open."

"Holidays?"

"Close enough to be holidays if you think of extended weekends. I'm also thinking some of those are vacation dates."

"So it's something they both did on Fridays. How about the McSweeny woman?"

"I found no calendars or appointment books in the house. I put a request in to the Myrtle Beach PD to get my hands on the evidence they collected. Haven't heard from them as yet."

"The letters, *mf*. What in the hell could those two letters represent, Tim?"

"Maybe she liked to curse once a week, but needed a reminder of what to say," replied Tim with a sly grin.

"Yeah, I'm sure that's it. Given a chance, might you have something intelligent to say?"

"My best guess is an organization of some type. Maybe a charity they both belonged to."

"Let's head over to the Annie Pott's home and see if we can find her calendar or appointment book."

Ten minutes later, both agents were cruising south on Route 17. Tim was driving due to Ron needing to finish eating one éclair and one Boston crème.

"Where we headed, Tim?"

"Litchfield. But to be more specific, Willbrook Plantation."

"Hey, that reminds me, keep next Tuesday open. The Hagan group is playing True Blue."

"Where are they today?"

"They are playing just down the road from Litchfield at the River Club."

"Let's stop while we're down this way and have lunch with the fellas."

"I doubt we'll have time, Tim. We need to get back to coordinate the preparations being made to catch our bank robbers."

"Can't Baxter, Proctor, and Buttocks do that?"

"I think you mean Braddock, Tim. He's our boss."

"Hmm, isn't that what I said?"

"Almost, but not quite."

"Well, can't they handle it?"

"They can, but I want our hands on it."

"Oh, so if something goes wrong, we can get our balls chopped off. Good thinking, Ron. Golly, gee whiz, I wouldn't want Buttocks taking any heat."

"His name is Braddock, partner. Braddock."

"Yeah, whatever. A pile of crap by any other name still smells like a pile of crap."

"I think you may have plagiarized Shakespeare, partner. Not too fondly, I must add."

"He's long dead. I doubt he gives a fuck."

"Point well taken, Tim."

As they passed the 15h hole at Indian Wells, the site of one of Ichabod's severed heads, Ron mumbled, "Some disturbing memories there, Tim. I don't think they come any worse than Ichabod."

"Yeah, well, now he's just alligator poop."

"Along with many of his victims," added Ron.

"That's true," nodded Tim.

They pulled into Annie Pott's home at 9:45. The house was closed up and surrounded by the obligatory yellow strands of crime scene tape.

"Got the key, Tim?"

"Yeah."

Upon opening the door, it hit them like a ton of bricks. The odor of rotting flesh had permeated the entire house. Robert Edge had calculated the woman had been dead for at least six days before being found. The killer had turned the home's thermostat up as high as it would go, which accelerated the body's decomposition.

"No air-conditioning, I suspect," guessed Ron.

"Seems that way."

"How was this woman killed again, Tim?"

"She fell and hit her head against a bookshelf about a dozen times. Remember?"

"That's right! This is Pam's acquaintance."

Ron took one more step before halting and turning to Tim, asking, "Did you say bookshelf?"

"Yeah, I did. Why?"

"There seems to be a pattern, Tim. Books and bookshelves."

"Lots of people, Ron, enjoy reading in their later years. I don't think it's unusual that these women all had libraries of books. My mom does."

"I guess I'm over-reacting," shrugged Ron. "Did she have her throat slit?"

"Post-mortem. Right down and through the larynx."

"Hmm, that's become a pattern, hasn't it?"

"A stupid detective could come up with that conclusion, partner."

"Even you?"

"Bite me," retorted Tim.

"Maybe later, but for now, let's find her calendar or her appointment book. You look in the kitchen. I'll look in the bedroom."

Less than a minute passed before Ron heard Tim call out, "Got something!"

Leaving the woman's bedroom, Ron rushed to meet Tim in the kitchen.

"What is it?"

"She had this calendar taped to the fridge. Look at the notations on Fridays."

Ron, taking the sheet of paper, glanced at the woman's Friday jottings. It read, starting on the 12th: TPC, Pawleys Plantation, Kimbles, and on August 2nd, Inlet Affairs.

"Golf dates?"

"These women are a little long in the tooth to be playing golf in 90 degree heat, Ron. Wouldn't you agree?"

"Yeah, I would, partner. Hey, I have an idea," Ron said as he pulled out his phone and dialed a number.

"Who you calling?"

"I'll put the phone on speaker."

The phone rang twice, and then they heard, "Good morning. Federal Bureau of Investigation."

"Hey, Pam, this is Colonel Ron Lee."

"Well, good morning, Colonel. What can I do for you, sir?"

"We are at Annie Pott's home. Since you knew her, I wonder if I might ask a few questions?"

"Fire away, sir."

"We found her calendar, and she had marked Fridays with names like Kimbels and Inlet Affairs. Do those names mean anything to you, Pam?"

"Yes they do, Colonel. They are restaurants in Murrells Inlet."

"Restaurants! Let me ask you another question. We found the notation 'mf' on the calendar of one of our victims. She wrote it on almost every Friday. Does that mean anything to you?"

"Oh, that's easy, Colonel. Those letters stand for *Movable Feast*. I'm a member. That's where I met Annie Pott. We meet almost every Friday during the year."

"*Movable Feast*? What do you do? Eat at buffets every Friday?"

"Buffets? Oh, no, Colonel," replied Pam, with an unseen smirk that was rapidly spreading into an enormous grin. In moments, that grin would burst into a guttural laugh that would leave her barely able to speak.

"So it's not buffets?"

"The members of the *Movable Feast*... hee-hee-hee...," said Pam, now giggling uncontrollably "... aren't a bunch... ha-ha-ha-ha... of buffet hunters."

"Then what the hell is it, Pam?"

"It's a... hee-hee... book club, Colonel."

As he hung up on Pam, Ron declared, "The Movable Feast is a book club! Where is the bookshelf that fell on Annie Pott a half-dozen times, Tim?"

"It's in the Carolina Room."

As they entered the sunlit room, two bookshelves, on either side of the room, presented themselves.

"You take the right, I'll take the left," ordered Ron.

"What am I looking for?"

"You'll know it when you find it."

Two minutes later, Tim announced, "Got it, Ron."

"Let me guess. There's a bookmark at the beginning of chapter three."

"Yeah, how did you know?"

"He's playing us, Tim. *Catch Me If You Can*. He's marking the chapters of his kills."

"What the ..." mumbled Tim.

"We need to go back to the judge's house. I'll bet you a dollar to a donut, that book is on her shelf and there's a bookmark placed at chapter four."

"No bet, Ron. Besides, like I've told you on numerous occasions, donuts cost more than a buck."

CHAPTER 22

It was just past 9:00pm when they left the parking lot.

"Where we headed, Aaron?" asked Nick.

He purposely planned a late dinner at Ruth Chris Steak House, just steps from the inn, so he and Aaron wouldn't arrive at the targeted dealership before it closed.

The meeting that morning at the Anchor Café brought smiles to every team member. Nick laid out the plan that would commence at 8:30 the next morning. Everyone had their assignments. If all went as planned, each of them would score a half-million dollar payout.

"There's a dealership up north in Little River. It gives us the best chance of snagging a vehicle they may not miss for a day or two."

"Why is that?"

"Their lot stretches for two or three hundred yards. They have a wide selection of used vehicles too. It's an excellent combination. Large lot and lots of vehicles."

"I assume they have security cameras?" said Nick, phrasing the statement as a question.

"I'll disconnect power to the building. The line feeding the building runs along the back of the lot. I'll drop myself off and disable the line. Once we have the vehicle we need, I'll reconnect the line so no one is the wiser."

"What the hell will I be doing while you're messing with the power?"

"Waiting in the car. I'll be back in ten minutes."

"Okay, Aaron, this is your baby. I'll just sit back and watch. I'm sure you know what you're doing, buddy."

Taking Route 31 north, it took about 20 minutes to reach Bell and Bell's car lot at the intersection of Route 9 and 57. It had a distinctive trademark: A huge bell, estimated to be 10 feet in diameter and standing 8 or 9 feet high, hung between two posts. Those motorists heading west on Route 9 couldn't miss seeing it.

"I wonder why they don't have two bells," muttered Nick. "Calling themselves Bell and Bell, you'd think they would have two."

"Yeah, you'd think so," agreed a disinterested Aaron.

Making a right turn onto Route 57, Aaron passed the lot's Rt 57 entrance. A drive of a quarter-mile had him turning onto Retreat Place. Another right onto Saye Cut and a left onto Cordgrass Lane had Aaron turning off his headlights.

"This road dead ends up around this curve."

"Damn, Aaron, there are lots of homes here. Don't you think someone will get suspicious of a car driving through the neighborhood with its lights off?"

"All these homes were just built, Nick. The majority are empty, and where we'll be parking, all the houses are still empty."

Reaching the end of the street, Aaron popped the trunk and exited the car, saying, "They gave this street the name it deserves, that's for sure. I need to put on some high-water boots."

"How come?"

"Behind all these new homes is wetlands. Cordgrass thrives in wetlands, Nick. Wait here. I'll be back in ten minutes."

Aaron had scouted the area earlier that day and knew a path to where the power line fed the dealership.

Slipping through the darkness, he found the power box that fed the dealership. It took him less than two minutes to disconnect the power. He was back at the car in less than ten minutes.

Nick was standing near the trunk. "Everything a go?" he asked.

"Yep," replied Aaron while taking off his boots and tossing them into the trunk, along with the tools he had used.

They both returned to the car with Aaron taking the wheel. He drove to the dealership's entrance off Route 57 and turned in.

"Less traffic means less noticeable," he told Nick, who nodded in agreement.

They arrived at 9:35. The sales staff had left at 8:00 and the cleaning people wouldn't arrive until 11:00. Time was not their enemy. It would take less than 20 minutes to accomplish what they came to do.

Aaron drove right up to the sales building and cut off his lights. They sat in the vehicle for five minutes looking for any signs of life. Other than a stray cat prowling the premises, there was none other.

"Let's look in the back, Nick," voiced Aaron as he removed two flashlights from the center-console.

Exiting their vehicle, they made their way to the rear of the lot where employees parked incoming vehicles. There were two Yukon XLs on the back line, one used, the other new, parked about 40 yards apart. Nick, eyeing the newer vehicle, made his way toward it, but stopped when he heard Aaron call out:

"We don't want that one, Nick."

"Why not?"

"It's covered in the protective plastic. I'm thinking they'll be prepping that one for sale come morning. Let's look at the used one."

The used XL was a 2017, V-8, and white. It had a used car sticker on it that read there were 36,000 miles on the vehicle. The dealership had already put new tires on it. Aaron tried the door.

Locked.

"Wait here, Nick. I'll be back in a couple minutes."

"Where are you going?"

"To get the key. This vehicle was just traded in. The key will be in clean up."

"Why don't you hot-wire it?"

"You can't hot-wire most vehicles made after 2004. They have a computer chip that makes it impossible."

Three minutes later, Aaron returned with the key.

"Right where I said it would be!"

He unlocked the door, climbed in, and started it up.

Rolling down the window, he said to Nick, "I'll need a plate. There are cars parked in the service lane where I can take one. What's the plan after we leave here?"

"I'll drive this one, Aaron, you drive the car. After you reconnect the power, drive to downtown Myrtle Beach and park about a block away from the Wells Fargo bank. I'll wait for you there."

"Okay, Nick, but do you mind if I ask, why?" asked Aaron as he exited the Yukon.

"Subterfuge, Aaron."

"Subterfuge? Okay, Nick, if you say so. Drive this over to the service lane. I'll get you a plate."

Aaron ran to the service lane and removing a plate off a truck, he put it on the Yukon.

As he returned to the car, he questioned Nick's decision to drive downtown, but knowing Nick always had a solid plan, he followed his orders.

The Wells Fargo bank sat on the corner of North Oak and 21st Avenue North.

It was nearing 11:00 when Aaron arrived and parked on 21st, a block from the bank.

Nick, seeing Aaron arrive, pulled in behind him and immediately left the Yukon and walked to the passenger door of the Camry and opened it.

"Will this spot do the trick, Nick?"

"Couldn't be better, Aaron."

"Now what?"

"I'm going back to the hotel, Aaron, but you'll be staying here in the car."

"What?" cried out Aaron as he turned toward Nick with bewilderment. "Now, why would I do that, Nick!"

"Because you'll be dead," answered Nick, as he raised the .22 pistol and put three muted bullets into Aaron's chest, two of which pierced his heart.

Aaron's body slumped forward against the steering wheel with his dead eyes, depicting astonishment, staring at Nick.

"Sorry, pal, but you were a liability."

Nick closed the passenger door and walked around to the driver's door, opened it, and sat the dead Aaron up so his head was against the headrest. Nick removed a roll of duct tape from his pocket, tore off a two-foot piece and wrapped it around Aaron's forehead and the headrest.

Aaron now appeared to be sitting in the car and watching the bank. It was just as Nick had envisioned.

He moved to the parking meter and put five dollars of time on the meter. Then, locking the doors, he returned to the Yukon and drove back to the Marina Inn.

Although Nick remembered to take Aaron's wallet, he overlooked something of importance: Aaron's room key.

CHAPTER 23

Tuesday, July 2, 2019 – 2:00pm

    It would be hours before Aaron Moore enjoyed his last meal at the Ruth Chris restaurant. Ron and Tim, back at their office, spent those same hours mulling over what they realized was the connection between the killings of four women.

    It was a book club called The Movable Feast. Its members would meet on Fridays to hear guest authors talk about their careers and their books. It was by no coincidence that Friday was also the day the Dispatcher killed.

    The only thing standing in their way to finding the murderer was determining his motive.

    "Determine the motive and you'll have your killer," Ron said matter-of-factly.

    "Motives, eh? How about a disenchanted author who the audience didn't like, and they let him know it?"

    "I can see that happening, Tim-o-thy. Who's the leader of that book club?"

    "According to our receptionist, Pam O'Dell, a lady by the name of Linda Ketron is the go-to gal."

    "Did you get her phone number from Pam?"

    "No, but I got her email address."

    "Send Mrs. Ketron an email saying we'd like to talk with her ASAP. Provide her our direct line into this office."

    "Time isn't on our side, Ron. Friday is just three days away. If we can't come up with a motive, chances are some poor book enthusiast won't have a need for her library card much past Friday."

    "Yeah, I get that. Send that damn email. Now!"

    Tim emailed the message, and while they waited for a reply, they began discussing the bank stakeouts.

    "Where do you think they'll hit, Ron?"

"I'll bet," he said with a shit-eating grin, "it will be someplace holding lots of money."

"Wow, you are omniscient, Ron!"

"Why thank you, partner. Here's another golden-goodie for you to marvel at. I believe it will be another downtown bank."

"Boy, oh boy, and golly gee whiz, Ron. The hits, they just keep on a comin'. I can't wait to hear another pearl of wisdom come from that pie hole of yours. Wait! On second thought, I take that back. I've heard enough."

"That's all right. I was running out of pearls, anyway."

"Do you think they'd hit Bank of America again?"

"I suppose it's possible, but unlikely."

"I hope your assumptions are right, Ron."

"Why? What do you mean?"

"That this gang is sticking around to rob another bank. If they don't, Buttocks will ridicule you forever for tying up all this manpower on the day before the biggest four-day weekend of the summer."

"Kind of ironic, isn't it, Tim?"

"What do you mean?"

"You hoping that someone robs a bank where someone might get killed, just so I don't get ridiculed."

"I didn't think of it in that way, partner."

"Neither did I until you said it."

A jangling phone interrupted the conversation.

"FBI," answered Tim. There was a pause and then, "Thank you for calling us back, Mrs. Ketron. My name is Agent Tim Pond and my partner is Special Agent Colonel Ron Lee. I will put you on speaker so we can both ask questions and hear your answers."

Tim put the phone on speaker, saying, "Can you hear us, ma'am?"

"Yes, I can hear you and please call me Linda."

"Very well, Linda," answered Tim.

"Now, tell me why I'm talking to the FBI, Agent Pond."

It was Ron who answered.

"Linda, this is Colonel Ron Lee. The reason we have called you is that we suspect someone is murdering women who are a part of your Movable Feast program."

"Oh, my, no!"

Ron could visualize the woman's legs giving out from under her as she struggled to find a chair.

"Are you sitting, Linda?"

"I am now, sir. I knew Annie Pott died, but the paper said she fell and hit her head."

"That is not exactly true, I'm sorry to say. Do you know Charlene McSweeny, Nancy Bracken, or Carol Holihan?"

"I don't recall those names, Colonel. Over the 23 years I've coordinated the Moveable Feast we have had over 4,000 people come by. People only attend if the topic or the author interests them. And of those 4,000, I know only a small percentage of them, I'm sorry to say."

Both men, upon hearing her state there were over 4,000 book enthusiasts, immediately knew that protecting them was an impossibility.

"Listen, we didn't expect you to remember all 4,000 names, but maybe you can recall occasions where something antagonistic happened between the audience and the authors."

"It's not a regular occurrence, by any means, but there have been spats and an occasional blowup involving the author and the audience."

"Might you be able to recall details of those incidences, especially any that may have arisen in the past two years?"

"There was an incident last October, when the author, not the most patient of men, lost control and began ranting. It occurred when a woman asked a question that others had asked three previous times. He went off at the poor woman, who, he didn't realize, was hearing impaired."

"Do you recall the author's name, Linda?" asked Tim.

"Give me a moment. I have my calendar right here."

The two men endured a few long moments of silence before Linda announced, "I'm sorry but I had the date wrong. It was in August that this occurred. August 24th, to be exact. The author's name is Wes Stapleton."

"Very good, Linda," replied Ron. "Any others you might recall?"

"Yes, there was a youthful man by the name of Allen Colby who became upset when his presentation didn't go well. Some women in the audience openly made fun of him. He used some profanity at the audience as they left the building. He was livid, as I recall. In fact... oh, no!"

"What is it, Linda?"

"Annie Pott laughed at him!"

"Might you know anything about him, Linda? Where he lives, works, etc."

"I think he's a locksmith, but I can't tell you who he works for. I don't know where he lives. His profile might tell me, but it will take me some time to find it."

"Profile, ma'am?" asked Ron.

"Yes, when an author agrees to come as our guest, I ask that he send me a profile of himself and his books. Some put their home address down. Some don't. In all honesty, I couldn't tell you if he did or didn't."

"Any others, Linda?"

"We had an author who had a hissy fit about the setup table we provided for her being too small. She screamed her frustrations at me and then walked off. Never seen or heard from again."

"Hmm, I don't think we are looking for a woman, but if you know her name, we'll check her out," Ron stated.

"I think she gave me her pen name only, Colonel."

"Why do you think that?"

"She told me her name was Ohso Alluring. Does that sound real to you?"

"Can't say it does, Linda."

"That was my take too."

"What percentage of your typical audience are men?" asked Tim.

"It's rare when we have over one or two men in the audience, other than our semi-regulars, although there have been exceptions."

"Can you tell us of an exception?" questioned Tim.

"A few years ago, Bobby Richardson, who played for the Yankees, was our guest speaker. Men packed the place that day. It's a pleasant surprise, however, if more than a handful of men attend on any given Friday."

"Have you ever had to ask an audience member to leave and not return?"

"One time in 23 years."

"What happened?"

"It was a woman. Middle-aged, I'd say mid-forties, and in superb shape. As they showed her the door, I thought to myself that she must work out daily to keep that body."

"What did she do? Why was she asked to leave?" asked Tim.

"She was berating our guest speaker and making her look like a fool. Two men in our audience tried to calm her down, but she took a swing at them, and hit one, drawing blood. She was a beast! Then she began cursing like a sailor. Oops, I trust neither of you were sailors?"

"Neither of us were sailors, Linda," answered Ron.

"But," interrupted Tim, "we often talk like one!"

"Excuse my partner's sense of humor, Linda. Do you recall the author's name or that of the woman?"

"I don't know the woman's name. She came alone and left alone."

"And the author?" asked Tim.

"The author was Joyce Melville. She lives in Pawleys Island. I've known her for years. She wouldn't hurt a fly if she was able."

"Why do you say that?"

"Joyce is wheelchair bound."

"You mentioned you had some semi-regular male attendees," Tim stated. "What did you mean by that?"

"We have two fellas who attend on a somewhat frequent basis. I'd say they might average two meetings a month."

"Do you know their names?"

"Yes, I do. Scott Skiles, and Ed Gooding. Ed comes with his wife, Mary Patten."

"What do you know about them?"

"Two nice guys. Ed, being retired, does a lot of fishing. It was Ed's face that stopped that woman's fist. Scott works at a hospital, but I don't recall which one. I think I heard him say Waccamaw, but I'm not positive."

"One more question, Linda."

"Let's hear it."

"How long ago did this fracas happen?"

"It was last June. It was the first Friday in June, to be exact."

"Linda, let us give you some advice. Be aware of your surroundings. Are you having a feast this coming Friday?"

"No, because it's the Fourth of July weekend. We don't have feasts on or around the holidays. We'll be back together the following Friday, though. You should stop by."

"We may just do that, Linda. Until then, you stay safe and let your audience know what's going on and to stay aware."

"All 4,000 of them!"

"Yep. All 4,000."

"Geez, you guys sure are demanding."

"Oh, yes, we are that and more," agreed Ron. "Hey, thanks for your help. We'll be seeing you soon."

As Tim ended the call, Ron said, "Tomorrow, after we nail those bank robbers, we'll get to work on these leads. I'll have Heather get us some addresses and phone numbers."

"Well, let's hope the bank thing is over in a hurry, because Friday is coming fast, Ron, and someone will die."

They didn't know it, but their worries about that day weren't necessary.

The Dispatcher wouldn't be killing anyone on Friday.

This week, Friday's scheduled kill occurred on Tuesday, and because it did, the police attributed Lillian Black's death to her trying to fight off an intruder.

Lillian never had her chance to tell the FBI her conclusions. Her premature dispatch would allow The Dispatcher to kill again.

CHAPTER 24

Wednesday, July 3, 2019 – 6:30am

It was 6:30am when Dan and Artie sat down to have breakfast in the Inn's dining room. Being pros, what was to transpire in less than three hours had no effect on their appetites. There were no rookie butterflies.

They had ordered coffee and were perusing the menu when Neil Tanner passed by their table.

Recognizing them from when they checked in on Monday, he stopped to say hello.

"Good morning, gentlemen. I hope you are enjoying your stay. Is there anything you need?"

"Good morning," the two replied in unison.

"We're just checking out the menu... Mr. Tanner," answered Dan as he strained to read Tanner's nametag.

"Very good, sir. And how about you, sir?"

"I could use some su-su-sugar for my coffee, ss-ss-sir."

If either man had looked up from their menu at Tanner's face, he would have seen the sudden realization in Tanner's eyes.

He stood frozen, recalling the words of the morning newscaster.

The FBI is still seeking the men who robbed the Bank of America branch in downtown Myrtle Beach last week. Their only clue is that one of the men had a noticeable stuttering problem with words starting with the letters, S and C.

Snapping out of his trance, he answered, "Yes, sir, I'll have your server bring it."

Tanner stopped to instruct their server to deliver more sugar, but then he made quick steps toward the front desk and his office. As he passed through the foyer, Nick stepped from an elevator and Tanner bumped into him.

"Oh, my! My apologies, sir. I don't know what to say."

"All is well, Mr. Tanner. No harm done. You seem to be in an awful rush, though."

"Yes, sir, I'm afraid I am," said a nervous Tanner, glancing back toward the dining room.

Nick's eyes followed Tanner's nervous gaze to where he saw Dan and Artie sitting at a table giving a waitress their breakfast order.

"You're looking at those two men with some anxiety, Mr. Tanner. Is there something wrong?"

"I shouldn't say this, sir, but I think they may be the men who robbed the bank last week."

"Really? Why would you think that?" asked Nick, with immediate thoughts that plans would need changing.

"See the man in the blue shirt?"

"Yes."

"He stutters."

"And that makes him a bank robber?"

"Yes! I mean, no, but yes, it might."

"How so, Mr. Tanner?"

"I heard on tv this morning that one man had a severe stuttering problem, especially with words beginning with the letters, S and C. When I asked if he needed anything, he replied with a pronounced stutter of the words, *sugar* and *sir*."

"I understand your thinking, Mr. Tanner, but you do realize that there are many people in this world that stutter."

"Oh, of that there's no doubt, sir, but I'm still calling the FBI."

The pistol was out of Nick's waistband and pushed hard against Tanner's stomach in a blink of an eye.

"I don't think so, Mr. Tanner."

Tanner, feeling his arm locked in the man's grip, looked down to see the pistol. He was about to yell out, but Nick stopped him cold.

"I'll empty this gun into your gut if you scream or draw any kind of attention!"

Tanner was sweating profusely as he nodded his understanding.

"Do you have the key to that penthouse elevator?"

Tanner nodded in the affirmative.

"Good. Let's you and I walk over to the elevator, real natural like. When the elevator doors open, we'll both step in and take a ride to the top."

"What going to happen then?"

"We'll step into that vacant penthouse."

"You're going to kill me, aren't you?"

"Kill you! Naw," Nick lied. "I'll just tie and gag you, hoping that my buddies and I can get far away from here before you get yourself free and warn the cops. Okay, Mr. Tanner?"

A nervous nod said that it wasn't okay.

It was just four steps to the elevator. Tanner entered the three-digit passcode, and the doors opened. It was Tanner's misfortune that it was sitting on the bottom floor where the cleaning crew always left it parked.

They stepped inside and Nick instructed Tanner to press the up button.

As the elevator whisked upward, Nick ordered Tanner to give him the key card.

Tanner knew deep in his heart it wasn't a good sign.

The thirty-second ride ended, at which time Nick asked, "Which penthouse is empty?"

Tanner thought about saying it was the Leftwich's, but he realized he would only put them in jeopardy.

"This one," said Tanner, nodding his head towards the Holihan's suite.

Nick reached over and slid the keycard into the slot. The doors opened wide, and they both stepped into the suite formally occupied by the murdered Carol Holihan.

After taking two steps into the suite, the elevator doors closed behind them.

"Now what?" asked Tanner, his voice filled with fear.

"I'm surprised you would ask that question, Mr. Tanner. I'm guessing you don't believe that I'm a man of my word."

"Are you?"

Nick didn't answer. He put the barrel of the pistol behind Tanner's right ear and pulled the trigger twice.

Tanner fell in a heap onto the floor, staining Carol Holihan's prized Persian rug with buckets of blood.

"No, I'm not, Mr. Tanner," whispered Nick as he stepped back into the elevator.

As the elevator descended, Nick glanced at his watch and saw it was 6:43.

"Good," he said aloud. "I still have time for breakfast."

CHAPTER 25

Wednesday, July 3, 2019 – 8:30

"Colonel, we have a suspicious vehicle parked on 21st. It's sitting a block from the bank, on the left side of the street."

Ron, sitting in the passenger seat of their surveillance vehicle, answered the call. From their position in the TD Bank parking lot, they could see all traffic coming and going on both North Oak and 21st. They also had an unobstructed view of the Wells Fargo Bank sitting diagonally across from their position.

Ron had projected the Wells Fargo Bank as the primary target for the bank robbers. It was the only bank in the vicinity holding the amount of money that would attract anyone looking to make a big score.

Radioing in the call was Bill Baxter, parked at the First Citizens Bank, which sat on 21st across the street from Wells Fargo.

"Is there someone in the car, Bill?"

"There's a man sitting at the wheel, Ron."

"That must be their getaway driver. It's only 8:33. We need to wait until they all get here," stated Ron.

The stakeout had been in progress since 4:00am. Chief Proctor placed unmarked police units on all streets surrounding the bank. Tim positioned the Bureau's top snipers on rooftops all along North Oak and 21st. Ron planted four FBI agents inside as bank employees. As soon as the robbery was underway, police would close off all exits.

For their own safety, bank officials had notified all their employees to stay at home until called.

When the clock outside the bank read 8:58, Ron got on the radio, saying, "Get ready, fellas. They should come any minute now. Bill, you and your people take the guy in the car."

"10-4, Ron."

"You guys inside ready?"

"We're ready, Colonel," replied Agent Jim Cooper.

A call came in from an agent parked on Legion drive. *"Colonel, there's a white van making a left turn off of Legion onto 21ˢᵗ."*

"Okay, let's keep our eyes on the van, fellas. No one does anything until I give the word."

A volley of *"10-4s"* responded.

Ron and Tim watched as the van made its way up 21ˢᵗ and turn into the bank's 21ˢᵗ Avenue entrance. They saw it park in front of the bank's front door, where it sat for a half-minute before the driver's door opened. A man in a white shirt, pants, and hat exited the driver's door and stepped to the rear of the van. He looked more like a milkman than he did a bank robber. It's doubtful that his physical appearance, 5'7" and 140 pounds, would have compelled anyone to turn over their money.

"Who's on him?" radioed Ron.

"I have him locked in, sir," replied an unknown voice of a rooftop sniper. *"One wrong move and he's history, sir."*

The driver opened the rear doors, reached inside, and extracted what appeared to be a 3 x 3 tray that had a white covering draped over it. Noticeable bulges in the white cover made it apparent that something occupied the tray.

The man, using both hands, carried it about shoulder-high, much as a waiter might when serving dinner to a table of four. He didn't appear as if he were laboring, however.

"What do you think he has under that sheet, Ron?"

"I don't know, Tim, but we can't take a chance."

Holding the radio's mic to his face, Ron barked, "If he attempts to open the front door, take him before he gets inside!"

Bounding up the steps to the bank's main door, the driver found himself knocked backward as he grabbed the door's handle. The four FBI agents inside surrounded him with weapons drawn. Two of the agents snatched the tray away, while the others patted him down and cuffed him.

Ron, seeing what was happening at the front door of the bank, screamed into the radio, "Bill, take that car now!"

Hearing Ron's orders to Bill, Tim fired their vehicle out of the TD Bank's parking lot and onto North Oak. A quick hundred yard ride had them turning into Wells Fargo's North Oak entrance. Moments later, they came to a screeching halt in front of the white van.

Rushing up the stairs to where the driver lay prone on the ground, Ron heard, "Would you like a bagel, Colonel?"

"What the hell are you talking about, Cooper?"

"The guy came to deliver bagels, croissants, and donuts. He said someone called in an order yesterday to have this tray of goodies delivered to the Wells Fargo Bank at 9:00am."

"Check out his story, and then let him go, Coop."

Ron's cell phone rang. It was Baxter.

"What is it, Bill?"

"Come on down here, Ron."

"Tim! Baxter wants us down the street."

Tim stopped in the middle of 21st, right next to a car surrounded by a half-dozen state troopers.

Exiting the car, Ron, greeted by Baxter, replied, "We have Aaron Morris, Ron."

"Where?"

"He's in the car. He's not talking."

"Oh, well, we'll see about that."

"No, Ron. He is not talking. Someone ventilated his chest with .22 slugs, two of which did a number on his heart."

"What!" screamed Ron. "How long has he been dead?"

"He's as stiff as a board. I'd guess at least ten hours."

"Ten hours... oh, shit!"

"What is it, Ron?" asked Tim.

"Those bastards set us up! I bet while we have been sitting here, they were doing their thing someplace else."

"But where?"

Ron's phone rang.

"I don't know, Tim, but I'm guessing this phone call will tell us."

It was Jim Braddock.

"Yeah, Jim."

"I hear you nabbed yourself a baker."

You could hear the hidden laughter in his voice.

"You're close, Jim. It was the baker's delivery man. Where did the real score go down?"

"Burroughs and Chapin at the Grand Dunes."

"How much?"

"Near three million."

"Jesus! Was anyone hurt?"

"No. The whole thing lasted five to six minutes. They show up, dressed in armored guard uniforms, in an armored truck, which they leave behind. They casually wheel the money out the door, say a fond farewell to the clueless security guard, whose employment, by the way, the company immediately terminated, and they drive off in a vehicle no one sees."

"Armored truck? Where did they get that?"

128

"They stole it, about 45 minutes earlier, from a company in Myrtle Beach. They found the real guards, tied up, gagged, and blindfolded, in the back of the truck."

"Well, that's good news at least."

"What now, Ron? These guys are probably halfway to Wilmington by now."

"Maybe, Jim. But I think not. I believe we have until Saturday to catch them."

He hung up as Tim approached.

"Who was that?"

"Buttocks."

Smiling at Ron's reply, Tim offered, "Bad news travels fast."

"Yeah, but terrible news travels faster."

"I got something for you."

"Tell me it's something good."

Tim extended his hand.

"What's this?"

"It a room key to a suite at the Marina Inn. I just found it on our dead bank robber."

CHAPTER 26

Artie and Dan were still eating when Nick sat down with them.

"Where's Aaron?" asked Dan.

"I think he's dead asleep behind the wheel of the car," chortled Nick.

"What's that supposed to mean, Nick?" asked Artie, somewhat afraid of hearing the answer.

"I told you guys that we needed to cut ties with Aaron. He was a hot potato. If the police caught him again, he'd crack like a dropped egg."

"What about that hotel manager?" asked Dan.

"What about him?"

"You mentioned that Aaron and you had a run-in with him last night. If he sees Aaron's face on tv, he'll have the cops here in no time," reasoned Artie.

"I'm happy to report that the manager is out of the picture also, Artie, but not for the reason you think."

"What! You offed the manager!" whispered Dan.

"What do you mean not for the reason we think?" asked Artie, also in shock.

"I'll let you know, Artie. But now is not the time."

"You're talking in riddles, Nick," expressed Dan, shaking his head while returning his attention back to the French toast he had ordered for breakfast.

The waitress approached the table, asking Nick if he would like something to drink.

"Yes. I'll have a glass of tomato juice, hi-test coffee, and a toasted bagel with creme cheese and strawberry jam, please."

Soon after the waitress brought Nick his juice and coffee, they reviewed what lay ahead, stopping only when the waitress brought Nick's bagel.

"Make sure you leave nothing in your room for the authorities to find," reminded Nick.

"Why would they look here?" asked Artie.

"One never knows, Artie, what might happen between now and then. It's always possible that one of us may screw up along the way. Who knows, but let's say, our waitress remembers us. Next thing you know, boom, the FBI is searching our rooms. They find something you forgot to pack. You left a fingerprint. Maybe you forget to flush the toilet and now they have your DNA."

Glancing at his watch, and seeing it was 7:00, Dan said, "Well, seeing that Aaron isn't part of the team anymore, how are we going to handle this, Nick? We have two hours before they unlock their doors. How we gonna do this now?"

"Simple, Dan. Artie will be the driver. He'll drop us off where we plan to pick up the armored truck. Once we have the truck, you and I will drive to the office. Once we're inside, Artie will bring the Yukon and park alongside the armored truck, so that no one inside sees our escape vehicle. You and I will go inside, get the money, exit into the Yukon and drive to the beach house I rented for the next three days."

"Can just the two of us handle what's inside the building, Nick?"

"We'll have AK-47s, Dan. Nobody in there will challenge us. If they do, we kill them."

"If there is as much money as you say, it may be a problem trying to carry it out."

"Sounds like a pleasant problem to me, Dan. What say you, Artie?"

"Ss-ss-sure does, Nick."

"Let's check out and get this show on the road, gentlemen. There's gold in them there hills!"

It was 8:20 when they pulled into the armored car company's lot. Nick and Dan, wearing clown masks, left the Yukon and proceeded to a side door where they had watched two uniformed armored guards enter. As Dan opened the door, Nick pulled a gun from his waistband and walked inside. Dan followed with his weapon in hand.

It took only minutes to locate the two employees they saw entering the building minutes earlier. They were busy reviewing their routes for the day and never heard Nick and Dan walk in on them.

Not until they heard, "Gentlemen, don't make a sound and you both might live to have dinner with your family tonight. Now, does that sound reasonable, fellas?"

Both men nodded as they stared down the barrels of two .45 caliber handguns.

"I'm glad you agree," said Nick. "Now, fellas, if you would take off your uniforms. When you're done, get on the floor and put your hands behind your backs."

A minute later both men were lying on the floor in their underwear. Dan, using zip ties, secured their hands behind their backs.

"Now gentlemen," said Nick, "I will ask you one time, and one time only, and whoever tells me first, doesn't get a bullet in the back of his head. Now, here's the question: what is the code used at Burroughs and Chapin to allow entry?"

"9-4-1-0-2!" both men screamed as loud as they could.

"Hmm, sounded like a tie to me, partner. How did you hear it?"

"I'd have to agree," said a beaming Dan. "So, should we shoot them both? I'll take the tall one, you get the other guy."

"Please, don't!" screamed the taller of the two men.

"They both called out the same code, partner. I believe they told us the truth, Nick. How about we just gag and blindfold them for now? If it turns out they lied, we'll have time to kill them."

"We didn't lie, mister! I swear, we didn't," yelled the taller of the two.

"I believe you, sir," replied Nick with a big grin on his face. "Okay, partner, gag and blindfold them. We need to get these uniforms on. Time is running short. We have five minutes."

A few minutes later, Dan and Nick had donned the two men's uniforms. Dan's uniform was tight in the legs but would suffice for the next hour.

"Okay, gentlemen, here's what's happening next. You will stand, walk outside, and get into the armored truck. Once inside, you will lie face down on the floor. We will tie your legs and you will remain in that position until they find you, which should be less than an hour from now. Don't give us a hard time, and we won't put a bullet in your head. Anyone have a problem with that?"

Both men shook their heads.

"Good. Let's proceed."

Dan had backed the truck up to the door and had the rear doors open. The chances of someone seeing the two half-naked guards climb into the back of the truck were near nil.

As the guards got down on the floor, Nick, just a moment before he closed the doors, reminded them of the consequences if they made a single peep.

Seeing that one guard had soiled himself convinced Nick they wouldn't be a problem.

It was 8:56 when the armored vehicle reached the traffic signal where vehicles turned to enter the Grand Dunes.

Burroughs and Chapin had scheduled the truck to be at the office at 9:00am. The light changed and Dan made the left turn, drove a few hundred feet, and then made a right into the driveway that led to the Burroughs and Chapin offices. They pulled up to the front door at 9:00, just as expected. Nick, holding his cell phone, sent a one-word text to Artie: Arrived.

Dan and Nick, both carrying AK-47s, exited the truck and went to the front door.

Nick entered the 5-digit code on a pad to the right of the double door. A click followed and the door unlocked. Dan opened the door, and both men walked in brandishing their AK-47s.

A security guard, whose name tag read *Ted*, greeted them at the door. He seemed surprised at seeing the heavy-duty weapons.

"What's with the firepower, fellas? You never carried like that before."

"We were told to be more careful, Ted," explained Nick. "The FBI says the guys who robbed Bank of America last week are still around. We're taking extra precautions."

"Seems like a reasonable thing to do," agreed the clueless guard. "I'll call down for the money. They tell me they have almost two and a half million this week."

"You don't say," said Nick, as he surreptitiously sent Artie another one word text: Now.

"I'm curious as to why the regular crew of Eddie and Smitty aren't here," stated Ted.

"They got suspended for a couple of weeks for violating company policy," answered Nick.

"You don't say. What did they do?"

"They got a speeding ticket while driving the armored truck."

"Damn!" cried Ted. "That was stupid."

"Don't mention it to them when they return. They're embarrassed enough as it is."

"I won't say a word, fellas. Say, do you fellas want me to help you carry it out to the truck?"

"No, that won't be necessary, Ted, but thanks for the offer," answered Dan.

An elevator dinged, and two doors slid open. A huge black man, pushing a cart, holding two large footlocker like containers, emerged.

"You guys may want to use this cart to take the cash out to your truck," suggested the man named Earl. "These boxes are heavy this week. They sold a lot of property over the past few weeks."

"Must be so," quipped Nick. "Ted says there's two and a half million."

"Closer to three," Earl stated with conviction.

"Well, we'll make sure this gets to where it's going," said Dan, as he flung his strapped weapon over his shoulder and lifted a box off the cart. "Mind getting the door for me, Ted?"

"Sure thing, fella," said Ted as he punched in a code to open the outside doors.

"Hold that door for me, Ted!" Nick pleaded as he removed the second box from the cart. "Thanks, fellas. We'll see you next week."

Artie parked across the street in the lot belonging to Pirates Voyage and The Carolina Opry.

When he received Nick's first text, he started up the Yukon and drove to the Grand Dunes Boulevard intersection.

When the second text came, he turned right onto Grand Dunes Boulevard, but a red light prevented his crossing Route 17.

Nick, however, had calculated for traffic signals in his plan, so Artie showed no concern at being delayed.

A moment later, the light changed and Artie drove across Route 17 and into the Grand Dunes property. He made the same right turn Dan had made minutes earlier. Driving up to the building, he parked parallel on the outside of the armored truck. For anyone inside looking out, the Yukon was invisible.

Artie, dressed in a uniform that closely matched that of the uniforms worn by his partners, exited the Yukon. He moved to the back of the armored truck and opened its left side backdoor.

"How you doing, fellas," he said to the two trussed up men. "Oops, it looks like one of you had the ss-ss-shit ss-ss-scared out of him."

Artie moved to the Yukon where he opened the side door behind the driver's seat.

After opening the vehicle's back door, Artie moved to stand behind the rear corner of the armored truck. From there, his partners, under the guise of putting the boxes inside the armored truck, would instead hand them to Artie, who would place them in the Yukon's back seat. The armored car's open rear door would provide the illusion that Dan was placing the boxes into the armored vehicle.

After handing both boxes off to Artie, Dan closed the armored truck's rear door and he and Nick returned to the cab.

But that was also an illusion.

Although it appeared as if Nick was heading to the cab, he instead climbed into the Yukon's back seat. Dan got into his driver's position, but then slid over and exited the cab via the passenger door. He then climbed behind the wheel of the Yukon and with Artie riding shotgun, drove off.

The armored vehicle would sit at the front door for ten minutes before Ted would notice it hadn't departed.

I wonder what's holding them up. He thought.

It took another ten minutes before Ted ventured out to determine the problem and discovered the tied up guards.

When asked about the men who had collected the money, a confused Ted replied, "They don't look the same in their damn underpants."

It was 9:09 when they pulled out of the Burroughs & Chapin offices. Nick instructed Dan to head south on Route 17.

"That went even smoother than I planned," laughed Nick, sitting in the back seat with two shiny aluminum boxes containing somewhere in the neighborhood of three million dollars

"This was the best heist ever, Nick," snorted Artie.

Dan agreed, saying, "Smooth, Nick. Ever so smooth. Now, we just wait until Saturday. Right?"

"Yep, we will leave Saturday morning along with the other quarter million people. The only difference is, we'll have three million bucks with us!"

"Damn, I almost feel like giving back Bank of America's measly quarter-million bucks," joked Artie.

"That beach house I rented in Garden City cost $6000 bucks for just three days! That damn owner saw me coming, that's for sure."

"You mean ss-ss-someone pulled one over on you, Nick? That's a first!"

"Where is this place, Nick?" asked Dan. "I'll put the address in our GPS."

Nick, eyeing Artie harshly, spit out the address. "It's 900 Pine Avenue."

Dan pulled up to the front of the beach house at 9:41.

"Back into the driveway, Dan," instructed Nick. "We don't need anyone seeing the plates. We'll get a rental tomorrow."

"That's a monster beach house, Nick!" exclaimed Artie, as he departed the Yukon's passenger seat.

"Just take our personal items into the house now," ordered Nick. "Leave the money and the AK-47's. We'll come get them when it gets dark. I don't want people seeing us caring two big-ass silver boxes into the house."

"You want us to just leave three million in the car, Nick! Are you mad?" asked a shocked Dan.

"I doubt that's the case, Danny. Relax, all will be okay. Pull down the rear seat, Artie," instructed Nick. "I'll slide the boxes and guns into the back. There's a retractable cover that hides whatever you have lying back there. When we get our bags from the back, just pull the cover closed."

A few minutes later, the three men entered the beach house, found a bedroom, and dumped their suitcases in them.

"Let's take turns watching the vehicle," suggested Nick. "We'll take two-hour watches. That gives everyone four hours between watches to sleep, eat, do whatever you can do that is within walking range."

"What are your plans, Nick?" asked Artie.

"I plan on taking a solid two-hour nap. You have the first watch, Artie. Dan will relieve you at noon, and Dan, I'll relieve you at 2:00."

"Sounds good, Nick," said Dan, flopping on a couch and turning on a tv. "Judge Judy comes on at 10:00."

Each man took two shifts of two hours, giving Nick the last watch at 8:00.

It was 9:20pm when Nick came looking for Artie.

"Where's Dan?"

"He ss-ss-sleeping in his bedroom," answered Artie.

"Let's not disturb him. You and I can get the money."

"Ss-ss-sounds good to me, Nick."

Nick opened the back hatch of the Yukon, reached in, and dragged one of the money boxes out to where Artie could grab one end of it.

"Let's take them inside one at a time, Artie. Damn thing has to weigh a ton!"

"There must be a helluva mix of bills, Nick."

"Why do you say that?"

"I read somewhere that a million dollars in hundred-dollar bills weighs less than 20 pounds, whereas a million in twenties weighs over a hundred."

"Damn, it may take us longer to split up than I thought."

"It might, but I can think of worse things," replied Artie with a gleeful smile.

Turns out, Artie was right. There was a mix of bills, including tens and fives.

After getting both metal boxes into the house, Nick suggested they get the guns as well. Artie obliged and went to retrieve the AK-47s. When he came back, he heard water running.

"Nick? Where are you?"

"In here, Artie. Look at this nice jacuzzi in my bathroom."

Artie made his way to Nick's bathroom, but when he entered, Nick, using the butt end of his .45, slugged him right between the eyes. Artie, bleeding like a stuck pig, went down like a tree.

Nick picked him up off the floor, placed him into the rapidly filling tub and, using all of his weight, held Artie's head under the water. Artie had swallowed a lot of water before regaining consciousness and, realizing he was on the verge of drowning, began fighting for his life. He fought hard, but it wasn't enough.

When Artie's kicking and flailing ended, Nick took his hands off Artie's head and stood up. A final bubble escaped Artie's mouth, only to burst when it reached the surface. Nick, exhausted, turned off the water, dried his hands on a towel, killed the lights, and closed the door as he exited the room.

An hour later Dan appeared from his long nap. Seeing the metal boxes, he said, "I see you guys got the money. You should have woken me."

"Artie and I handled it," said Nick, his eyes on the 60-inch tv that was playing a west coast baseball game.

"Where's Artie?"

"He's in the jacuzzi imitating a rock."

"What the hell does that mean, Nick?"

"I drowned him."

"You drowned… but why?"

"Don't you read the papers or watch the news, Dan? The cops, the FBI, or anyone else wearing a badge is looking for a man who stutters. That manager at the Marina Inn was about to call the FBI when I stopped him. He realized Artie was the stuttering man the FBI is looking for. Artie was a liability, Dan! He needed eliminating."

"Do I have any liabilities I'm not aware of, Nick? I need to know because it seems you enjoy disposing of liabilities."

"Think of it this way, Dan. Your share of those two boxes is now one and a half million."

"That's great if I live long enough to spend it, Nick. I think I'll lock my door tonight. It seems we have the boogeyman on the premises."

CHAPTER 27

"We'd like to speak with Mr. Tanner, please."

They had left the Wells Fargo Bank and driven straight to the Marina Inn. As they turned into the Grand Dunes off of Route 17, they saw the driveway leading to the offices of Burroughs and Chapin.

"We'll stop by on our way out, Tim."

"Good idea, Ron. It must be a damn Chinese fire drill in there right now."

"I don't doubt it. I don't know who's planning all this, but he has his act together, that's for certain."

"Well, we know our boy back at the bank wasn't in on it."

"I disagree, partner. He made us believe that Wells Fargo was the target. That was a genius move. While they have a stiff holding half the law in the county at bay guarding a bank, they knock off a private enterprise to the tune of three million bucks. That, my friend, is the signature of a fucking genius!"

"I haven't seen Mr. Tanner at all this morning. He's in the building because his thermos is sitting on his desk. I'm Karen Hart, the assistant manager. How may I help you, gentlemen?"

Ron, holding out his badge, said, "FBI, we are here about three men that stayed at the inn. I'm Agent Ron Lee. This is my partner, Agent Tim Pond."

"Three men?"

"Yes. They may have checked out just a few hours ago. Is this is a room key for this hotel... oops, I meant, inn?" Ron asked while producing the key.

"Why, yes it is, sir."

"What room?"

"Let me have it, Agent Lee."

Ron handed her the key, and she slipped it into a reader of some type.

"It's suite 419, sir. A Mr. Thomas Bidwell and another unnamed man checked in on Monday at 3:00."

"Who else checked in around 3:00, Ms. Hart? It would have been two men."

She scanned the check-ins and saw that two other men checked in just 15 minutes later.

"A Mr. Norm Sedgefield and a man friend checked in at 3:15. They were in suite 502."

"Did you see these men?"

"I didn't, and our security tapes won't have them checking out either."

"Why the hell not!" Ron barked.

"They self-checked out in their room."

"Can we see the tapes when they checked in?"

"I'm afraid we only keep those tapes for 24 hours, sir. Someone on staff would have erased them by now."

"Oh, damn! Please, tell me there's someone who might recall seeing these men."

"I can ask the wait staff. If they ate in the hotel, someone might recall them."

"Ask! And find Mr. Tanner for us."

"Yes, sir," said Karen Hart as she scurried off to the dining room.

As they stood waiting for Karen's return, a young Latin-looking man stepped behind the counter.

"Do you work here?" asked Tim.

"Yes, sir. May I be of service?"

"What's your name?"

"Carlos Alvarez."

"Have you seen this man in the past two or three days, Carlos?" asked Tim as he held up a photo of the late Aaron Moore.

"I'm sorry, sir, but who are you to ask?"

"Sorry, Carlos. We are the FBI," said Tim, while showing his badge.

"FBI. Oh, my."

"So have you seen this man?"

"Oh, yes, sir. He is in room 419 with Mr. Bidwell."

"That's an amazing memory you have, Carlos,"

"Yes, sir. I just remember faces and names. I don't remember hearing his full name, but I remember Mr. Bidwell calling him by Aaron."

"Can you describe this Mr. Bidwell for us?"

"Yes, sir, but better yet, you can see him on tape talking with Mr. Tanner this morning by the elevator."

"Mr. Tanner was talking with him this morning?"

"Yes, sir. I saw them talking by the elevators. I looked again a few minutes later, and they weren't there."

"We'd like to see those tapes, Carlos."

"Yes, sir, but I must ask Mr. Tanner's permission."

"Mr. Tanner isn't around, Carlos."

"Then you will need Ms. Hart's authorization to view the tapes, sir. Here she comes now."

They both looked up to see the returning assistant manager. She had a young girl in tow.

"Agent Lee, this is Darlene Davis. She said she waited on the man you are seeking. He joined two other men for breakfast around 6:45."

"Thank you, Ms. Hart. Carlos has something he needs you to do. And I would ask that you please do it now," Ron said, with his trademark bluntness.

Turning to Darlene, he asked, "Did you talk with those men or overhear anything they were saying?"

"Can't say I spoke with any of them other than to take their orders."

"Did you notice any quirks they may have had?"

"They were great tippers, that I can tell you!"

"That's nice, but we're looking for things more specific, like looks, weight, tall, short, accents, how they talked…"

"Oh, the one guy, the smallest one, had a stuttering problem. Couldn't say words like salt and sugar."

"That's our boys, all right," whispered Tim.

"Agent Lee?"

It was Ms. Hart, calling out to them from Tanner's office.

"Yes, miss," answered Ron.

"I have that footage of Mr. Tanner and the other fella talking at the elevator."

"Tim, call Heather. Ask her to send a sketch artist to sit with Darlene. Try to recall the features of those three men, Darlene. If you think of anything that seems important, give my partner a yell. We'll be in Mr. Tanner's office."

As they stepped into Tanner's office, Karen said, "This is where Mr. Tanner runs into, literally, Mr. Bidwell. If you go back a few seconds, you'll see Mr. Tanner leaving the dining area. He seems in a hurry and doesn't notice Mr. Bidwell coming out of the elevator."

"Let's take it back, Ms. Hart, to where you first see Mr. Tanner."

"Very well, sir."

Karen ran it back a few seconds and then hit the play button. They watched as Tanner exited the dining room. As he walked, he continuously looked back toward the dining room. His face looked worried.

"Are there cameras in the dining room also, Ms. Hart?"

"Yes, sir. Mr. Tanner had two cameras placed in there."

"Do you still have this morning's activities?"

"Oh, yes. They won't erase those until tomorrow evening."

"I'd like to see those tapes before we go any further."

"Won't take but a minute, sir."

Shortly after, they watched as Tanner entered the dining area. He stopped at numerous tables to say good morning to the guests. They saw him stop and speak with two men sitting at a table near the dining room exit. It appeared to be a pleasant ongoing conversation between the three men. That all changed when the shorter man held up what appeared to be an empty sugar packet. The man said something to Tanner that changed the manager's entire demeanor.

"Look at his eyes, Ron," said Tim. "He looks like he just saw the alien from the movie by the same name!"

"The look of recognition and fear," Ron stated.

At first Tanner appeared to have frozen up right where he stood. A moment later, he nodded and scurried away to speak with Darlene.

"Stop the tape!" commanded Ron. Looking out toward the front desk and seeing the dining room waitress, he yelled, "Darlene! Come in here, please."

Darlene, hearing the gruffness in the big agent's voice, became afraid. *What could I have done to piss off the FBI,* she wondered.

Hurrying into Tanner's office, she approached Ron, saying, "I admit I didn't report all my tips, sir!"

"I'm FBI, Darlene, not the IRS, and I don't give a rat's ass if you reported your tips or not. In fact, if I were you, I wouldn't report them either."

"Oh. You called me?"

"Yeah, I want you to watch this tape, and tell me what Mr. Tanner said to you."

Darlene watched the brief ten-second tape, then said, "He told me to take some sugar over to table ten."

"Anything else you may have noticed?"

"Yeah, his voice."

"What about his voice?"

"It wasn't strong and filled with assurance."

"It was… weenie-like. I never heard that tone from Mr. Tanner before."

"That was very descriptive, Darlene," said Tim.

"Okay, Darlene, you can go back to the restaurant. Thank you."

"I recalled something, sir."

"Oh, and what is that?"

"The man with the stutter."

"Yeah, what about him?"

"Well, he tried to call me sweetie, but he couldn't get it out and his friend said, 'Artie, she's way too young for you, so give it up.'"

"They called him Artie?"

"Yes, sir."

"Thank you, Darlene," Tim said with a smile. "If you recall anything else, come running!"

"Let's watch the elevator tapes from where we left off," said Ron.

"What did that dining room tape tell you, Ron?"

"I think when that guy held up the empty sugar pack, he asked if Tanner could get him more. I'm guessing that Tanner has been watching the news or reading the papers. The guy must have stuttered when asking for the sugar, and it set Tanner to believing these guys are the wanted bank robbers. He was hi-tailing it to his office when he bumped into the guy walking out of the elevator."

They continued to watch the tape and saw the two men collide.

Although it amounted to nothing more than a minor fender-bender, Tanner, embarrassed, goes about apologizing profusely.

The tape continued with the two men carrying on a conversation with Tanner continuously looking toward the dining room. Then, as Tanner makes a move to get past Bidwell, he stops and looks down at his waist.

"What's happening, Ron?"

"I'm not sure, Tim. They're talking, but their faces are close. Way too close for a friendly conversation."

"Yeah, I agree, Ron. And look at Tanner. He looks under duress and although the camera doesn't capture it, I believe he's sweating."

"I believe you're right, partner."

"They're walking toward the elevators, Ron."

"Yeah, the penthouse elevator."

They watch as Tanner punched in the code and the elevator doors slid open. Both men stepped into the elevator and the doors closed.

Less than four minutes pass when the elevator doors open again.

Bidwell walks out and turns toward the dining room and walks out of the camera's range.

"Put the dining tape back on, Ms. Hart."

"Okay, but where is Mr. Tanner?"

Ron and Tim exchanged knowing glances.

"I'm afraid that Mr. Tanner may be dead, miss."

Hearing a loud thump behind them, they turned around to see that Ms. Hart had fainted.

"Carlos!" Ron yelled. "Ms. Hart has fainted. Attend to your manager."

"She is my assistant manager, sir."

"Yeah, well, I think there's an opening that needs filling. A promotion is in the wind, Carlos. Think about that."

Turning their attention back to the screen, they saw Bidwell enter the dining room and sit with the two men who were already well into their breakfast.

"That prick is the leader, Tim. You can see it in his eyes. I'll bet you a dollar to a donut he shot his own man and left him in that car."

"Yeah, well, I'll bet you a buck and a quarter to a donut, that you're right, Ron," Tim said with a laugh.

Ron gave his partner the single-finger salute, then said, "Cancel the sketch artist. Take this tape to the lab. Our labs guys can garner some still photos of those three bastards. We'll have their damn faces all over the news before dinnertime. I want these fucking bastards dead or in cuffs before the day ends!"

It was a nice goal, but it wasn't to be.

CHAPTER 28

Thursday, July 4, 2019 – 8:00am

    Tim pulled into Ron's driveway and beeped the horn twice. The passenger seat held a bag of Krispy Kreme donuts. Two cups of coffee, one medium, one large, sat in the cupholders between the front seats.

    A third beep of the horn had Ron opening the door and giving his partner the single-digit salute.

    "Patience isn't one of your best attributes," Ron said as he opened the door and climbed in.

    "Being punctual ain't anywhere near the top of your list of attributes, pal."

    "Damn, Tim, it's only 8:03. Three minutes makes me... what, unpunctual?"

    "It's the friggin' fourth of July, Ron! It's a day off for every American except for you and me. Not only do I have to pick you up at your house, as if I'm your personal driver, but I'm also required to bring the obligatory coffee and donuts. And at no charge to you, I may add. Then, I must wait while you do who knows what! Am I pissed? You bet your big fat ass I'm pissed. I expected to spend the fourth with the family."

    "Did you remember to have cream put in my coffee?"

    "Yeah, I remembered."

    "Did you get those chocolate-covered crème donuts?"

    "Three of them."

    "Oh? What are the other two?"

    "Sour crème."

    "Oh, yeah, I like those! Did you get yourself a peanut donut?"

"I ate my donut. Everything in the bag is yours. Where the hell are we going?"

"I want to go to Judge Nancy Bracken's home."

"We've been there."

"I know. I'm betting that there's something we missed when we were there last. Wait! That's an unfair statement to make. On our previous visit, we didn't know what we were looking for. Now, I think we do."

"Will it help us catch the killer?"

"All I can say, it's similar to the Lady Justice scenario."

"How so?"

"Let's get there first to re-verify my suspicions."

Twenty minutes and four donuts later, Tim pulled into Nancy Bracken's drive.

Two minutes after their arrival, they were inside the house, and Ron was perusing the judge's bookshelves.

"What are you looking for, Ron?"

"This," as he pulled a book down from the shelf and handed it to Tim. "Notice the book's title, partner."

"Okay, I'm holding a book. Now what?"

Tim looked down to see it was a copy of *Catch Me If You Can.*

"Damn, Ron, this book has been at every murder scene."

"Open it. If I'm right, there should be a bookmark at the start of chapter four."

Tim opened the book and sure enough, there it was!

"You have yourself a bingo, Ron!" announced Tim.

"He's putting the bookmark at the chapter matching his number of kills."

"That's right. The judge was the fourth."

"We couldn't be sure of how many he had killed, but he indicates the number with these bookmarks."

"So what now?"

"Remember what I said about it being similar to the Lady Justice scenario?"

"Yeah, so."

"What did we do after we collected a few of the Lady Justice figurines, Tim?"

Tim gave thought to Ron's question and after a moment or two, his face lit up.

"We found the store that sold them!"

"Bingo, partner."

"I guess we're off to bookstores."

"We are," affirmed Ron. "Are they open today?"

"Hell, I believe all but government buildings are open today. That, Ron, includes our building."

"That's why I had you pick me up, Tim-o-thy!"

CHAPTER 29

Thursday, July 4, 2019 – 6:00pm

"What are we going to do with his body, Nick? If we leave it in that tub of water, it will bloat. I don't want to mess with a bloated body."

"He isn't bloating, Dan. I emptied the tub last night. In fact," Nick paused to look at his watch, "in another 75 to 80 minutes, there will be no sign of Artie in the tub."

"What the hell are you saying, Nick?"

"I went out last night and bought several containers of Drano. It's a sodium hydroxide, which, if you knew your chemistry, will dissolve a body in three to four hours."

"God, Nick. What are you? I never knew you were this…"

"Brilliant?"

"I was leaning more toward… sadistic."

"Interesting you would say that Dan. We being best of friends and all."

"Yeah, but that's when I didn't know how fucked up you are."

"I guess this means we are no longer friends, Dan?"

"Well, I won't be inviting you to any more of my birthday parties, providing I live long enough to have another birthday."

"You're not a liability, Dan. Aaron and Artie were. If they had gotten caught, they would have hung us out to dry. I had to do what I did."

"Yeah, well, when we leave on Saturday, we will be forever parting, Nick. No hard feelings, I hope," expressed Dan as he turned on the television.

"None here, Dan!" answered Nick as he headed toward the kitchen to get a beer.

"Oh, shit!"

"What is it, Dan?"

"It looks like we're both a liability now, Nick."

Nick looked at the tv screen and saw three headshot photos of Artie, Dan, and himself.

"Yeah," he muttered, "it seems we are."

CHAPTER 30

Thursday, July 5, 2019 – 4:40pm

They started at the north end of the beach and worked their way south, but after visiting the Conway Barns and Nobles, Ron made a call. He put his phone on speaker so Tim could join in on the conversation.

"Hello."

"Linda Ketron?"

"Yes, this is she."

"Linda, this is Special Agent Ron Lee calling."

"Oh, how you doing Agent Lee?"

"Doing fine, ma'am. I've got a question or two for you."

"Ask away, sir."

"When you hold your Feasts, is it always at the south end of the strand?"

"I'd say it's held 99% of the time down this way. I know the restaurants down here, and they know me."

"What percentage of the attendees are from the south end?"

"That's hard to quantify, Agent Lee, seeing that I'm not all that familiar with most of the attendees, but if I had to guess, I'd say 75% or better."

"What's the biggest bookstore at that end of the beach?"

"I'd say it was Books-a-Million at Inlet Mall. Are you familiar with it?"

"Oh, yes, I am. It's quite familiar, in fact," said Ron while recalling Bill Baxter's close encounter with death at the hands of the murderess, Vivian Hanson.

"I think many of our ladies buy their books there. Are there any more questions, Agent Lee?"

"Not at the moment. Now, remember what we told you about staying alert."

"How can I not? Look what happened to poor Lillian."

"I beg your pardon, Linda? Who is Lillian? And what happened to her?"

"You don't know? Her name is Lillian Black, and she was 92 years of age. Someone killed her Tuesday afternoon. Bludgeoned her to death with a tire iron!"

"And you knew her how?"

"Lillian has been a regular Movable Feast attendee for over twenty years!"

"No one informed us, and I think I know why," said Ron, hanging up the phone without saying goodbye.

"Head to Inlet Mall, Tim."

"There's a Barnes and Nobles in The Market Commons. Shouldn't we stop there first?"

"If Books-a-Million is a bust, we'll stop on our way back," Ron said with a curtness Tim wasn't used to hearing from his partner. "Right this minute though, I need to speak with Baxter."

The phone rang twice before Bill Baxter answered.

What he heard was a seething, *"Why the fuck weren't we notified about Lillian Black!"*

"Whoa, take it easy there, Ron. I'm not one of your subordinates you're talking to."

Ron, ignoring Baxter's reply, barked, *"Why?"*

"Because it wasn't the Friday Night killer. That's why!" Baxter screamed back.

"So you concluded it wasn't the Friday night killer, because it occurred on a Tuesday?"

"No, I concluded that because the woman's throat was still intact."

Ron sat silent for a moment, pondering Bill's words. *"What was it then?"*

"Appears to be a break-in. The woman, using a knife, put up a fight, but it wasn't enough to overcome her intruder. He beat her with a tire iron."

"How many blows?"

"What? Why would that matter?"

"God dammit, answer my damn question, Bill! How many blows?"

It wouldn't be difficult to interpret the silence at the other end of the phone as anything but Baxter sitting there seething.

"At least seven," he muttered with reluctance.

"At least seven blows! An intruder beats a 92-year-old woman at least seven times with a tire iron. At her age, she had to be dead after two. But he kept going. Why? Seven indicates anger, even hate. He knew her, Bill! That's why!"

Baxter, realizing Ron had run him over like a truck, asked, "So what are you saying, Ron?"

"I don't know the bottom line yet, Bill, but I'll see you tomorrow, and we'll discuss it. Oh, and Bill, I'm sorry I lost my temper."

Click.

"While we're at Books-a-Million," suggested Tim, "maybe you should pick up a copy of *How to Win Friends and Influence People*."

"While I do that, why don't you pick up a copy of *Keep Your Fucking Yap Shut*," snapped Ron.

The rest of the ride to the Books-a-Million store was as quiet as a graveyard.

"May I help you, gentlemen?"

"FBI," snorted Ron while flashing his badge. "We need to know if someone bought a large quantity of a specific book. Is that something you can determine?"

"I might, sir, but I can tell you that buying books in bulk is not unusual. School and library personnel do it all the time. What is the title of the book?"

"Catch Me If You Can," answered Ron.

"We do carry that book, and it doesn't sound like a book a teacher would purchase in bulk. Let me check its inventory history. Excuse me, I'll be back in a few moments."

"What's our options if this doesn't work out, Ron?"

"We check out all those people Linda Ketron gave us."

"What about our bank robbers?"

"You ask too many damn questions, Tim."

"I could be wrong, but you seem agitated, Ron."

"Your detective skills are as sharp as ever, partner."

Tim was ready with another quip, but the clerk returned, saying, "We had ten copies sold to an individual just last month. It was on June 1st to be exact."

"Might you have the name of the person who purchased those books?"

"Yes, I have it right here. It was a lady…"

"A lady! Are you sure?" asked Tim.

"I'm assuming that Charlene is a woman's name."

"Charlene who?"

"Charlene McSweeny."

"His first kill," murmured Ron.

"How many copies did you say she bought?" asked Tim.

"Ten."

"He's got six remaining, Ron. The man has ambitious plans."

"Who sold the books to her?" asked Ron of the clerk.

"Sonya Redding. She's stocking books in row 9," said the clerk, pointing to a spot over Ron's shoulder.

"Thanks for your help," said Tim as he turned to catch up with Ron, who had already headed in Sonya's direction.

High on one of those sliding ladders used to reach higher shelves, was a woman Ron judged to be in her early thirties. She was tall, blond, and had legs that went on forever.

"Sonja? Sonja Redding?" asked Ron.

Looking downward at the two men, she asked, "May I be of service, gentlemen?"

She looked like a movie star. Her face was stunning, highlighted by a pair of blue eyes that would make a man's knees buckle.

Tim, seeing those legs, bit his tongue.

"Hopefully, you can," answered Ron. "We're from the FBI."

"FBI? Whatever could I do for the FBI?"

Her voice purred. Tim bit his tongue again.

"You sold a woman ten copies of *Catch Me If You Can* about a month ago. Do you recall that sale?"

"Yes, I do," she replied as she stepped down from the ladder.

She was indeed tall. At the least, four inches taller than Tim.

"Did she mention why she needed ten copies?"

"No, she didn't, and I didn't think it was my place to ask. She did mention that she was buying them for a close friend who was having back issues, as I recall."

"Male or female?"

"I beg your pardon?"

"Her friend. Was it a man or a woman?"

"She did say, 'he was having back issues.'"

"Can you recall anything else she may have said?"

"I know she was happy that she only had to carry them to Poppy's. I'm guessing she was meeting him there for lunch and to give him the books."

"Poppy's?"

"Yes, it's a small sandwich shop right out there on 17 business," she said, pointing out the window. "It's almost directly across from where we are."

"Is there anything else you can recall, miss?"

"It's Mrs. Redding, and that's all I can remember."

"You've been a great help. Thank you."

As they exited the door, Ron whispered, "You can stop drooling now, Tim. It's not befitting of an FBI agent."

"Did you see those legs! And how about that voice!"

"No, Tim, I guess I didn't. I must be the blind and deaf one. Dumb, I leave to you."

They headed to Poppy's deli, where no one would recalled seeing the woman.

"Dead end, Ron?"

"I wouldn't say that. At least we know our killer has a double signature."

"Double?"

"He leaves a copy of that book with a bookmark designating what number kill it is."

"And?"

"He has a propensity to slice the victim's larynx after they are dead."

"He's silencing them, isn't he?"

"Yes, he is, partner. The question, however, is what the hell could they all have said, that makes him want to kill them?"

"Look, it's going on 7:30, Ron. It's been a long day and I'm bushed. Let's call it a day."

"I'm in agreement, Tim. Pick me up at the house around 9:00 tomorrow morning."

"What! It's Friday! The second day of the long weekend!"

"Yeah, it will be a long weekend, no doubt about it. Tomorrow, being Friday, is the day our killer strikes. Also, let's not forget those three bank robbers are still in town, but no doubt preparing to leave Saturday morning."

"How do you figure that, Ron?"

"Saturday is moving day. About 200,000 people will leave town on Saturday and another 200,000 will arrive. They know we can't stop every vehicle. I guarantee you they will be somewhere in that flow of traffic."

"So what are we going to do?"

"Their pictures are all over tv and the papers," explained Ron. "Someone will see them and call. When we get that call, and I know we will, we have to be ready for what's coming."

"And what might that be?"

"I doubt we'll be taking them alive, Tim. They've killed and they have three million dollars plus."

"Oh, shit."

"Yeah, oh shit."

CHAPTER 31

Friday, July 5, 2019 – 10:00am

Judi Kiernan was dusting the living room furniture when she heard the back door open. She peeked around the corner to look into the kitchen to see that her husband, Bob, had come home.

"Bob, what are you doing home at this hour?" asked Judi. "I thought you and Bones had an all-day job to do at Jinny Stacy's house."

Bones' proper name was Jimmy Greer, but everyone called him Bones on account of his being six-foot three and weighing about 130 pounds. He looked like a walking skeleton with hair.

"We do," he answered as he marched toward her. "We ran short on some pipe. I told Bones I'd go back to the shop and pick it up. But I was lying."

It was then that she noticed he was wearing one of those cheap full-length see-through plastic raincoats with a hood and a face shield.

"Why are you wearing that raincoat, Bob?" she asked. "It ain't raining."

"No, it's not, and I have plenty of that pipe on the back porch."

"What are you saying, Bob?" asked Judi, her fear growing as she saw the look in his eyes.

"I've had enough, Judi," replied Bob. And with those words, the boxcutter he held in his hand swept through the air and across the throat of his hated wife.

Blood spurted everywhere, including onto Bob's see-through raincoat.

Judi fell to the floor with death just seconds away. Bob, emotionless, watched her die, then reached down and slit her throat again, slicing her larynx.

Bob took one last look at his dead wife, before walking out the back door. As he exited the back porch, he grabbed the extra length of PVC pipe he had left there earlier that morning.

He had parked his truck behind a grove of trees, some two hundred yards away. As he made his way toward it, he stripped himself of the raincoat, bunched it up and put it and the boxcutter into a bag.

As he drove back to the Stacy's, he added two bricks he had put in the truck earlier that morning to the bag.

Two miles from the Stacy's was a small creek. Bob stopped the truck on the small two-lane bridge that crossed the stream. After checking and seeing no one, he exited the truck and tossed the bag into the creek. The bag sunk in six-feet of water.

Bob had planned it well. He knew the job required 40 feet of PVC pipe, but when he carried the supplies inside to do the job, he only took in 30 feet.

He also suggested to Jinny that the two couples go to the Carolina Opry the next night.

"Should I call Judi and run it past her, Bob?"

"That would be a good idea, Jinny."

Jinny did just that and spent a good twenty minutes talking with Judi.

When Bob announced they were short of pipe, he sent Bones out to his truck to look for more.

Bones returned, saying, "There ain't no more pipe in your truck, Bob."

"Damn!" Bob cursed, faking the inconvenience. "I'll run back to the shop," he said. "I'll be back in 30 minutes."

The shop was only 12 miles away, as was Bob's house, but in opposite directions.

After killing his wife, Bob returned to the job site, extracted the pipe from the back of his truck and carried it inside. There he stayed, working until the police showed up at 2:30 to inform him of his wife's murder.

A FedEx driver, delivering a package, found her. The package, forgotten in the chaos that followed, remained unopened. If opened, someone would have found a bottle of rat poison Judi planned on feeding Bob at all the upcoming meals until he dropped dead.

But Bob, as the saying goes, "beat her to the punch."

His alibi was rock solid.

Jinny Stacy could attest to talking with Judi long after Bob had left for work, and who, along with Bones Greer, could attest to Bob's being on site all day.

Bob would never have come up with a way to kill his wife if it hadn't been for a late-night call he received two weeks earlier.

State Trooper Dennis Wade called one night with an emergency plumbing problem. Bob answered the call and as he worked, the two men talked.

"How's the police business going, Dennis?"

"I don't know if you've been following the news, Bob, but we got someone killing old women with a boxcutter."

"Hadn't heard about that," Bob answered.

"Well, the news isn't saying how he killed the women. Captain Baxter, that's my boss, calls the son-of-a-bitch, the Friday Killer."

"I'm guessing that all the killings happened on a Friday, Dennis?"

"Hey, you could be a detective, Bob," kidded Dennis.

"No thanks. I'll stick with plumbing."

"I don't blame you, Bob. Police work can be gruesome. For instance, this guy kills them and then slices their throat after they are dead, right down to the larynx."

"Sounds like a real sicko to me, Dennis. I hope you guys catch him soon."

"It won't be happening soon, Bob. They can't find a connection between the women, and that makes it difficult to determine a motive."

"All done!" announced Bob.

"What do I owe you?"

"Nothing. Next time you catch me speeding, just give me a warning."

"You got it, Bob. Thanks."

Bob had arrived at Dennis's house with no hope of getting out of his marriage. He left with a plan for the perfect kill.

Nope, trooper Wade didn't owe Bob Kiernan a damn thing.

CHAPTER 32

About an hour before Bob Kiernan would kill his wife, Tim was once again pulling into Ron's driveway. He blew the horn once, waited a minute, and blew it again.

No Ron.

A third toot of the horn saw the door open and Ron come trudging out.

"Good afternoon," Tim said with more than a bit of sarcasm as Ron opened the passenger door.

"Up yours, partner. You caught me dropping the browns off at the pool."

"Gee, thanks for sharing. I really needed to know that."

"I thought you'd want to know."

"Did you wash your hands?" asked Tim as he handed Ron the bag of donuts. "Maybe if you didn't eat so many donuts, you wouldn't need to spend the entire morning sitting on the throne."

"Maybe if you didn't talk so much, I wouldn't have to listen to your drivel. Is there anything new to report?"

"Yeah. Bell and Bell. It's a car dealership on up on Route 9."

"I know it. What about them?"

"They reported that someone stole a white Yukon off their lot and a plate taken off a vehicle parked in the service lane."

"Anything on their security tapes?"

"Nothing, but they had a 30 minute gap."

"Ahh, so our clever thieves disable the security system, steal the vehicle of choice, and hoping no one notices a vehicle is missing, they reconnect the security system."

"That's how I read it, Ron."

"Now, does that sound like your typical car thief to you, Tim-o-thy?"

"No, it does not!"

"It sounds like something a sophisticated bank robbery team might do, though."

"Agreed." said Tim.

"So?"

"So I put out an BOLO for a white 2017 GMC Yukon with SC plates reading FGU-5597."

"I doubt they will use that vehicle to get out of town. They know that we know they have stolen it. They'll be finding something else to drive if they haven't already."

"Okay, Ron, what's the plan for today?"

"Let's go check out the woman's... Lillian Black... murder scene while we wait."

"Wait? Wait for what?"

"The next kill. It is Friday, isn't it?"

"It is," acknowledged Tim.

They were approaching Lillian's house in Queens Harbor when Tim asked, "How are we going to get in?"

"I called Baxter last night. He said he'd have a trooper there."

"What's the address, Ron?"

"It's 409 Pennington Loop."

Tim pulled up in front of the house at 9:45. A state trooper vehicle was sitting there. As Ron and Tim emerged from their car, a trooper emerged from his.

"Federal agents Lee and Pond?"

"Yes, Officer," the two answered, while flashing their badges.

"I unlocked both the front and back doors, gentlemen."

"Thank you, Officer," said Tim with a nod of his head.

"If you enter through the back door, you'll walk right into the murder scene. I suggest you enter through the front door."

"That's an excellent suggestion, Officer," replied Ron.

Tim opened the front door and seeing light switches on the wall to his right, he flicked them all on. Lights in the hallway, living room, an overhead ceiling fan, and the outside lights that lit the entrance all came on.

Lillian Black may have been 92 years-of-age, but her furniture was even older.

"Damn!" exclaimed Tim. "I'd bet furniture gurus would classify most of this stuff as antiques."

"I must agree, Tim, although it looks in pretty good shape."

They made their way through the house of two bedrooms, two baths, a living room, a small sunporch, a kitchen, and a laundry/mud room where the killing occurred.

The living room and sunroom both had bookshelves filled with books. As Ron perused the books, he made a mental note to ask Linda Ketron for a list of the past year's Movable Feast authors and the title of their books.

"Tim, check her bedroom for an appointment book or calendar. I'll check out the kitchen."

Ron entered the kitchen and found it to be far more up-to-date than he expected. The stainless steel appliances appeared to be almost new. The small four-seat kitchen table, however, was more in line with the rest of the furniture in the house.

He opened the laundry room door. Seeing a wall switch on his right, he flicked it on and the small room lit up.

A tipped over ironing board and an iron lay where they fell during the struggle.

Ron took one step inside. His mind tried to replay the killing scene. It couldn't. Not yet. He needed more information.

Another step took him within four feet of the blood-stained floor. He could see in his mind, the enraged killer, tire iron in hand, striking the woman's frail head over and over. Blood spraying in all directions. To the right he saw the chalk outline of a large knife lying next to the door.

He turned and looked back at the fallen ironing board and iron. He saw the tipped over box of detergent and only then noticed the spilled detergent on the floor.

Now, in his mind, Ron played the scene as it may have happened.

This is where she surprised him. He must have gotten in somehow. Maybe she heard him. She grabbed a knife and swung open the door, catching him by surprise. She swung the knife at him, two or three times. While driving him backward, the ironing board tipped over and the box of detergent overturned and spilled onto the floor. She drove him against the door. Trapped, he swung the tire iron and hit her, causing her to drop the knife. Then, seeing her disarmed, he beat her to death.

He advanced no further. If he had advanced, a blood trail would have indicated it to be so. No, he left. He didn't come to steal. He came to kill.

Ron opened the back door and stepped out onto the small concrete slab. Three brick steps led to the ground. He stepped down and looked around. Lillian's trashcan was occupying a space to the right of the steps. He walked over to it and lifted the lid. A single bag of garbage lay inside.

He was about to walk the perimeter when he heard Tim call from inside, "Hey, Ron. Where are you?"

"I'm out back, Tim. You find something?"

"Yeah, I did, and it is strange."

Ron rushed back inside and saw Tim leaning against the counter below the cupboards.

"What do you have?"

"This," said Tim, holding up a small writing pad.

Ron walked over, took the pad from Tim's hand, looked at it, and saw nothing written on it.

"Okay, I give. What's the joke?"

"No joke, Ron. Look at the indentation in the paper."

"I see an indentation, but I can't make it out. What is it?"

Taking the pad from Ron, Tim took a pencil and scribbled over the indentation. When done he handed the pad back to Ron.

"It's a phone number. So what?"

"Look at the number, Ron," encouraged Tim.

Ron read the number aloud, "843-555-7476."

"Ring a bell? No pun intended."

Ron studied the number and one could see his mind whirling. Then, "Damn!"

Tim, laughing, said, "At last!"

"That's the number of the FBI. She called us."

"Either she did, or she was going to," agreed Tim.

"I wonder why?"

"She knew something, is my guess."

"Tell me, Tim, what are the chances that a Movable Feast regular attendee gets murdered by someone who was not responsible for the previous Feast victims?"

"Unlikely, in my estimation."

"Mine too. Do me a favor. Have her recent phone calls checked. Find out who she called and who called her in the 24 hours preceding her death. Tell them to send a lab team too."

"Lab team? How come?"

"I think she surprised the intruder in the laundry room. She backed him up to the door. Maybe he left some DNA behind."

"Do you think a 92-year-old woman backed him down, Ron?"

"Maybe. She was wielding a big knife. It's possible he's had a previous unpleasant experience with a woman, and when confronted, he backs down and runs. Look at his previous kills. He didn't kill them face-to-face. He ambushed them all from behind."

"I'll make the calls. What's on your agenda?"

"Checking her book collection for what I know isn't there."

"I presume you mean *Catch Me If You Can.*"

"That's a bingo, Tim-o-thy!"

"Why are you saying it won't be there?"

"There's no blood trail from the laundry room into the house. I think he killed her and then ran."

"Well, if neither of his signatures are present, why do you think the Friday killer did this?"

"It comes down to not believing in coincidence, Tim. You even agreed with that just a minute ago."

"Hmm, so I did."

"Make your calls. Then come help me go through this litany of books Lillian collected over the years."

"Hey, Ron, there's always the chance that the book is in her collection."

"Maybe, but I'll bet a dollar to a donut, there won't be a bookmark at the start of chapter five."

"A dollar for a donut. I wish I bought donuts wherever you buy donuts. I'd save about eights bucks a week," said Tim as he walked off to make some calls.

Ron had gone, without success, through the three bookcases in the living room, searching for the book. He had been at it for twenty minutes when Tim came in, saying, "Someone called her at 7:05. That was twenty to thirty minutes before the kill."

"Did they trace the call?"

"It was a burner."

"He called her before he killed her. Have we checked previous victims to see if that may have happened with them?"

"We haven't," answered Tim, "but we are now. I ordered a check on all the others."

"He called at 7:05 and was in the laundry room 15 to 20 minutes later. What might that tell you, partner?"

"It tells me one of two things."

"Please," said Ron with a flair of a hand gesture, "Elaborate."

"There's a couple of 'ifs'."

"Which are?"

"The first is, if her killer the Friday killer."

"Okay. And the second if?"

"If it was her killer who made the call."

"True, but, please, give me your take."

"Well, it could mean he was very close when he made the call."

"And your second assumption?"

"He lives close by."

"Anything else?"

"Yeah. If it was him that called, then she said something to him that knocked him off his routine. That's why no neck slicing and, most likely, no book."

"Damn, you are good, partner!"

"Let's hear your version, Sherlock."

"It's very much like yours, Tim, with a few things added that my snooping around makes possible."

"Well, let's hear it."

"Lillian had two bolt locks placed on the back door. Neither show signs of tampering. So the obvious conclusion is she left the door unlocked."

"I know you don't have any proof, but do you have a theory that supports that conclusion?"

"Why yes I do, and I'm glad you asked. I'm guessing that Lillian took out the garbage, and while she was out there, the phone rang. Hearing the phone, she rushed into the house, forgetting to lock the doors."

"I wouldn't have known that as you had me checking her bedroom."

"I'm a master at giving myself opportunities to look good, Tim. Shall I proceed?"

"Yeah, continue, but tell it with a little more relish, and a lot less mustard. I almost fell asleep with your back-slapping ramblings."

"I'll try to do better."

"That would be nice," Tim replied with his patented shit-eating grin.

Ron began. "Okay, he calls."

"Who calls?"

"Our Friday killer! What? Did you just walk in the room?"

"I warned you that you were putting me to sleep."

"Cut the crap! Now pay attention."

"I'm listening with both ears, Ron."

"He calls and says something to her. She responds. Whatever it was she said, and I believe she told him she was going to the FBI, puts him in panic mode. Without thinking, he rushes over and almost gets ambushed by a 92-year-old woman. He's out of sync in his haste to kill this woman. He's unhinged. The indications of that being true is his forgetting his boxcutter and his book."

"Unhinged, you say. Well, I believe five dead women make that an easy diagnosis, partner."

"Are you capable of saying something nice for once, Tim?"

Tim, glancing at his watch and seeing it was 12:50, was about to suggest they grab some lunch, when Ron's phone rang.

It was Baxter.

Ron answered, listened for a moment, and while nodding his head, said, "We'll be there in about an hour, Bill."

"Just where is it we'll we be in an hour, partner?" asked Tim.

"Conway."

"What's in Conway that needs our attention?"

"A dead woman with a slashed throat and larynx."

"Hmm, so much for our theory that the Friday killer now works on Wednesday's."

"Yeah, damn it," moaned Ron. "I still think we're on to something, Tim. I just don't know what!"

CHAPTER 33

They walked in the Kiernan house at 2:00 on the button. The drive from Lillian Black's to the home of Bob and Judi Kiernan in Conway had taken almost an hour. It would have been shorter but for a 15-minute stop at Jersey Mike's for Ron to grab a sub sandwich.

Bill Baxter and Robert Edge were there, talking with a man who Ron immediately assumed was the deceased woman's husband.

Parked outside were two news vans. Competing reporters waited hungrily for someone to make a statement.

Seeing the blood-soaked sheet covered body lying on the floor, Ron asked, "What time did this occur, Bob?"

"Less than four hours ago, give or take an hour, but I won't know for sure until I get her on a table. She had very little rigor, even with the massive loss of blood."

Ron bent down, drew back the sheet, and saw the usual two slices of the neck. Peering at the cuts, Ron thought he perceived something different from those on the other victims but couldn't put his finger on what it was.

"Robert, did you notice anything different from these cuts, then those on previous victims?"

"Can't say I did, Ron. What are you seeing?"

"That's the problem, Robert, I don't know, but something is different about these cuts."

"I'll look at photos of the others, Ron, and if I see something, I'll call you."

Ron stood and gazed around him. Blood spatter was everywhere but for a swath where he stood and behind him.

"I'm guessing the killer stood here when he sliced her throat open. He was looking at her straight on, it seems."

"Yes, that was my conclusion also," said Bill.

"He must have gotten blood on his clothing."

"I agree," said Bill.

"I take it the husband was clean of blood."

"He was. They located him at work about 12 miles west of here. He's a plumber and he and his assistant were doing an all-day job at the home of Jinny Stacy. Mrs. Stacy also vouches for Mr. Kiernan's presence. She also talked with the victim for about 30 minutes while the victim's husband was working."

"You don't say. So the wife gets herself killed while her husband is at an all-day job just 12 miles away. Did the Stacy woman mention why she was talking with the victim? Was she a good friend?"

"They were friends. Jinny said that they often do things together. She called Judi to see if she would like to go to the Carolina Opry tomorrow night."

"The husband wanted to go, but I'm guessing he wanted the wife's okay. Is that about right, Bill?"

"Mrs. Stacy did say it was Bob Kiernan's idea."

"I see. Are these two witnesses available, Bill?"

"They are at the Stacy's house. Bob's partner, Bones Greer, is finishing up the job."

"Bones?"

"You'll understand when you see him."

"Bill, I'd like to look around a bit."

"Be my guest."

A walk into the living room brought a bookshelf into view. Ron walked over to it and scanned each shelf but didn't find what he knew wouldn't be there. The books were, excluding a dictionary, all paperbacks, whereas hard-copy books dominated the libraries of previous victims.

Stepping outside, he called Linda Ketron.

"It's you again, Colonel."

"It is. Am I interrupting?"

"Don't you always? It's not like I sit here by my phone waiting for you to call."

Ron laughed aloud at her reply, then said, "I have a question. Does the name, Judi Kiernan, ring a bell?"

"Can't say it does, Colonel. Is that it?"

"No, that's not it. One more question."

"You mean for this current call."

"Yes," replied Ron with a laugh. "Do your author's sell paperbacks at your Feasts?"

"Hell, no! I don't run a damn second-rate show!"

"Sorry, Linda. Just wondering is all."

"Do you have a sensible question to ask, Colonel?"

"Can't think of one, ma'am."

"May I go back to living my life now?"

"Go right ahead, Linda. I'll try not to call again."

"Gee, I'll hold my breath," she said as she hung up.

"What's up, Ron? Who were you talking with?"

"Linda Ketron. She insinuated that we're taking up too much of her time."

"Well, you gotta admit you call her as much as some high-school kid who's got it bad for some girl."

"Nice analogy, Tim. What have you been doing?"

"Checking out their books. Did you notice most of them are paperbacks?"

"I noticed that. Did you find…"

"No. *Catch Me* wasn't there."

"Let's go talk with the husband."

"Baxter told me he has an air-tight alibi, backed up by two witnesses."

"So I hear. Let's go see just how air-tight this alibi is, Tim."

CHAPTER 34

His wife had just served him a grilled cheese sandwich and a glass of iced tea when a news bulletin interrupted the program he was watching.

A dark-haired female reporter stood with her back to the Kiernan home as she reported that the Friday killer had struck again.

I'm here in Conway where, in this house you see behind me, the Friday killing of women continues. A delivery man found a woman murdered, with her throat slashed, replicating the four previous female victims of the Friday killer. The woman's husband, a plumber, was at a job site when he received the news of his wife's murder. They have not yet released the identity of the victim. Just moments ago we saw two FBI agents enter the house. We will remain on the scene and bring you updates as they occur. Reporting for WMBF news, this is Melissa Connors.

He sat seething in his chair. Hearing them refer to him as the Friday killer enraged him. Didn't they know that he was the Dispatcher!

His anger was such that he hadn't noticed the grilled cheese sandwich had slipped from his plate onto the rug. By the time he noticed it, Fritz, his four-year-old bulldog, had already cleaned up the mistake.

As he sat there staring at the tv, which had returned to its regular programming, his other voice spoke to him. *"They will forever discredit you with any death that occurs on a Friday. What can I expect you to do about it?"*

As he rose from the chair, he realized he had an empty plate in his hand. He looked down at Fritz, whose tongue was slapping at his jaws as he savored the last bit of the sandwich.

He smiled at his bulldog.

Whispering, he said, "Good boy, Fritz. I hate grilled cheese sandwiches. I hate almost anything she makes. It won't be long before she won't be making me any more meals. She will pay for her traitorous act."

His rage was building. Someone, trying to get away with murder, had copied him.

So they think I kill only on Fridays, do they? It's apparent I'm getting no credit for Lillian's Black's death. My list has five more names on it. Adding a sixth won't be a problem. I do have an extra book. Oh, to see their faces when they find the next victim. I think the Dispatcher shall blow the minds of these not-so-clever cops.

Forgetting himself for a moment, he barked, "A bouquet should do the trick!"

Lucky for him, only Fritz heard the bark and he didn't know what it meant.

CHAPTER 35

They found Bob Kiernan in the backyard, sitting on the edge of a dried-up well he had covered with plywood so no living thing could fall in.

"Mr. Kiernan, I'm Special Agent Ron Lee of the FBI. This is my partner, Agent Tim Pond."

"FBI! I didn't know the FBI would get themselves involved in a case like this."

"It's a long story, Mr. Kiernan," Ron stated. "Let's just say, we have our reasons."

"I reckon you need to ask some questions. That Baxter fella sure asked a lot. Can't imagine anything new comin' out of your mouth, Agent Lee."

"We might ask a few of the same questions, sir, but bear with us. Let me start by asking you what time you left for work this morning?"

"It was 7:15."

"Where did you go at 7:15?"

"I went straight to the shop. I picked up some supplies we needed for the job Bones and I had lined up for the day."

"Bones being Mr. Greer?" questioned Ron of the strange moniker.

"Yep. That skinny rascal and I have been partnering for almost 15 years."

"Where is the shop located, sir?" questioned Tim.

"About 25 miles west of here."

"That's quite a distance to drive each day."

"Oh, I don't normally go there every day. Our jobs take us toward every point on the compass. We try to load our trucks up with what we'll need for the entire week on Monday mornings."

"Excuse me, sir, but you said just a moment ago that you load all of your materials you'll need for the week on Monday. Why did you go to the shop?" asked Ron.

"The Stacy's called us on Tuesday to do their work. We didn't have all the materials we needed, so I had to stop at the shop and pick them up."

"I see," said Ron, disappointed he hadn't caught the man in a lie.

"What time did you arrive at the Stacy's?" asked Tim.

"Well, let me see now. I drove over to the shop, which takes, give or take, about 40 minutes."

"Forty minutes to drive 25 miles, Mr. Kiernan? You must drive like a turtle," stated Ron.

"I follow the speed limit, Agent Lee. That entire route, scattered with traffic lights, is 45mph. Been driving it for years and forty minutes is about what it takes."

"Taking that long would drive me crazy," commented Ron with a laugh. "I would have busted the speed limit every trip, that's for sure."

Tim gave Ron a strange look, knowing that his partner drove like someone's grandmother, rarely exceeding the speed limit.

Bob Kiernan continued his story, saying, "Stayed at the shop for, oh, maybe ten minutes. And then I took off for the Stacy's house. I reckon I got there about 8:20, give or take a minute or two."

"And that's where you stayed until the police showed up. Correct?"

"Yeah... well now, wait a minute, fellas. I had to leave for about forty minutes."

"Oh? Why's that, Mr. Kiernan?"

"Well, Bones and I were laying some pipe when we came up about ten feet short. I had to drive back to the shop and pick up the additional pipe. I drove straight there and back."

"How long did that take, Mr. Kiernan?" asked Tim.

"I reckon it took 35-40 minutes."

"Did you mention what time it was when you left?" asked Tim.

"I didn't look at the clock, but Jinny was still talking with Judi when I left."

"How about when you returned?"

"It may have been around 11:45, but I couldn't swear to it."

"Can you think of anyone who would want to kill your wife, Bob?"

"Can't think of a soul, Agent Lee. She was a friendly gal who had a lot of friends."

"We see lots of books in the house."

"Yeah, we both read a lot."

"Belong to any book clubs?"

"No, we stick to paperbacks we pick up at the flea markets or the discount bookstore."

"Well, that's it for now, Mr. Kiernan. We are sorry for your loss, sir. I can assure you we will catch your wife's killer."

"Thank you, fellas."

As they walked back inside, Ron murmured to Tim, "Something ain't right. I want to talk with this Stacy woman and Bob's partner, Mr. Bones."

"I believe the name is Greer, Ron. Bobby 'Bones' Greer."

"Yeah, whatever. Get the directions to the Stacy residence. I'll wait in the car."

When Tim returned, Ron said, "I want you to drive the speed limit all the way to the Stacy's house."

"Yeah, I've been meaning to ask you what that crap was back there about you being a pathological speeder. You drive like my grandmother walks."

"I don't drive that slow, and that back there was me trying to distract him."

"Distract him? From what?"

"The leading questions I was asking."

"Okay, enough of the double talk. Let's get to the Stacy's."

"Speed limit, Tim. Speed limit."

As they drove, Ron talked his thoughts.

"This Stacy home is 12 miles from the Kiernan's house."

"That's correct."

"The shop is 25 miles from the Kiernan's house."

"That's correct."

"Therefore, it sounds like the shop is 13 miles from the Stacy's house."

"If everything is a straight line, then yes," agreed Tim.

"If the speed limit is 45 on all the roads, then it would take about 15 minutes to drive 11 miles. But the shop is another 2 miles, so you add, what would you say, two minutes?"

"Two minutes to travel two miles is sixty miles an hour, Ron. Make it three."

"Okay, let's make it three. So 18 minutes to the shop from the Stacy's house. Add 18 minutes for the trip back, that's 36. Kiernan said he left the job site for about 35-40 minutes. Let's split the difference and call it thirty-seven and a half."

"That seems fair, for now," quipped Tim.

"Agreed," replied Ron with a sneer. "In 90 seconds, he exits the truck, unlocks the shop, grabs ten feet of pipe, leaves the shop, locks the door, loads the pipe, and gets back into his truck."

"Okay, so what's your point?"

"Either he's lying about the time, or he speeds when he needs to."

"I know there's a bigger 'or' so let's hear it."

"Or, he didn't drive west to the shop and pick up pipe but drove east and killed his wife. It's about four minutes shorter. Then his saying he left for 35-40 minutes fits."

"He also said the Stacy woman was still talking with his wife when he left. Knowing how women can get to gabbing, wouldn't it have been a risk for him to walk into the house while his wife was talking to the Stacy woman?"

"Hearsay."

"What's hearsay?"

"He said they were still talking. Let's hear it from the horse's mouth, then we'll deal with that possibility."

The 12.3 mile trip took 17 minutes with one stop for a traffic signal.

"Double that, plus five minutes to kill, and you have about 40 minutes," Ron stated as they headed toward the front door of the Stacy home.

"That's not in line with your timeline, Ron."

"That's because of the 45mph speed limit factor. Change that factor to 55mph, and everything fits."

"That's nothing more than supposition, Ron."

"I know he killed his wife. He had to make a mistake somewhere. We'll find it."

CHAPTER 36

    "Come in, gentlemen," greeted **Jinny** Stacy. "I received a call from Captain Baxter saying you were on your way."

    "Good afternoon, ma'am. I'm Special Agent Ron Lee, and this is my partner, Tim Pond. We'd like to ask you and Mr. Greer a few questions. I assume Mr. Greer is still here?"

    "Yes, he's finishing up in the basement."

    "Let's start with you then, ma'am."

    "Please, I prefer you call me Jinny."

    "Okay, Jinny. Tell us what time it was when you called Judi Kiernan and how long the call lasted."

    "I'm pretty sure it was about 10:00 when I called her. I had the television turned on. My favorite game-show, *Let's Make a Deal*, was just beginning."

    "And Bob was here while you talked?" asked Tim.

    "Oh, yes. Bob's the reason I called Judi. He suggested that the four of us go to the Opry tomorrow night. He had me call Judi to clear it with her."

    "Did she agree to go?"

    "She did, but she didn't sound enthused about it."

    "Why was that?"

    "I don't know. It's just the vibe I got over the phone."

    "We understand that Bob left while you were talking with his wife. What can you tell us about that?"

    "I'm not sure what happened, but Bones went outside to Bob's truck to get something. I believe it was PVC pipe. When he returned, he told Bob there was no pipe in the truck."

"Then what happened?"

"Bob took his truck and left for the shop."

"And you were still talking with Judi when he left?"

"I was. I mentioned to her that Bob had to go back to the shop because they ran out of pipe. She seemed surprised."

"Did she say why?"

"She thought it surprising that Bob would forget something. He's so detail-anal."

"Do you recall what time it was when Bob drove off, and the time when you ended your call?"

"I'm guessing Bob left around 10:15. He said he'd be back in 35 or 40 minutes. I know he walked back into the house at 10:50 because they had just begun doing the big deal of the day."

"I beg your pardon, Jinny. They who? Big deal?"

"You don't watch too many daytime game shows, do you Agent Lee?"

"Can't say I do, Jinny. Too busy catching bad guys."

"The big deal of the day happens in the last ten minutes of the *Let's Make a Deal* game-show."

"So he left at 10:15 and returned at 10:50?"

"Don't hold my feet to the fire on that one, Agent Lee. It could have been a minute or two either way, although I'm pretty sure about when he came back."

"Because of the big deal of the day," mumbled Tim.

"That's right."

"So when did you end your conversation with Judi Kiernan?"

"I'd say about 10:25."

"So you spoke with her for 20-25 minutes?"

"I guess I did. It didn't seem that long, though."

"We'd like to talk with Mr. Greer now. Would you mind getting him for us?"

"I'll have him up here in a jiffy, gentlemen."

As they waited for Bones Greer, Ron said to Tim, "How often do you go out with your wife?"

"I think the last time was my junior year in high school."

"Yeah, and I bet it was Dutch-treat."

"It involved no money. We went to the town park. Spent the day on a blanket. I had a snicker's bar with me. I think I shared it with her."

"It sounds like you were quite the guy with the womenfolk, Tim."

"Oh, yeah, I was a real womanfolker, that's for sure."

Ron grinned at his partner's double-entente, before asking, "So you haven't suggested to Wilma, 'Hey, let's go to the Opry.'"

"Hell, no. it's too expensive. If I did that, I wouldn't be able to buy you your donuts for a week!"

"Hmm, I'm glad to see you have your priorities in order, partner."

"Gentlemen, I'd like to introduce Bobby Greer. He goes by Bones."

The reason for the strange moniker was immediate to both agents. Greer made a skeleton look chubby.

"Mr. Greer, I'm Agent Ron Lee of the FBI. This is my partner, Agent Tim Pond."

"Never spoke with any big time FBI guys before. I see you on the tv a lot, though. You guys are on tv shows every night. You're always gettin' shot at or shootin' someone. Ain't that excitin'!"

"Yeah, that's us all right," said Ron, his voice riddled with sarcasm.

"I hear you got some questions that need answerin'."

"That we do… Bones. We understand that you and Bob Kiernan have been working partners for a long time."

"Yep, it's been, oh, let's see," said Bones, while rubbing his chin. "I'd say we've been together goin' on 15 years."

"Do you enjoy working with Bob?"

"Oh, sure do. He's all business, but he's easy to work with though."

"What do you mean, 'he's all business', Bones?"

"I mean when we go do a job, he has it mapped out down to the last screw we'll need. But today was a surprise."

"Surprise? What was the surprise?"

"Us not having the correct length of pipe. That's the first time in all the years we've been together that we came up short on a part, much less a 10-foot piece of pipe."

"Are you saying Bob always makes sure you guys have everything you need to do the job when you get to the job site?"

"Bob's the brains of the outfit. I'm the brawn," Bones said, laughing as he made a muscle with his arm.

Ron's immediate thought was that he'd seen bigger pimples.

"Today was the first time you came up short on materials in 15 years, Bones?" asked Tim. "Are you positive of that?"

"Oh, yeah. First off, a body don't forget somethin' historic like that!"

"How long was Bob gone when he drove to the shop to get the pipe? What's your guess, Bones?"

"When he left, he said he'd be back in 35-40 minutes."

Then Bones held up his left arm and showed them a silver-banded watch dangling from his wrist. "I took a gander at the watch and it was 10:12."

"Did you notice what time it was when he returned?"

"Can't say I did, fellas. Why is you askin' all these questions about Bob? You're not thinkin' he killed his wife, are ya? I know he wasn't happy with her, but he wouldn't kill her."

"How do you know he wasn't happy, Bones?"

"Cause he told me he wasn't."

"When did he tell you that?"

"He told me plenty of times in the last year or so. He said she was a frigid woman. Even I know what that means."

"Explain to us what that means, Bones," ordered Ron.

"You fellas are in the FBI and you can't figure out what that means? Shoot, I don't give you fellas a snowball's chance in hell of solving this case!"

"Humor us, Bones. What did he mean when he said she was a frigid woman?"

"She didn't give him no sex for over a year!"

"Oh, my! That poor man!" whispered Jinny Stacy, who overheard the last question asked of Bones.

CHAPTER 37

Friday, July 5, 2019 – 7:30pm

"Dan, leave the water running in the jacuzzi for about an hour or two. We need to wash Artie down the drain."

"This is the most disgusting thing I have ever seen or been a part of," replied a gagging Dan Lucas. "I can't imagine how you came up with this idea, Nick."

"Using the jacuzzi to dispose of Artie's body seemed like the right thing to do, Dan. It doesn't seem all that bad an idea now either, what with our faces plastered all over the news. It's one less face the public or the police might recognize."

"Have you been outside, Nick?"

"Just on the back deck. It's hot, but there's a pleasant breeze."

"Did you stock anything besides beer in this place? I'm starving, and like you said, we can't go out to eat."

"There's a bag of pretzels in the kitchen, and that's it. I must admit I didn't expect our mugs being on display."

"How about we order a pizza?"

"That sounds good, Dan, but tell them we'll leave the money on the porch. We can't take a chance on being recognized by the delivery guy. You might as well order two. We'll take one with us to eat on the road tomorrow."

"What time do you figure we'll be leaving, Nick?"

"I'd like to get on the road no later than 5:00am. It's tough getting out of this town on a Saturday during the summer months. It may take us two hours or more just to get to I-95."

"What the hell we gonna do, Nick? We can't go home. We're national news."

"I bought a radio at Wal-Mart that picks up police bands. At least we'll know what they are up to. It may help us bypass the sticky spots."

"That was smart, Nick."

"If we can make it to northern Virginia, I have a friend who will fly us and our wives out of the country. It will cost us, but it's better than life in jail."

"We could go straight up Route 17 to Wilmington and pick up I-40, to I-95 north," suggested Dan.

"It's a six of one, a half-dozen of the other situation, Dan. Let's see what tomorrow brings. Have you called in those pizzas yet? I want pepperoni and sausage on mine."

Remembering seeing a menu from a restaurant attached to the fridge, Dan went into the kitchen and using his cell phone called Marco's pizzeria.

"Marco's Pizzeria. This is Leo. What would you like?"

After ordering the two pizzas, he told Leo to have the delivery guy leave the pizzas on the porch where the money will be.

"Ahh, sorry buddy, but we don't deliver after 7:00 on Fridays. Too many people who are leaving town, like to play gags by ordering pizza deliveries to houses who didn't order them. Tourists have burned us way too many times this summer."

"Where are you located?" asked Dan.

"We're in Garden City on Business 17 at the corner of Cypress. Where are you?"

Dan hesitated for a moment, then replied, "We're on Pine and Elizabeth."

"Oh, hell, fella, you're two minutes away. Just head north on Elizabeth, make a left onto Cypress, and drive up

to where it meets Business 17. We're in that little strip mall on your left next to the Krispy Kreme."

"When will the pizzas be ready?"

"Fifteen to twenty minutes. It will be $22.50."

"Okay, I'll be there."

"Hey, fella, what's the name?" asked Leo.

Dan hesitated for a moment, then answered, "The name is Artie."

After hanging up with Leo, Dan returned to the living room where Nick was watching television.

"They don't deliver. We need to do a pickup."

"The hell you say!" screamed Nick.

"It's right at the end of the street. Right next to that donut place, Krispy Kreme."

"I don't give a rat's ass if it was across the damn street! There's no goddamn way you're going to pick them up. Think, Dan! If someone recognizes you, they'd lock down this neighborhood and search it house-by-house."

"I'll wear a hat and sunglasses, Nick. No one will recognize me."

"Oh, is that right? Well, what about the SUV? It's stolen and so are the plates. What if a cop is sitting at Krispy Kreme? Cops, I hear, love donuts. What if he sees the vehicle and recognizes it as stolen? Then what, Dan?"

Dan didn't answer. He knew Nick was right, but damn, he was hungry!

"What if I walk up there?"

"Are you hearing me! Your fucking face is all over television. I don't care if you got dressed up like Santa Claus, you're not going out that damn door!"

"I'm hungry."

"Call a pizzeria that delivers."

"Okay, Nick."

Dan was about to dial another number when his cell phone rang.

"Who the hell is calling you?"

Dan looked at the phone. It was Marco's.

"It's the pizza place."

"You'd better answer it."

"Hello?"

"Hey, Artie, this is Leo. Your pizzas came out earlier than I expected. Come get them before they cool off."

"Sorry, Leo, but I can't. Haven't got a vehicle. I didn't realize that one of the other guys staying here took off in it."

"What the hell do you mean you can't pick them up?" screamed Leo.

There was silence for a few seconds, then Leo said, *"Okay, I'll bring the pizzas to you. What's the address?"*

"It's 492 Pine. I'll leave the money on the small table on the porch. Just leave the pizzas there."

"Okay, sure thing," responded Leo. *"I'll be there in two minutes."*

"He's delivering the pizza."

"Yeah, so I heard," nodded Nick. "How much is the bill?"

"$22.50."

"Turn on the outside lights. Put two twenties on that small table sitting between the two rockers. Hurry!"

Dan did what he was told. He had no sooner closed the door than did Leo pull into the driveway. Dan failed to secure the money with a weight, and the draft of closing the door blew the two twenties onto the floor and under a rocker. A moment later, the "pleasant breeze" Nick had mentioned lifted both bills off the porch and out into the wind.

Days later, a young boy would find one bill in his backyard. The other bill would linger for months in a tree just yards from where it had departed.

Leo left the small delivery van running as he grabbed the two pizzas off the passenger seat. As he exited the vehicle, he saw the Yukon parked under the house.

"No vehicle, my ass," he mumbled.

Bounding up the stairs, Leo saw the small table, but he saw no money. He immediately pressed the doorbell. Leo heard it buzz, but there was no response from inside. He buzzed it again, yelling, "Hey! I got your pizza, but there's no money on the table!"

Dan, his head pressed against the door, glanced at Nick for advice.

"You left the money?" whispered Nick.

"Yeah. Two twenties, just like you said," Dan answered, also in a whisper.

"Damn! They must have blown off the table. Tell him to look on the floor."

A perplexed Dan stepped away from the door, saying, "It must have fallen off the table, Leo. Look on the floor for two twenties."

A minute had passed when Leo reported, "Sorry, Artie, but there are no twenties in sight. These pizzas are getting cold."

Nick rose from the couch and marched to the door, taking two bills from his wallet while on his brief journey.

"Sorry about that," said Nick as he handed the delivery man two twenties with his left hand while grasping the two pizzas with his right. "Keep the change."

During the brief encounter, Nick never looked Leo in the eye. If asked to describe Leo, he couldn't. Nick hoped the same was true from Leo's side.

Leo, seeing the $18 tip, was about to say thanks, but the door had already closed.

The next morning, multiple events would occur.

The man who sold the Drano to Nick would see the photos of the three bank robbers the next morning. Recognizing Nick's photo as the man he waited on the previous day, he called the police tip line at 5:27am.

Leo, an early riser, turned on the local news and while enjoying his second cup of coffee, also saw Nick's photo. He wasn't sure, but he thought it may have been the guy who gave him a big tip last night. Leo hesitated with uncertainty because he never saw the man's entire face. But after toying with the oddness of the whole situation involving the pizza delivery, he too called the tip line. The police tip line registered Leo's call as received at 5:39.

Dan and Nick waited until 4:00am before slipping out of the house. They were seeking another vehicle and found an SUV parked in the driveway of a nearby rental beach home. Its tailgate was open. Two suitcases lay inside.

"Someone is leaving early, Dan. I'm assuming they went back inside to get more luggage. Let's give them a hand."

The older model SUV belonged to a young couple who, after being interrupted by Nick at the doorway, would get no older. Taking the vehicle's key from the pocket of the dead man, they drove back to their rental, collected their suitcases of money, their weapons, and the remaining pizza. They were on their way north at 5:45.

The police arrived at 5:51.

Nick and Dan didn't know it then, but there would be plenty of potholes dotting the road to North Carolina.

CHAPTER 38

Saturday, July 6, 2019 – 5:30am

Ron was already on his second donut when the phone rang at 6:00 sharp.

"Would you mind getting that call, Tim? My hands are sticky from that chocolate éclair I ate earlier."

"By earlier, don't you mean like two minutes ago?"

Ron had arrived at the office at 5:30. Tim, because he had to wait for the donut shop to open, arrived at 5:50. They had a busy day ahead of them. Today was the day they expected the bank robbers to attempt their escape from the Grand Strand. Ron would coordinate the blanketing of the area. They knew they were looking for a white 2017 GMC Yukon with SC plates reading FGU-5597.

"I doubt that's the vehicle they are driving now," Ron commented as he took his first bite into the éclair. "Let's get a list of all stolen vehicles in the past 48 hours, Tim, and add those to the watch list."

Ron also had Bob Kiernan on his mind. Everything he had was circumstantial, but it all pointed to Bob as the killer of his wife, Judi.

"Hello, FBI. Agent Pond speaking."

"This is Sergeant Sam Brewer with the state police. Captain Baxter asked that I contact you about the bank robbery suspects, sir."

"What do you have, Sergeant?" asked Tim, as he placed the phone on speaker.

"Two callers reported seeing suspect number one in the Garden City area."

"What were the circumstances, Sergeant?"

"The first call came in from the local Wal-Mart. A clerk there says he sold ten containers of Drano to the suspect we labeled as number 1."

Not knowing their identities, when the FBI sent out photos of the suspects, they assigned each of the three men a number. Nick was number one.

"I believe we now only have two suspects on the run," Ron stated after hearing the sergeant's words about Drano. "I'm betting the guy who stuttered isn't stuttering any longer."

"The second call also came in this morning. The caller says he's sure the guy who paid for the pizzas he delivered was also suspect number one."

"Did you check out the address, Sergeant?"

"We did. We found the stolen 2017 white Yukon parked under the house. The inside of the house was clean except for the jacuzzi. It appeared to have a sticky substance in it."

"That, I'm willing to bet, would be what's left of suspect number three," quoted Ron. "Sergeant!"

"Yes, sir?"

"Has anyone, in the last few hours, reported a stolen vehicle in that neighborhood?"

"I'll check on that, sir."

"If there has been a stolen vehicle reported, send out a BOLO, and then call us back."

"Understood, sir."

The sergeant hung up, and Tim turned to Ron, asking, "Which way do you think they're heading, Ron? North, south, or west."

"Good question, Tim. Here's my opinion. It's all but certain that these guys, based on their accents, are from the north. Now they could throw us off by heading south, say down to Jacksonville, then turn west on Interstate 10, before heading north. It's the long way home, that's for sure. I'm estimating it would add eight to ten hours to their journey. I'm guessing they won't do that though."

"Why not?"

"Three reasons I can think of. First, they are driving a stolen vehicle. The longer they drive it, the better the chance someone spots them. Second, the longer distance might mandate getting a room for a night. That also betters the chances someone will recognize them. And last, they are carrying about three million dollars. If it were me, I'd want to get home fast and do something with that cash."

"Okay, so you're ruling out the southern route. How about west?"

"Not a terrible choice, considering that you'll have the company of about 200,000 others. It would be akin to a needle in a haystack."

"Hey, didn't you climb all over my ass for using the word akin awhile back?"

"Yeah, I did, but it sounds… professional."

"You told me it sounded stupid."

"No, I said you sounded stupid."

"Oh, yeah, that's right. I think you mumbled that between eating donuts four and five that morning."

"I think it was three and four."

"So you think they are heading west, then."

"No, I don't. With traffic trickling out of town, the chance of drivers in other cars spotting them is almost a certainty. It also gives our guys a better chance to see them. I'd rule out going west based on the lack of speed."

"So that leaves…"

The phone rang.

"FBI. Agent Pond speaking."

"Agent Pond, this is Sergeant Brewer."

"What do have for us, Sergeant?"

"We found a couple was found murdered in their rental two blocks from where the suspects stayed. Their 2003 dark blue Ford Explorer is missing. The vehicle carried an Illinois plate reading… now get this, fellas… BAREFAN#9. That's bare spelled b-a-r-e."

"Well, hell, that won't be hard to spot, Sergeant," voiced Ron. "Did you get the BOLO out?"

"It went out at 6:17, sir."

"Good. Have the northern units be on alert. I have a hunch they left heading north, right up Route 17."

"Will do, sir."

The phone call ended and Tim asked, "Why so sure about them heading north, partner?"

"It's the smart move. They know hiding amongst 100,000 cars heading west is smart, but they know we know it too. If they head north, they get into another state the fastest, which will give them all kinds of outs. Buses, Ubers, trains, picked up by friends, you name it. We need to stop them before they cross the state line."

"And if we don't stop them?"

"I suspect that within a week, they'll be living somewhere in Costa Rica, drinking margaritas, and wearing nice tans. I know I would."

CHAPTER 39

Saturday, July 6, 2019 – 8:00am

Ron had ordered a 24-hour stakeout on Bob Kiernan's home.

Assigned to the 8:00am to 4:00pm watch was Agent Brandon Elliot.

Arriving at the scene a few minutes early, he approached Agent Angela Patrick, who drew the short straw known as the graveyard midnight to 8:00am shift.

"Anything happening, Angie?"

"I was told he went to bed at 10:00pm. He awoke at 6:15. I saw him step out the front door, scratch his crotch a few times, then return inside. At 7:12 he appeared again, holding a cup of coffee. He walked down the driveway to fetch the paper and returned inside. I saw a light being turned on. I'm guessing he was reading the paper."

"Anymore scratching?" asked Brandon with a mile-wide smile.

"What do you think? Men are animals."

Brandon Elliot was head over heels in love with Angela, but she didn't know it. He was too shy to ask her out. What he didn't know was she would have eagerly accepted.

"I'll take it from here, Angie. Go home and get some sleep."

"I'll see you tomorrow morning, Brandon."

"I'll be here."

It was 9:12 when the panel truck came up the road and turned into the Kiernan's driveway. Printed on the driver's door were the words, *'Brenda's Boutique'* along with an address location and a phone number.

The driver, for whatever reason, lingered in the vehicle for about a minute before exiting. He walked to the back of the truck and opened the rear doors.

Brandon jotted down the license plate number but hesitated calling it in after seeing the man extract a gigantic bouquet from the truck.

He dressed as a delivery man would dress, with that typical bluish-gray jacket and slacks, and a matching cabbie hat. Brandon guessed his height at slightly under six-feet and his weight somewhere just south of 200. He looked to be in his late 50s or early 60s.

"You're a little old to be delivering flowers, ain't you, pop?" murmured Brandon.

The agent watched as the man carried the flowers to the front door and rang the doorbell.

A half-minute passed before Bob Kiernan opened the door.

Brandon, well over a hundred yards away, could see Kiernan's surprise when the delivery man thrust the flowers toward him.

He watched as they exchanged words, and then, to Brandon's surprise, Kiernan invited the delivery man inside.

That's weird, thought Brandon. *But hey, maybe he knows the guy.*

"Those are beautiful flowers!" exclaimed Bob Kiernan. "Who sent them?"

"There's a card here, sir," said the delivery man, handing the small envelop to Kiernan.

Kiernan opened the envelope and pulled out the small card that had a red and gold flower on the front, along with the word, *Condolences*.

Turning toward a lit lamp to better see the writing, Kiernan read the card aloud.

"You killed her and tried to blame me – The Dispatcher."

Bob hadn't noticed that the flowers lay on the floor and that the delivery man had stepped behind him.

"Who the hell is The Dispatcher?" shouted Bob. Those words would be his last.

The arm of the delivery man encircled Bob's neck, and the blade of the boxcutter slid across his throat, and blood, spouting like a crimson water fountain, followed.

As The Dispatcher stood watching, Bob sank to his knees. His hands clutched his throat as he attempted to stop the bleeding. The blood, however, just filtered its way between Bob's fingers and ran down his arms. Fifteen seconds later, he was just as dead as his wife.

Something isn't right here, Agent Elliot told himself. He called in the panel truck's plate number.

A response came back a minute later.

"That is a 10-71" reported the FBI dispatcher.

"Stolen vehicle," said Brandon aloud.

Then, speaking into his radio, Elliot said, "We have a situation here. Send backup."

A moment later, Bob Kiernan's killer exited the front door.

"Suspect is leaving the scene. I will confront him."

"Stand down until backup arrives," warned the FBI dispatcher.

Elliot had closed his vehicle's door and didn't hear the command to abort his pursuit.

He unbuckled his revolver but left it in the holster.

When the two men were twenty feet apart, Elliot shouted, "Sir, I'll need you to stop and put your hands out to the sides where I can see them."

"What's going on? Who are you?"

"I'm FBI Agent Elliot, sir, and you are driving a stolen vehicle."

"Nonsense! I own this vehicle and I have the papers to prove it," said the Dispatcher as he stepped to the driver's door and grabbed the door's handle.

Elliot, in his very first confrontation as an FBI agent, made the mistake of stepping, unarmed, toward his suspect.

It was a rookie mistake.

It was also a fatal mistake.

The weapon came out of nowhere! The flash of the blade slashed the agent's face just below the left eye. Blood filled the socket just enough that Agent Brandon Elliot never saw the killing swipe that severed his carotid artery. He was dead before he hit the ground.

After glancing at the dead agent with total indifference, The Dispatcher climbed behind the wheel and drove off.

Backup arrived ten minutes later to find two brutal murder scenes.

Angela Patrick would never know Brandon Elliot's love.

CHAPTER 40

They had been on the road for 20 minutes and hadn't gone over three miles, when an agitated Nick asked, "How much gas in this piece of shit?"

Dan glanced at the display and found the gas tank reading just above empty.

"Almost on empty, Nick."

"Damn! We'll be out of gas before we get through this damn light!"

The early morning traffic was already heavy with vacationers heading back home. The majority would head west on route 501. However, to get to Route 501 all the beach traffic first had to traverse 14 miles of Route 544 and it was already bumper-to-bumper.

Nick's plan had them taking 544 to Route 31, a journey of 9 miles from the beach house. The 30 mile trip on 31 would have them exiting onto Route 9. A quick drive past the Bell and Bell car lot would have them turning onto Route 57. Five miles northeast on 57 would have them in North Carolina, leaving them just five miles from Route 17 north. Once on Route 17, they would have about an hour's drive to Wilmington, where they would complete arrival plans to the private airfield in Virginia.

The twenty minutes they had been driving had only taken them to the intersection of Business 17 and Route 544. The line to make a left onto 544 was at least 70 cars long. It would take at least a half-dozen changes of the light before they could make the turn.

Vehicles could make the left turn onto 544 from two Business 17 lanes. But the left turn lanes where cars merged were 100 yards further on from their position.

A 40-yard median separated the north and south lanes of Business 17. Pacing up and down the median were two Horry County deputies.

Each time the traffic stopped, they would walk the median with one perusing the inside lane vehicles and the other those in the outside lane.

Two deputies, posted on the opposite side of the road, inspected the occupants of vehicles heading north on Business 17.

"Oh-oh!"

"What is it, Dan?"

"There are two cops standing on the median up near the intersection. I think they're looking for us, Nick."

Ahead of Dan and Nick was a large pickup.

"Dan, stay behind this pickup. There's the left-hand turn lanes about a hundred yards ahead. If he turns into the far-left lane, pull up alongside and stay parallel with him."

"What if he stays in this lane?"

Nick twisted around in his seat to see what vehicles were behind them. A panel truck was two cars back.

"There's a truck behind us. It might move into the left lane. If not, we'll just have to take our chances."

The light changed, and traffic began moving. They had moved about 20 car lengths when the traffic light changed and traffic stopped. The pickup truck, however, had made it far enough to merge into the far left turn lane. Dan pulled forward and stopped alongside him. There was, however, a problem. Dan had at least two open car lengths in front of him, and the people behind him, with horns beeping, took no time to let him know it.

The cops had returned to the start of the median to await the next stop of traffic. Once it stopped, they once again began their journey down the median inspecting every car as they passed them. The blowing horns caught their attention. They looked ahead, but they were at least 15 cars from where the commotion was being heard.

"Some dumbass is looking at his cell phone and hasn't moved ahead," said one cop to the other.

"Stay with your lane, Harry. I'm guessing it's a woman gabbing with someone. She'll get the message eventually and move up."

"What should I do, Nick? We're pissing off the cars behind us. Their horn blowing may draw the cops."

"Yeah, you're right, Dan. You better move up. We'll wait for the truck after the light changes."

"I think we're too far away to get through the light, Nick. The next time we're stopped, we'll be able to carry on a conversation with those two cops."

As Dan crawled forward, they saw the two cops were just four vehicles ahead of them.

"They'll be here in seconds, Nick. Any ideas?"

Nick had none. But as luck would have it, the light changed and the two officers reversed themselves and headed back toward the intersection.

Dan began moving ahead, and a moment later the pickup was alongside him. The turning arrow, a good twelve cars ahead, was green and vehicles were rapidly streaming through it.

Eight cars and it was still green. Six cars! Five! Four! The arrow turned yellow, but cars continued turning. Three cars! Two! It looked like they would make the turn, but those hopes vanished when the Impala in front of Dan stopped as the arrow turned red. They were second in line.

Beside them sat a Subaru Outback that wasn't big enough to hide them. It was 6:12. It would be four minutes before the traffic signal would change in their favor.

"Look to your right. Don't let them see your entire face," said Nick, who was staring at the car to his right.

The taller of the two officers was surveying the outer lane, his partner, the lane closest to the median.

Although they were to watch for a 2017 white Yukon, they understood that the bank robbers had more than likely switched vehicles. All law enforcement was told to peruse each car they saw for the three suspects.

His name was Cpl. Sidney Segal. His fellow officers called him Sid, as did all his acquaintances, all that is but his mother. To his mom, he would always be Sidney.

Seeing the Impala occupied by two women, Sid's eyes moved on to the old Ford Explorer, where two men filled the front seats. Both had their heads turned to the right, making a total scrutiny of their faces impossible.

Sid stopped and stared at the two men for a full 15 seconds or more. Neither, however, turned to face forward.

"Sid! What are you doing?" asked his partner, Harry O'Leary, who was a full six vehicles ahead.

Sid moved along but kept looking back at the Explorer.

Three minutes passed, and both Sid and his partner had checked out the next twenty cars in line when their radios crackled.

"Attention all units. Be on the lookout for a blue 2003 Ford Explorer. We believe our suspects, now numbering two, are using a vehicle of that description to escape the city."

"Damn!" yelled Sid. "I saw them, Harry, up near the head of the line! C'mon!"

Sid and Harry, running as fast as they could, were ten vehicles from the traffic light when it changed.

Cars poured out of the inside lane like kids escaping the school when the last bell rang. The outside lane remained dormant because of two women in the Impala having a heated conversation on how to raise their grandchildren. The driver, too busy arguing, didn't notice the light had changed.

Dan, seeing the oncoming cops, laid on the horn.

"Those cops are coming fast, Nick."

Hearing the horn blast, the driver of the Impala looked up at the light and seeing it green, panicked, and hit the gas.

The Impala didn't move. She had put the gearshift in park while waiting for the long traffic signal. The woman, now in panic mode, and with her foot on the gas, threw the gearshift into drive. The Impala shot forward a car-length before she panicked again and slammed on the brakes. The Impala stalled in the middle of the intersection.

Dan, having nowhere to go, glanced in the rearview mirror, and seeing the two cops just three cars back, said, "We got trouble coming our way."

Nick didn't hear him.

He had stepped out of the car with an AK-47 in his hands. Raising the barrel of the weapon above the Explorer's roofline, he let loose a burst that cut down the two pursuing officers.

"Push that fucking Impala out of the way, Dan, and let's get our asses out of here," screamed Nick.

Dan pulled up behind the stalled vehicle and as two 70-year-old women sat screaming inside, the Explorer pushed the Impala out into the middle of the intersection.

"There's a Chick-fil-A up the road about a mile. Pull in there."

"We're not stopping for lunch, I hope," replied Dan.

"This is no time for humor."

Officer Harry O'Leary lay in the second lane of Business 17 with wounds to his shoulder and forearm. His partner, Sid Segal, lay beside him. He also had two bullet wounds. Sid's wounds, one in the right eye, the other in the jaw, were mortal. A hole, the size of a baseball, in the back of Sid's head clarified that he would no longer be walking the earth.

Harry, sobbing, radioed in, "Officer down! Officer down! Business 17 and Route 544. Suspects heading west on 544 in blue Explorer."

Dan pulled into Chick-fil-A.

"Drive around to the drive-through window side," ordered Nick.

"What are you doing?"

"Park over there and stop asking questions. Grab the money and the weapons. Then follow me."

Nick, after leaving the Explorer, stood and examined the line of cars in the drive-through. A small Toyota was picking up an order, and behind it was a 4-door Chevy Silverado.

"Perfect," Nick said in a whisper.

As the Toyota pulled away, the Silverado moved up to the drive-thru window. While the driver was exchanging a twenty-dollar bill for a giant-sized bag of food, Nick opened the passenger door and climbed inside.

The driver, collecting his change, didn't hear Nick get in the car. He turned to place the bag of food on the seat but froze when he saw a handgun pointing at his chest.

"I'll take that bag," Nick said, snatching it from the man's hands.

"What the hell is this all about?"

Waving the gun at the driver, Nick replied, "This is about you living or dying. Now, do you see that fella standing over there holding those bags? He needs a lift too. Let's drive over there and pick him up."

Shocked by the turn of circumstances, the man appeared dumbfounded. He just sat there, unable to move.

"DO IT NOW OR DIE!" screamed Nick.

The driver snapped out of his semi-state of unconsciousness and pulled forward forty feet.

"Stop!"

The rear door opened and Dan tossed two suitcases inside, followed by a bag of weapons. Climbing in, he said, "This is crazy!"

Nick didn't reply to Dan. Instead, he told the man to head west on 544.

"Do what we say and we may let you live."

"Whatever you say, mister."

"Dan, look what… I'm sorry, what is your name?"

"Russ."

"Dan, look at what our newest friend, Russ, bought us. Breakfast!"

As Russ drove toward the Route 31 entrance, Nick and Dan enjoyed a lunch of chicken sandwiches, waffle fries, and a cold orange juice.

"Ahh, shit!" voiced Dan.

"What's the matter?"

"I forgot the pizza."

CHAPTER 41

"What the hell!" screamed Ron.

He had just answered the phone and heard Sergeant Brewer inform him of the shootout between the suspected bank robbers and two Horry County Sheriff deputies.

"We had one deputy killed and the other wounded, sir."

"What about the shooters?"

"They were last seen driving west on Route 544. The shootout caused a panic at the intersection of 544 and business 17 that resulted in a horrendous tie-up of traffic. Pursuit was impossible."

"So you're telling me we don't know where they are?"

"No, sir, we don't."

Ron hung up the phone.

"I take it that was about our bank robbers?"

"Yes and no," answered Ron. "Our bank robbers are now cop killers."

"Jesus!" yelped Tim. "What the hell happened?"

"Two cops spotted them at a traffic stop, and in trying to make an arrest, one got killed and the other wounded."

"Last seen?"

"Heading west on 544."

"Does that knock out your theory of them heading north?"

"On the contrary, Tim-o-thy. Knowing they were last seen heading west, they will head north. My guess is they turned onto Route 17 or onto Route 31."

"What about the car?"

"They'll change cars as soon as they can, no doubt."

The phone rang.

Ron picked up, mouthing a gruff, "Yeah?"

"Sergeant Brewer, Agent Lee."

"What is it, Sergeant?"

"We found the Explorer, sir."

"Where?"

"They left it in the Chick-fil-A parking lot on 544."

"They stole another vehicle?"

"Not that we can determine, sir. No one reported their car stolen."

Ron stood mum for a moment, then said, "Let me guess. You found the Explorer near the drive-thru lane?"

"Why, yes, it was," answered Brewer, his voice registering a tone of amazement.

"They commandeered a vehicle that was in the drive-thru lane."

"No one reported anything like that, Agent Lee."

"That's because they also commandeered the driver. They have some poor bastard driving them out of harm's way and we ain't got a fucking clue who it is!"

Tim, overhearing the conversation, asked, "Ron, ask if Chick-fil-A has security cameras covering the drive-thru."

Ron asked Tim's question.

"Hang on, sir. I'll ask the manager. He's standing right here."

Seconds later Brewer reported, *"Yes, sir, they do. I'll look at them and get back to you."*

Three minutes passed before Brewer called back.

"You were right, Agent Lee. They took a Chevy Silverado. I'm having the plates checked... wait, here it is.

The truck belongs to a Russell Burke, who lives in Socastee."

"Issue a Bolo on the vehicle, Sergeant!"

"Already taken that step, sir."

"They have a head start on us, Sergeant. Any idea as to how much?"

"The videotape shows them climbing into the vehicle at 6:20. It is now 6:30."

"Have all the exits on Route 31 closed and blocked off. Set up a quiet roadblock on Route 17 North at 38th Ave."

"Only at 38th, sir? Why only 38th?"

"It's walking distance from our office."

CHAPTER 42

When they exited the Chick-fil-A, Nick had Russ turn onto Route 17 North.

"Why are we taking this route, Nick?"

"I got to thinking about our choices, Dan. If the cops determine we got on Route 31, they will close all the exits. Getting caught on 31 would be suicide. There would be no place to hide. We'd be open targets out there on that long slab of concrete. For the cops, it would be like shooting fish in a barrel."

"If you don't mind my asking," voiced a nervous Russ, "what the hell did you guys do to have the cops after you?"

"Well, damn, Russ, that's mighty nice of you to ask. I'm guessing you mean besides stealing your truck and kidnapping you?"

"Yeah, I guess that's what I mean," replied the shaky driver.

"Well, let me see," said Nick, as he held up his left hand and started counting by popping up a finger as he detailed each act of crime.

"One, we robbed the Bank of America last Friday, and two, we robbed Chapin and Burroughs on Wednesday. Three, I killed a hotel manager who caught on to who we were. We had two partners I had to kill due to their becoming liabilities. They account for numbers four and five. Although, hindsight being 20-20, we sure could use them now. But we cannot undo what I have done."

"Don't forget the couple and the two cops you shot about 20 minutes ago, Nick," reminded Dan from the back seat.

"Ahh, yes. That too! I guess that brings the count to… nine!"

Russ, hearing the list of egregious acts told in such a flippant manner, almost wet himself. He didn't see himself coming out of this alive. He began begging for his life.

"Hey, I've got two little girls, ages 2 and 5, and a wife who needs me. I'll do whatever you ask, but I'm begging you not to kill me."

"Kill you!" snorted Nick. "The thought never crossed my mind, Russ. Did it cross yours, Dan?"

"You're the one doing all the killing, Nick. I never gave it a thought."

"You just get us to Wilmington, Russ, and you'll see your wife and kids. I have no reason to kill you. The cops have pictures of us, so they don't need you to give them a description. You have nothing to tell them that they don't already know. You can relax and just drive, pal."

Russ didn't believe a word Nick said, and there were no reasons that he should.

CHAPTER 43

"**We have spotters both on** foot and in unmarked cars, partner, at the 707 and Farrow Parkway interchange. We also have coverage on both sides of 17 at Harrelson Boulevard, both sides of 17 at 501, 10th, 21st and 29th Avenues."

Both agents and a dozen State Troopers, Horry County Sheriffs, and Myrtle Beach Police had gathered at the 38th Avenue and Route 17 intersection.

They were all in 'quiet mode' with no sirens or lights.

"If we don't hear something soon, then they already passed us or they have taken Route 31."

"Maybe they went west, Ron."

"Yeah, maybe so, Tim. We have limited resources on that route, though. If I'm wrong about this, I'll have my ass roasted."

"They'll need a lot of firewood," smirked Tim.

Radios crackled.

"Suspects have just passed the Harrelson intersection."

"Either the Farrow spotters missed them or they had already passed," stated Tim.

"What's next, Tim?"

"501."

"They'll be going straight through."

"What makes you say that?"

"If they wanted to get onto 501, they could have done it at Harrelson. That route offered more escape routes. They're coming our way."

Radios crackled.

"Suspects caught by Pine Island light. They are in the left-most lane."

"How far away are they, Tim?"

"I'd say four miles. If they come to us, they should be here in 7-8 minutes."

"We're all set on the blocker."

"Check."

Radios crackled.

"They are on their way to 10th."

"Hey, mister."

"Russ, you can call me Nick. What is it?"

"I have less than a quarter tank of gas. Now, I love this truck, but I know there's not enough gas for her to get us to Wilmington."

"So you're suggesting we stop for gas?"

"Yeah, I am. There's a Sam's Club up ahead at the 10th Avenue intersection. I'm a member there. You pump your own gas."

"What do you think, Dan?"

"We're going to need gas, so let's get it now."

"Okay, Russ, but Dan will pump the gas. You just give him what he needs."

Russ, while nodding yes, slid over to the far right lane to make the turn onto 10th. As he did, so did a half-dozen other vehicles at various lengths behind him.

Radios crackled.

"Suspects are making a right onto 10th. What are the instructions?"

"What the hell!" barked Ron. "Give me that damn mic."

Handing Ron the mic, Tim reminded him that there are six units following them.

Nodding his understanding, Ron spoke into the mic, "I want only two units to follow. The rest are to pull into the first available space and await further instructions."

Sergeant Brewer, in unit one, was in charge of the roadblocks and it was he who responded.

"Understood, sir."

Ron listened as the sergeant directed units one and four to make the turn, and all others to pull aside into a nearby service station at the intersection.

Seconds later Russ made the right, drove about a hundred yards and moving to the left, turned on his left turn signal.

"The suspects appear to be turning into Sam's Club, sir," reported Brewer.

"Sam's Club? What the…?" a confused Ron was saying when Tim interrupted.

"Gas. I'll bet that they are stopping for gas."

"Let's take them there, Ron," suggested Bill Baxter.

Ron took a minute to ponder Baxter's suggestion. After giving the situation some thought, he replied, "No. We don't have enough manpower."

"We have four other units sitting in that gas station, which can't be more than a few hundred yards away."

"Bullets, Bill, travel faster than do cars having to drive a few hundred yards. Let's see what they do after they gas up."

Tim was right. The truck pulled into the Sam's parking lot and drove straight to the gas pumps.

"They stopped for gas," reported Sergeant Brewer.

"Good call, Tim," said Ron, with an approving nod.

Five minutes later, after Dan had filled the tank, they left the lot with Russ making a right turn onto 10th Avenue. Seconds later they were again heading north on Route 17.

"Suspects heading your way, Agent Lee," radioed Brewer.

Two minutes later the spotter at 21st radioed, *"Passing 21st."*

The drive to the next intersection took the truck and its unknown followers past Broadway at the Beach. The light at 29th turned yellow as the truck was a half-dozen lengths from the intersection.

"Don't stop, Russ," ordered Nick.

Russ didn't stop, but the entourage of lawmen behind them had to stop, due to the law-abiding citizens in front of them.

"We got caught by the 29th traffic light, Colonel," radioed Brewer. *"They ran the light. They'll be on you inside a minute. There may be up to eight other vehicles in their pack."*

"Blocker be ready," instructed Tim into his mic.

"I'm ready, sir," replied the driver of a 30-foot rig.

"Don't fire into the cab of the truck," instructed Ron. "Make sure you take out the tires."

"Let's kill these sons-of-bitches, Ron."

"Sounds good to me. I hate going to trial. Messes up my golf days."

A stream of lights appeared, no more than a quarter-mile away. Mixed in that stream was a truck carrying a pair of madmen and a scared out-of-his-mind individual.

In less than ninety seconds, two of them would be dead.

CHAPTER 44

"Block the road!" Tim screamed into his mic.

"Units one, two, and three, fall in behind them!" ordered Ron. "No lights! No sirens!"

They were in the right-hand lane behind two other vehicles when Russ slammed on the brakes and barely avoided rear-ending the car in front of him.

"What in the hell is happening!" shouted Nick.

"A big-ass truck pulled out into the highway. He's got three lanes blocked," stated a fearful Russ.

"Asshole!" yelled Dan. "He could have gotten us all killed."

Glancing at his side mirror, Nick saw three vehicles pull in behind them.

"Where did they come from?" he asked.

Russ, looking in his rearview mirror, shrugged, suggesting, "I'd guess they were the cars caught by the last light, catching up."

"Just three of them? Look! Further back! There must be a dozen cars a half-mile back. I'm guessing those are the cars caught by that last light. Something ain't right, Dan!"

A volley of bullets hitting the truck's tires confirmed Nick's suspicions. The truck sagged at least six inches. It wasn't going anywhere.

"Cops, Nick! They have us surrounded! We gotta make a run for it!" yelled Dan as he opened the back door.

"NO!" screamed Nick. "You go out there, you'll be dead before you get ten feet. Stay in the truck. Having our buddy Russ here with us provides us with some real good leverage. Out there, we got nothing."

Nick was right about his second point, but a sniper's bullet that tore half his face off made his leverage option a moot point.

Dan, sitting in the back seat, covered with Nick's blood and bone fragments, panicked, and leaped from the car, yelling, "I didn't kill any…"

They would have honored his surrender, but in his hurry to do so, he forgot to leave the AK-47 he was holding in the car.

Dozens of bullets of various calibers ripped Dan to shreds. Nick was right about him not getting ten feet from the truck. Dan only made it six.

Ron and Tim, using extreme caution, approached the incapacitated truck.

The extreme caution was unnecessary. They had vanquished all chances of harm.

Nick Jonas remained in a sitting position, but the entire right side of his face was missing.

Dan Lucas lay outside, a few hot-lead ounces heavier than when leaving the truck.

Russell Burke was sobbing as he sat in the driver's seat, his head on the steering wheel.

Ron opened the driver's door, saying, "Are you all right, Russell? You can relax. It's all over now."

The man was so wrought with emotion, he couldn't answer.

Tim, grabbing Russell by the arm, said, "Come out of there, Russ. We'll have a doctor look at you. You're fine now, although your truck could use some tires and a new windshield. Your passenger seat might need a little cleansing too."

"Bill, I'll leave you to clean up," said Ron. "I'm going for breakfast."

"Gee, what a guy," said Bill, slapping Ron on the back. "I get all this! A guy with half a head…"

"Don't forget the three million dollars."

"Hey, who gets to pay for the damages to the guy's truck, Ron?"

"Not the FBI. Let's hope he has good insurance."

As Ron was walking away, Baxter called out, "Good plan, Ron."

"Yeah, but we were lucky. They could have gone west."

"It's obvious they didn't listen to some excellent advice!" exclaimed Bill.

"And what excellent advice was that?"

"A few years back, a guy named Horace Greely said, 'Go west, young man, go west!'"

"Horace didn't say that, Bill. John Babsone Lane Soule said it."

"Who?"

CHAPTER 45

"They have good crisp bacon here and excellent home fries. The best in town."

They were sitting in Mammy's Kitchen enjoying a long breakfast-Ron already had three cups of coffee-as they celebrated the capture and elimination of the bank robbing team.

"You would know, Ron. I dare say you have eaten in all 5,781 restaurants along the Grand Strand."

"I think you may have missed one or two, Tim-o-thy, but I didn't," replied Ron with a twinkle in his eye.

"So Colonel, are we taking the rest of the weekend off now?"

"Neg-a-tory, partner. We have two killers to corral."

"Two?"

"Yeah. The guy killing these women and the person who killed Mrs. Kiernan."

"You're set on Mr. Kiernan as the killer of his wife, aren't you?"

"No doubt in my mind, partner. As soon as we finish breakfast, we're going to take a ride out there and have a long discussion with Mr. Bob Kiernan."

"No, we are not," Tim replied.

"Are you disobeying my orders, Tim?"

"First off, it wasn't an order, and second, I just received a text from Buttocks, saying he wants us back at the office, pronto."

"I'm guessing he wants to award us the Silver Star or maybe even the Congressional Medal of Honor for our early morning exploits."

"His message doesn't quite read that way."

"How so?"

"He texted three words in caps followed by an exclamation remark."

"What was it, 'WAY TO GO!'"

"No. I'm assuming it reads, 'WHAT THE F*CK!'"

"What do you mean, you assume?"

"He put an asterisk between the F and the C. Maybe he can't spell."

"That's a possibility, I suppose," acknowledged Ron.

It was 8:45 when they walked into Captain Braddock's office looking like two Cheshire cats.

"Morning, Captain!" said Ron. "I'm guessing you heard we caught our bank robbers."

"Disposed of them, too," added Tim.

"Oh, yeah, I heard about it, all right," replied Braddock. "I heard about it from all kinds of people who want your asses hung out to dry."

"What!" yelped Ron. "What the hell for?"

"They say you shot a man in cold blood."

"Cold blood? What the hell are you talking about, Jim?"

"Others are saying you killed two men without even verifying they were the men you were seeking."

"This is nuts!" exclaimed Tim. "These guys, besides being bank robbers, were cop killers and kidnappers."

"They say that one of men you killed was trying to give up. What's your response to that accusation?"

"Oh, yeah, right! The guy was giving up, eh?" asked Ron, with emphatic sarcasm. "The bastard jumps out of the truck with an AK-47 and we're supposed to interpret that as a surrender! Are you shitting me, Jim?"

"How did you know the guys you were tracking were the same guys who shot those cops, Ron?"

"The state police found the car they were driving when they killed the deputy sheriff. They parked it at the Chick-fil-A on Route 544."

"I know that place. Stopped there a few times," interrupted Braddock.

"Yes, sir," responded Ron, irritated that Braddock's useless drivel had interrupted him.

Waiting to ensure Braddock had said all he would say, Ron continued his explanation of events.

"They confiscated the truck and kidnapped the driver as he was waiting in the drive-thru. We caught the entire encounter on the Chick-fil-A camera. After tracing the plate, we issued a BOLO which resulted in picking them up on 17 heading north. I had teams placed at various positions along Route 17 who monitored their route. We set up the blockade at 38th, and that's where the story ended."

They went on talking for another 45 minutes before Braddock's ringing phone interrupted the conversation.

Ron and Tim talked quietly while Braddock took the call.

Their attention pivoted to Braddock when they heard him ask, "Who is the downed FBI agent?"

There was another pause and then they heard Braddock ask, "What was he doing there?"

He followed that question with, "Who authorized the stakeout?"

Another moment of pause and Braddock slammed down the phone!

"Ron, did you authorize a stakeout at the Kiernan home?"

"Yes, I did."

"Well, it got one of our agents killed."

"Kiernan killed our agent?" voiced an angered Ron.

"No. Kiernan's dead as well."

"What? What the hell happened out there, Jim?"

"I don't know, Ron. Get your asses out there before I take your badges for all the shit you've caused."

"The shit we've caused! Well damn, Jim, I'm saying that we should discuss that point at another time," said Ron, with visible sternness. "But it will have to wait. As you said, we're needed elsewhere."

"Keep me informed of your every move, Colonel!" screamed Braddock, as the two agents were walking out the door.

"Roger that, Captain…" replied Tim as he stepped from the office. Then, as the door closed, he added, "Buttocks."

CHAPTER 46

Saturday, July 6, 2019 – Noon

Ron and Tim were investigating the crime scene at the Kiernan home, when The Dispatcher was knocking on Linda Ketron's front door.

"Hang on! I'll be there in a minute," yelled Linda in a shrill voice. She was arranging a date with a restaurant owner to hold her Movable Feast Book Club meeting.

"Thanks, Harvey, I'll talk with you later to firm up the date and the arrangements. Appreciate you doing this for us. Goodbye."

There was another knock on the door and Linda answered with, "I'm heading your way! Hold on!"

Reaching the door, she flung it open, only to see an old acquaintance standing there.

"Hey, Ed, whatever brings you here? Where's that girl of yours?"

"She couldn't make it, Linda. She decided she would just hang around the house. May I come in?"

"Why, of course! I was just about to pour myself some iced tea," she said as she made her way to the kitchen.

Removing glasses from a cupboard, she poured two glasses of iced tea, saying, "Here, Ed. I just made this fresh this morning."

"No, I won't be staying that long."

"Okay. You're here for a reason, so tell me, what's on your mind?"

"Linda, do you remember that meeting where Joyce Melville was the guest speaker, and the woman who just kept ragging on her?"

"I do, Ed. I remember you trying to calm her down and she struck you. Bloodied your nose if I recall."

"That she did," acknowledged The Dispatcher.

"Why are you bringing that up, Ed?"

"You laughed, Linda. So did many others. You all ridiculed me for getting beaten up by a woman."

"Oh, Ed, we weren't laughing at you," shushed Linda with a wave of her hand.

"No? Then why did I hear about it for weeks? Crass remarks, like, 'Hey, Ed, is that the first woman you lost to?' Or 'Hey, Ed, do you need a corner man?'"

"Everyone was just joking, Ed. Don't take things so serious."

"Annie Pott gave me the nickname, 'Punching Bag Ed.' She won't be calling me that anymore, though."

When she heard that and saw the sadistic look of craziness in Ed's eyes, Linda's blood ran cold.

"You... you..."

"Yes, I killed her and a few others. I have a long list, Linda, and guess what? Your name just came up."

Linda didn't see what was in his hand, but she saw his arm swinging up at her.

She raised her left arm to ward off whatever was coming. The boxcutter blade rewarded her quick reaction with a six-inch gash in her forearm and the removal of two fingertips.

She stared, her mouth agape, her eyes filled with shock, at the bleeding fingers. She tried to scream, but she didn't have time. Another swipe was coming her way. She put up her bleeding arm in front of her face but saw the blade slice through her shoulder and then felt it cut her forehead, just below her hairline.

Blood flowed from the head wound and filled her eyes. She tried to wipe away the blood with the fingers that weren't there anymore. She fell back against the kitchen counter and as she did, both her hands grabbed the counter. Her throat, now fully exposed, was an easy target.

She heard his voice, not sounding like the voice she had known for over 25 years, but one filled with evil, ask, "Linda, Do you believe in God?"

"Yes," she murmur.

"Good," he replied. "When you see him, tell him I sent you."

Her blood filled eyes never saw it coming. It was probably a blessing.

The blade sliced through her carotid artery, and blood began spurting from her throat like a miniature geyser. She sank to the floor in a sitting position. The spurt of blood was now just a trickle as her heart stopped beating. She fell over sideways, dead.

The dispatcher knelt next to her, lifted her head back and sliced through her larynx.

"Your days as Movable Feast Coordinator are over, Linda. Maybe next time, you won't laugh."

The Dispatcher, now as mad as a hatter, walked out the front door, covered in the blood of Linda Ketron.

The next name on his list was Robin McCall.

Linda Ketron was his seventh kill.

His sixth was at his home, hanging from a rafter in his garage.

CHAPTER 47

Saturday, July 6, 2019 – 11:00am

Just about an hour before The Dispatcher would kill Linda Ketron, Ron and Tim reached the crime scene at the Kiernan home.

They stopped at the sheet-covered body of Brandon Elliot lying halfway up the driveway. A large puddle of blood had seeped from under the sheet and had coagulated on the concrete.

"Pull back the sheet," ordered Ron to the FBI forensic specialist who stood nearby.

"His gun is still in his unsnapped holster, Ron."

"Yeah, that I see, partner."

"What happened to his arm?" asked Ron, noticing the flattened portion of the agent's jacket.

"The van ran over it."

"Van?"

"Yes. Agent Elliot called in the plate of a vehicle that had pulled into the driveway."

"What kind of van was it?"

"It belonged to a nearby boutique. The owner reported it stolen at 8:33. Elliot's call came in at 9:24."

"I'm guessing the van got here much earlier than that," said Ron with certainty in his voice.

"What gives you that idea?"

"For one, Elliot's body is lying here in the driveway. Ask yourself, what made him get out of his car and approach the suspect?"

"And the answer is?" asked Tim.

"He sees a florist van pull in. He watches the driver take flowers out of the van and walk to the door. Knowing that the man inside the house had just lost his wife, he concludes that condolence flowers is not unusual. Using that logic, he doesn't react, as would most, given the situation. But he sees the driver go inside, which is unusual, and realizes he's inside for an abnormal amount of time. So he calls in the plate. Now knowing he is dealing with a stolen vehicle; Elliot confronts the driver as he exits the house."

"He didn't follow protocol, and he didn't wait for backup, and now he's dead," lamented Tim.

"Yes, he is. C'mon, let's go inside."

As they entered the front door, they first saw Bill Baxter and Robert Edge, the Horry County Coroner, conversing as they stood over the sheet-covered body of Bob Kiernan.

"What do we have, Bill?"

"We got a mess, Ron."

"Please, elaborate."

"The killer slashed Kiernan's throat from behind with a boxcutter," reported Edge. "A bouquet was lying on the floor behind the body."

"What does that tell you, Robert?"

"I'm not sure why, but it tells me the victim turned his back to the killer who I presume was acting as a floral delivery man."

"That is a given, Robert."

"Okay. Then, when the victim turned around, the fake delivery guy drops the flowers, and slits the victim's throat from behind."

"Was there a second cut, Bob?"

"No."

"That's what I would have guessed," said Ron.

"Why?" asked Baxter.

"He didn't kill Kiernan for the same reason he's killing the women. He killed Kiernan because Kiernan killed his wife and made it look like our Friday killer did it."

"Who says Kiernan killed his own wife?" asked Baxter. "There's no proof of that!"

"I do, and your proof is lying under that sheet."

"There's a question needing answering, fellas," voiced Tim.

"What's that, partner?"

"Why did he turn his back on the killer?"

Ron scanned the room, then turning to Baxter, asked, "Is this the condition of the room when you arrived, Bill?"

"Yep! No one has moved a thing."

"That light was on?"

Baxter turned to look at the lamp in question and responded, "Far as I recall it was. It is a bit bright for it to be on. Wouldn't you agree?"

Ron, glancing at his watch and seeing the hour was approaching noon, replied, "It is now, but maybe at 9:00 he needed a light to read by. I see the morning paper is lying on the table under the lamp."

"I just had a thought," remarked Tim.

"Are you going to share it?" asked Ron.

"I might if you buy donuts tomorrow."

"No deal. I am now ordering you to share your thoughts."

"Cheap bastard," mumbled Tim.

"I beg your pardon, Tim-o-thy?"

Ignoring Ron's veiled threat, Tim asked, "What normally accompanies a bouquet?"

"I'm not in the mood for twenty questions, partner. Spit it out!"

"A card. In this situation, a sympathy card, I would think. Maybe he turned toward the lamp so he could read it."

"Did you find any such animal, Bill?"

"Can't say we did, Colonel."

"Did you look under the furniture? He had to drop it when his neck was being sliced open. It could have flittered away under a chair or table."

"We looked."

"Have you turned the body over, Robert?" asked Tim.

"I just turned his head to verify the cut."

"Let's turn him over, boys!" shouted Ron.

Two interns from the morgue reacted immediately.

Pulling the sheet back to expose Kiernan's entire body, one intern grabbed the knees, and the other took hold of the shoulders. They rolled the cadaver over and in doing so, blood sputtered from the wound, much like a thick soup might on a slow boil.

There, stuck to Kiernan's chest, was the condolence card. Ron bent down and lifted the card off the chest. Blood covered both sides.

"Give me something to wipe the blood off," ordered Ron to no one in particular.

An intern provided a clean white cloth.

Ron wiped the card and although stained with blood, he could read the inscription.

He looked up at the men surrounding him and announced, "We have an ego-maniac on our hands, fellas. Our killer refers to himself as *The Dispatcher*. And with what's happened here, I think we have ourselves a whole new ballgame."

CHAPTER 48

The Dispatcher, his mind now far beyond insane, made his way in the stolen florist van to Robin McCall's home on Pawleys Island. As he drove, he could vividly recall her sparkling blue eyes regaling in laughter as the Feast members made fun of his being taken down by a woman. Soon she would pay, as seven others already had.

As he drove, his thoughts drifted back to a scant three hours earlier.

He had just returned home from killing Bob Kiernan and an FBI agent whose name he didn't know. Parking the van in his garage, he exited, and on his way to the door leading into the house, grabbed a vinyl clothesline his wife used on occasion. Covered in blood, The Dispatcher made his way into the house and entered the kitchen.

His wife, Mary, standing at the kitchen sink, was rinsing off vegetables she would use to make tonight's dinner salad.

Seeing her husband walk in with blood covering his clothes, hands, and face, her knees buckled, and she had to grab the sink to keep from falling over.

"What in God's name has happened to you, Ed! Why are you covered in blood?"

"To me? Nothing. I'm fine, although for two other fellas,… hmm, not so much. They are… oh, how can I phrase this? Oh, I know! They're dead!"

"Dead! Are you saying you killed two men?"

"Yes, I did, and now, Mary, it's your turn… you bitch!"

"Ed! Whatever is wrong with you? Why are you talking crazy like that!"

"I should have killed you first. You betrayed me!"

234

"What are you talking about? I never betrayed you."

"Oh, but you did," he said as he made his way around the island bar toward her. "You laughed, just like the others as they belittled me for getting beaten up by that woman."

As he came around the bar she saw the vinyl clothesline in his hands.

"What are you doing with that clothesline, Ed?" the fear in her voice undeniable.

"We're going to play a little game, Mary. It's called Hangman! But guess what? You won't need to guess the letters."

She screamed, but a mighty right-hand uppercut, not only cut it short, but knocked her out cold. The blow also removed three teeth and split her mouth open to where, if she had lived, the cut would have required multiple stitches.

Grabbing her feet, he dragged her into the garage. Her bloodied mouth left a trail of crimson along the route as well as one of her loosened teeth.

He left her lying on the floor while he attempted to toss the clothesline over a beam in the garage's rafters. A dozen unsuccessful attempts had him angrily fetching a stepladder.

He was babbling to himself as he tied one end of the line into a noose. After placing the noose around Mary's neck, he tightened it and hoisted her upward. Once her feet lifted off the garage floor, her survival instincts revived her and she began struggling.

He hadn't tied her hands, and although she tried desperately to remove the cord from her neck, it was a futile effort. The cord, well past tight, was cutting deep into her neck. Her fingers had no chance to get under it.

Her wildly dancing legs quickly burned the thirty seconds of breath her lungs had held. He watched as her face turned blue and her eyes bulged.

She was still fighting when the cord cut into her carotid artery and ended her misery and her life. The blood shot out all over the garage walls and floor, then petered out as her body went limp.

Ed tied the other end of the cord to a workbench and left her hanging there while he showered and changed clothes.

The cord continued to cut into her neck, and if they had not found her a few hours later, the cord would have decapitated her.

Finding a decapitated body is never on anyone's bucket list.

CHAPTER 49

Saturday, July 6, 2019 – Noon

"He didn't cut the larynx, Ron," observed Tim.

"No, he didn't. I believe it's because this guy never did to him what the women did."

"What do you think that is?"

"The women must have belittled him. I think we need to go talk with Linda Ketron again, Tim."

"Why? What are you thinking?"

"Remember her telling us about an author who the audience dissed? I don't recall his name. Did we ever follow up on him?"

"Yeah, I had Agent Foster check on the guy. He was a locksmith, but he moved to Dallas about a year ago where he works at a Home Depot. He's not our guy."

"Let's go see, Linda Ketron. I think she can help us. I'm convinced that the killer has a Movable Feast connection. Linda doesn't realize it, but she has to know the killer. We just need to pump her brain until something clicks."

Forty minutes later, they were standing at Linda Ketron's front door and ringing her doorbell. It was when Tim rang the doorbell for the third time that Ron noticed the bloody footprint.

"I don't think Linda will be answer the door, partner."

"Oh? Why not?"

Ron pointed downward.

"Damn!" hissed Tim as he turned the doorknob. The door swung open. As they stepped inside, Tim called out, "Linda Ketron! FBI!"

No reply.

They scurried through the house and found the bloodied body of Linda, her throat slashed twice on the kitchen floor. A copy of *Catch Me If You Can* was lying on her bloodied chest. Tim called for the coroner and a forensic team.

"I think he killed her within the last two hours, Ron."

"Based on?"

"She's still warm, and the blood hasn't coagulated."

"Good observations," agreed Ron, as he stood in the middle of the kitchen, surveying the room.

"She knew her killer, Tim. She invited him in."

"Proof, please," said Tim.

"Two glasses of tea."

Tim gave Ron a quizzical look and then, seeing the two glasses sitting on the counter, realized what Ron was saying.

Two state troopers entered the room.

"Troopers McCall and Andrews, sir. Baxter sent us. What do you need us to do?"

"Glad you came as fast as you did, men," replied Ron. "I'd like you to canvas the nearby neighbors and see if anyone saw a man entering or leaving this house. If they did see someone, ask if they saw the vehicle the man was driving. Hurry!"

"What are we going to do, Ron?"

"Search the house and see if there is a list of Movable Feast members. We need to find someone who recalls a confrontation."

It took Tim only minutes to locate Feast members on Linda's computer.

"She has an email list."

"Print it out, Tim. We need to know their addresses."

"I'll send out a notice to all of them, saying to beware of anyone coming to your door. He's there to kill you. Lock your doors and call 911."

"That will work!"

As Tim was typing out the message, Ron's phone rang. It was Bill Baxter.

"Your guys showed up, Bill. They are out talking to the neighbors."

"That's good, Ron, but that's not why I called."

"Why did you call?"

"We put out a news bulletin about the florist's truck. It's been all over the news since 10:00 this morning."

"And?"

"A woman called in saying she saw a florist truck in the driveway of her neighbor. It was there for almost 45 minutes."

"What's the address?"

"It's 1400 Windemere."

"What's the woman's name who lives there, Bill?"

"Here name is Mary Patten."

"Tim!" yelled Ron. "Is there a Mary Patten on Linda's email list?"

It took Tim only seconds to reply, "Yes, there is."

"Ron, there's a kicker here."

"What's that, Bill?"

"The neighbor saw the woman's husband leave the house, get into the florist truck, and drive off."

"What's his name?"

"Gooding. Ed Gooding."

"Son-of-a-bitch!" roared Ron.

CHAPTER 50

Ron and Tim were watching a forensic team lower the hanging body of Mary Patten from the rafters at the same time Robin McCall was answering her door.

"Ed! Whatever brings you by? Where's Mary?"

"Oh, she hanging around the house today, Robin," he replied while smiling at his private joke.

"Why the shitty grin, Ed?"

"Inside joke, Robin."

"C'mon inside, Ed. It's too hot to be standing out in this heat. I made some lemonade. Could I interest you in a glass?"

"You could," answered The Dispatcher.

Robin was on her way into the kitchen when she heard her computer chirp. Ed was two steps behind her with his boxcutter in hand.

Robin stopped and whirled around to face Ed, saying, "Oh, excuse me a minute. I'm expecting a message from my daughter. That might be it. Have a seat in the kitchen. Make yourself comfortable. I'll be just a moment."

Ed smiled and nodded his head as he held the boxcutter behind his back.

He watched as Robin made her way to the study where her computer sat. She seated herself and opened the email message. He was about to go into the kitchen when he noticed her body stiffen as she put her hand to her mouth.

"Bad news?"

"Wh... what?"

"I don't mean to pry, but I saw your reaction when you read your email. I hope it's nothing serious."

She turned toward him, and he could see the fear in her eyes. She knew.

"No… nothing serious. Listen, Ed, I have to leave. My daughter needs me."

"Doesn't she live in Charlotte, Robin?"

"Yes, she does."

"Well, you won't be going there. You'll never see your daughter ever again. It's time for you to pay."

"Pay? Pay for what, Ed?" Robin asked, as she rose from her chair.

"You disparaged me about being beaten by that woman last year. I had to listen to your laughter and insults for weeks and weeks. The chickens have come home to roost, Robin."

"Ed, you have it wrong. We weren't laughing at you."

"That's funny. That's what Linda Ketron said before I slit her throat."

Then flashing the boxcutter, the Dispatcher hissed, "Now it's your turn, Robin."

He came at her with an unusual agility for a man in his seventies, but Robin, herself only 65, also possessed unexpected agility. While dodging his first swipe, she grabbed a stapler off her desk. As she stepped aside, she brought the stapler down with all she had on his head.

Ed fell to his knees as blood poured from a substantial head wound.

Robin went flying out the front door, screaming for help. She didn't stop running until she was a full block away from her house. She looked up the street and saw she wasn't being chased. All she saw was a florist truck slowly coming her way.

She ran to the nearest home and banged on the door. A man opened the door and seeing her distress, helped her inside.

"Call 911! He's trying to kill me!" she screamed.

"Who is trying to kill you, ma'am?"

The question did not go unanswered. But before Robin could provide the answer, the homeowner's front door flung open. The answer now stood in the doorway. It carried a boxcutter in its hand, and its head spewed blood.

The homeowner, both fearless and careless, approached what was a formidable figure, asking, "What in the hell are you doing, fella. Get out of my home!"

"That's him!" screamed Robin. "He wants to kill me."

The homeowner turned to Robin, saying, "What?"

It would be the last word he would ever utter.

The boxcutter swished through the air and sliced the man's throat wide open. Gushing blood snaked around the room as the man spun in a circle before falling to his knees, his hands clutching his throat. Ten seconds later he was dead.

It's true, he thought just before he died. *No good deed goes unpunished.*

Robin didn't stay to watch the proceedings. She ran through the house attempting to find another exit. A rear door leading to the garage presented itself.

She entered the garage and closed the door behind her. A quick scan told her that the garage had no door leading to the outside. Panic seeped into her mind, but then she saw the switch on the wall just a few feet from where she stood. She punched the button and waited as the double-car garage door opened at what seemed a snail's pace.

Not waiting until the door fully opened, she ran and ducked under it.

The Dispatcher was waiting for her.

"I said it was your turn, Robin."

She kicked him in the balls and ran for her life.

It seems adrenaline knows no age boundaries.

Robin, at 65-years of age, although not setting any speed records, ran another quarter mile before finding safety at an insurance office.

Someone called 911, but when the police arrived, neither The Dispatcher nor the florist truck was still around.

CHAPTER 51

They left Linda Ketron's murder scene and drove like hell, with lights flashing and siren howling, to the Mary Patten murder scene.

As Tim drove, Ron recalled Ketron talking about the scuffle with the harassing woman who, while being restrained, punched the man attempting to restrain her.

"I remember Linda saying that it was one of the regular male attendees. When Baxter said the name, Ed Gooding, it set off the alarms."

"So you think he's our guy?"

"I'm 99% sure. I'm guessing he took a lot of ribbing from the women. Although I'm no psychologist, I'd be willing to bet a shilling or two that he has always lacked an abundance of self-esteem. It's obvious that the ribbing was too much for him to handle, and so…"

"He went over the edge."

"Pretty much."

They pulled into the Gooding driveway at 1:30. Bill Baxter and Robert Edge were already there.

"I hope you guys catch this bastard pretty damn soon," growled Edge. "This running back and forth cleaning up this guy's messes is flat wearing me out."

"There's another one about ten miles from here, Robert," reported Tim.

"I know. I sent Cathy to oversee that one. I'm sure it's another sliced throat scenario."

"You're right, Robert, although she put up some resistance that cost her two of her fingertips," informed Ron. "This one, however, looks way out of character."

"Very observant Special Agent Lee. What was the first hint? Was it the cord around her neck, the dangling from the rafters, or was it that her head was about to depart from her body?"

"I must admit, Bob, the body appears to have some loose attachments," expressed Tim.

"Loose, you say," remarked Edge. "I'd say that if we had gotten here an hour or so later, we would have found her body on the floor and her head dangling on that cord. Although it is in the realm of possibility that it could have slipped off and rolled under the car."

"What did you find inside, Bill?"

"It seems, Ron, that our killer showered and changed clothes before driving off in the stolen florist van."

"Any guess as to how long she's been hanging up there, Robert?" asked Ron.

"I'd say three to four hours."

"So he killed her before killing Linda," murmured Ron.

"Yeah, and before killing Linda," said Tim, "he took time to shower and change clothes. She must have been special to him."

"Don't forget, he had already killed three others earlier," offered Edge. "Those were bloody kills, and I'm sure a lot of that blood found its way onto the killer. He knew he had to clean up, if he had any hope of getting to his next target. No one would get anywhere close to him, much less invite him into their homes, appearing as ghastly as I can imagine he looked."

"You know, Bill, it seems The Dispatcher, as he likes to call himself, has gone off the deep end. Until recently, he was killing once a week, but as of... 1:30 in the afternoon, he has killed four people since 9:30 this morning."

"Busy bastard, ain' he?" murmured Tim.

"Yes, partner, he is a busy bastard, but I doubt he's anywhere near done. We need to check the house, Bill."

"Be my guests, fellas. I don't think the lady of the house will give a damn."

The two FBI agents entered the house with Tim asking, "Anything in particular we should look for, Ron?"

"I'm wondering if this guy had a working list. If he did, maybe we can narrow down who he intends to kill."

"Linda Ketron estimated that over 4,000 people have attended the Movable Feast over the years, Ron."

"Yeah, well, I doubt he intends on killing them all. Remember, the incident in question happened over a year ago. He's targeting the women from that period."

"I'll check his office, assuming there is one, and if there's a computer, maybe we'll get lucky again," said Tim.

"I'll check the bedroom," replied Ron.

Only five minutes passed before Tim called out, "Ron! In here!"

Rushing from a rear room, Ron met Tim in the kitchen.

"What did you find?"

"This list of ten names. Seven names are dead."

"Who are the remaining names?"

"There's Donna Drouin, Cybil Rankin, and Robin McCall. Drouin and McCall are on Ketron's Movable Feast members list. Rankin is not."

"Find out which one lives closest to Linda. That's where he'll go next!"

Ron's phone rang.

"Hello!"

"Agent Lee, this is Captain James Hardin with the Georgetown County Sheriffs."

"Yes, Captain. What can I do for you?"

"Thought you'd like to know, sir, that a Mrs. Robin McCall had a run in with a man named Ed Gooding. He tried to kill her twice, but she escaped. She said he's driving a florist van."

"Where did this happen, Captain?"

"Pawleys Island, sir."

"Captain, close all exits off the island. Get the state troopers to help you. Do it now!"

Ron hung up the phone and went to find his partner.

"Tim! Where are you?"

"In here, Ron, on the computer. I'm getting the addresses of these three women."

"I know that McCall lives on Pawleys Island, so don't waste your time looking for her address."

"How do you know that?"

"Because Gooding just tried to kill her."

"Tried?"

"Yes, but she escaped. Where do the other two live?"

"Rankin lives in Murrells Inlet, and Drouin lives in Pawleys Island."

"Let's go! We need to get to Drouin's house. She's his next intended victim."

"Intended is being optimistic, Ron," declared Tim. "I'd say there's a better chance she could be his latest."

Ron didn't argue what he knew could be a strong possibility.

They jumped into their vehicle and headed to Pawleys Island, where people would soon die.

CHAPTER 52

Donna Drouin was an attractive woman. Her sparkling blue eyes and her soft blond hair belied her 72 years of age.

An hour earlier she had just stepped off the 18th green at The River Club golf course. Now, as her doorbell sounded, she was extracting herself from her jacuzzi where she had soaked for 30 minutes.

Grabbing a towel, she patted herself dry, grabbed a robe hanging on the back of the bathroom door, tied it around her waist, and went to the door.

Peering through the peek hole, she recognized the visitor as Ed Gooding. She knew him as a frequent attendee at the Movable Feast and the man who got punched in the face by an inconsiderate bitch who was harassing the guest speaker.

Keeping the door chain locked, she opened the door and speaking through the small opening, greeted The Dispatcher, saying, "Ed! What a surprise! I'm sorry I can't let you in. I just stepped out of the jacuzzi and I'm not dressed. What can I do for you?"

"Do you remember that altercation I had with a woman at a Movable Feast meeting last year, Donna?"

"Why, yes I do, Ed," she replied while thinking it was a strange question to be asking. "Why do you ask?"

"You thought it was quite funny that she bloodied me, Donna. You got a big kick out of it," said Ed with his voice sounding more dangerous with each pronounced syllable.

Donna knew she was in trouble. She made a move to close the door, but Ed put his shoulder into it, and the chain gave way as if made of putty.

The door slammed into Donna, knocking her to the floor. Her white robe came undone, and she hurriedly closed it with her two hands, as Ed, looking wildly crazed, stepped through the busted doorway.

"Get out!" screamed Donna as she scrambled on her back, along the floor, using her legs and one hand.

The Dispatcher slowly stepped toward her. His eyes, filled with evil, never left hers.

Even though she knew death was only five feet away, her modesty had her right hand holding the two sides of the robe together.

Her scrambling ended when the back of her head bumped into a wall. Ed now stood right above her. His expression never changed as he reached into his right-hand pocket and extracted a boxcutter. His thumb pushed the slide and the blade, dulled by the blood of others, slid out to its full length.

Donna screamed as she used the wall to stand. Seeing the blade, her modesty evaporated, and the robe fell open. A doorway leading to her bedroom was just a few feet away. She bolted for the door, but she couldn't outrun the flashing blade.

Ed raised the weapon and made a left-to-right sweep that caught Donna across the back, slicing open the back of the robe, and putting a 10-inch gash in her back. The robe turned crimson around the wound, and then blood began filtering down the entire back of the garment.

The wound was painful, but it wasn't debilitating. Donna kept running toward the open doorway. Reaching it, her left hand caught the doorframe as she turned into the room. A second slash of the boxcutter sliced through the door-grasping hand, severing the ligaments of three fingers.

Donna, seeing her bloodied hand, opened her mouth to scream, but it never escaped her lips. A third slash of the blade ripped through her face, removing a piece of her nose and some of her upper lip.

Instead of a scream, Donna went into shock. But it was short-lived. A final slash opened her carotid artery and seconds later she fell over dead, face-up, onto her bed. The robe, now fully open, revealed all her secrets.

"Hmm," said Ed as he sliced the woman's larynx, "it appears as if Donna was indeed a true blond."

Tossing a book onto the bed, he turned and left.

As he approached the busted front door, he saw a set of keys lying on a side-door table. Picking them up, he mumbled, "These may even the odds."

He was 100 yards up the street when a Georgetown County Sheriff's vehicle turned the corner and blew past him. He watched in the rearview mirror of Donna's Honda Accord as the cop car turned into her driveway.

As he made a turn onto Route 17 North, more law enforcement cars blew past him, including a black Yukon containing two FBI agents.

Ed started laughing. He could visualize the officers, seeing the florist truck parked in the driveway, huddling behind their vehicles, guns drawn, and barking out orders to *come out with your hands up.*

They couldn't know that the only person in the house was incapable of hearing, much less obeying, their surrender commands.

CHAPTER 53

Saturday, July 6, 2019 – 3:11pm

When Tim pulled up to the house, police vehicles jammed the street. Behind each car was a cop, hunkered down and holding a weapon.

Ron jumped from the Yukon, yelling, "Who the hell is in charge?"

"That would be Captain Hardin," offered a nearby officer. "Who's asking?"

"FBI Special Agent Ron Lee."

"Oh," replied the officer, sheepishly. "I'll get him for you, sir."

A minute later Captain Hardin was standing in front of Ron answering questions.

"What's going on here, Captain?"

"When we arrived, we saw the suspect's stolen van parked in the driveway, sir. We have the house surrounded. We have made overtures to him to come out numerous times."

"Overtures?"

"Ahh, yes, sir."

"And?"

"There's been no response, sir."

"Call your medical examiner. Tell him or her you have a murder victim."

"I do? How do you know that?"

Ignoring the captain's question, Ron instead dictated, "Find out the make, model, and the plate number of the car this woman drove. Do it now, Captain!"

Hardin ran off to make the calls. Ron and Tim, with their weapons holstered, entered the house through the busted front door.

"No car in the driveway and this front door busted open told me all I needed to know, Tim."

Walking into the front room, they saw the blood trail made by Donna Drouin's back wound heading toward an open door. Blood on the door frame told them what they would find next.

They walked into the bedroom and saw Donna stretched out on the bed with her robe open. Blood leaking from her neck wound had bloodied the bed in a three-foot radius around her head.

"Cover her up, Tim."

"The jacuzzi is still full of water, Ron."

"She must have been in it when he arrived," Ron surmised. "She donned that bathrobe and then made the fatal mistake of answering the door. It looks like she had it chained, but he busted it open. He chased her in here and…"

"Yeah," acknowledged Tim.

A moment later Captain Hardin entered the room, and seeing the bloodied body of Donna Drouin, turned his head away, while hissing a derogatory term.

"What kind of car, Captain?" asked Ron.

"She drives… drove… a 2018 Honda Accord. White. Plate is JPP-056."

"Did you put out a BOLO?"

"Yes, sir."

"Good. You take over here, Captain. My partner and I have business to take care of in Murrells Inlet."

"May I ask what business might that be, sir?"

"Killing the prick who did this."

CHAPTER 54

"Don't you think it odd that Rankin's name is the only name on his list who is not on Linda Ketron's list of Movable Feast members?"

"He's saving the best for last, Tim."

"What do you mean? He hasn't killed Robin McCall yet. She's still alive."

"True, but he gave his all in his attempt. Believe me, partner, Cybil Rankin will be his last victim."

"But why her?"

"I'm just throwing out a guess here, partner, but I'm thinking she's the woman who punched him out at the Movable Feast get together last year."

"Linda stated they never saw her again after that confrontation."

"True again, partner, but I'm guessing that Mr. Gooding, after a long search, tracked her down."

"Explain, 'after a long search?'"

"Remember when I mentioned the guy had low self-esteem?"

"Yeah."

"I think the berating got so bad, at least in his mind, that he said, 'the hell with it.' I now believe the guy has given up on life and will off himself… but not before he exacts his revenge. He didn't start exacting that revenge until after he found Rankin."

"Okay. Now get to the punchline."

"He wants to die."

"Well," said Tim, "if he makes any threatening moves, we will do all we can to oblige the son-of-a-bitch!"

"That's the plan, Tim. Remember our motto."

"Ahh, remind me."

"Avoid trials when given the opportunity."

"Ahh, yes. How could I forget!"

Ten minutes later, they made the turn into Murrells Inlet.

"What's her address?"

"1401 Key Largo Avenue."

"Never heard of it. You know where it is?"

"It's down near the Inlet Crab Shack and the Beaver Bar," responded Tim. "She lives in the Key Largo Mobile Home Park."

"Sounds fancy."

"No, Ron, you're talking about the Key Largo 'Deluxe' Mobile Home Park."

"Ahh, yes. I do get them mixed up. What's the difference?"

"The Deluxe provides every home with a backyard view of a dead possum."

"Well worth the extra five bucks a night, I'm sure."

Although the speed limit through most of Murrells Inlet is 35, Tim was racing along at 70.

When they reached the heavy traffic areas near Drunken Jacks and Dead Dog Saloon, Tim slowed to 50 due to heavy tourist foot traffic.

It took five minutes to travel the last mile to the turn onto Key Largo Avenue. They headed straight to Cybil Rankin's trailer, but when they arrived, found it locked.

"Break the lock, Tim," ordered Ron.

"If I ever retire from the FBI, I might go into the cat burglar business," Tim said while picking the door lock.

"You do know that cat burglars don't steal cats."

"They don't! Damn. Whatever am I to do with all my Meow Mix?"

"Feed it to your dog. He's nothing but a big pussy."

"You're amazing, Ron. You have this knack of finding the perfect solution."

"It's a gift, Tim."

The door opened, and they both entered expecting to find the throat-slashed body of Cybil Rankin, but they found nothing but a filthy living space.

"Are you getting the vibes, Ron, based on the surroundings, that Cybil never heard of a broom or a mop?"

"Or trash cans and hangers," added Ron.

"Hey, would you look here!" announced Tim. "Someone broke in through the back door."

Seeing the broken glass lying on the floor, Ron looked around, saying, "No sign of a struggle."

"How the hell could you tell? The place looks like a trash dump."

"Let's talk with some neighbors," suggested Ron. "I want to get out of here. It smells bad."

"Bad? Hell, that's a compliment."

As they exited the back door, Ron ordered Tim to canvass the homes to the right.

Tim knocked on the door of the house to the immediate right of Rankin's. A woman dressed in a mustard and ketchup stained sweatshirt and a faded pair of jeans answered.

"Who might you be and why are you staring at my sweatshirt? You some kind of pervert or somethin'?"

Tim, flashing his badge, answered, "FBI agent Tim Pond, ma'am. Sorry to be staring, ma'am, it's just the stains looks like Yoda…"

"You like looking at stains, do ya? Maybe you'd like to take a gander at the stains in my underwear!"

"Thank you, ma'am, but I'll pass."

"FBI, eh? I suppose you want to know where Cybil is. Right?"

"How did you know that?"

"I saw you and another fella breaking into her front door. Another fella, a lot older than you, broke into the back door about a half-hour ago."

"Describe him for me."

"Tall, old, and balding."

"Did you see him leave?"

"He came out the back door and walked toward Stella Stankowski's house."

"Might you know where we can find Cybil, ma'am?"

"She's working."

"Where does she work?"

"A place in Surfside called Crabby Mike's. Do you know it?"

"I do. What's her job there?"

"Don't know. I think she's a server, but I can't swear to it."

"Do you know her hours?"

"Do I look like a walking dictionary to you?"

Dictionary? thought Tim, as a smile creased his face.

"No, I don't know her hours, but she normally leaves around 3:30 and comes home around 9:00."

"Thank you, ma'am. You may have just saved a life." With one last look at the stained sweatshirt, Tim ran off to find Ron.

He found him just two doors down. He was standing in the driveway, talking on the phone.

As Tim approached, he heard Ron say, "Thanks for the update, Jim. That may come in useful."

"What's that all about, Ron?"

"Braddock. Gave me an update on our guy. Did you find out anything?"

"I know where Cybil Rankin is, Ron."

"Where?"

"She works at Crabby Mike's."

"Are you shittin' me, partner!"

"Why? What's up?"

"Braddock told me our guy got a job a month ago."

"Let me guess. Crabby Mike's."

"Bingo, buddy!"

"He's gonna kill her at work."

"Yeah, this is his big send-off. What time does it open?"

"4:00, I believe."

Ron, looking at his watch, said, "We got 20 minutes. Let's go!"

"He has a twenty-minute head start on us, Ron."

"Then let's make up some time. It's less than five miles from here."

They were in the car and speeding up business 17, blowing through every traffic light they came to.

"He may try to kill her before they open for business."

"Neg-a-tory, partner."

"Why do you say that?"

"He wants to go out with a bang. He's going to put on a show. Witnesses to the finale of his grand plan. He'll wait until we get there."

"Why wait for us, Ron?"

"He wants us to bring down the curtain."

"Well, let's not make him wait."

CHAPTER 55

Crabby Mike's was never at a loss for customers. On any summer night, the parking lot was full long before they opened the doors. If you weren't a local, you could expect a wait ranging from 15 to 60 minutes. Some might argue, however, that whatever the wait, it was well worth it.

Tim pulled the black Yukon into the lot at 3:48 and stopped right in front of the main doors where a large crowd had already congregated.

Ron and Tim exited the vehicle and pushed their way toward the front door. As they made their way to the door, they could hear murmurs trickling through the crowd. Most were worried someone was cutting ahead of them.

Tim reached the door first and, tugging on it, found it locked. He pounded on the door, yelling, "FBI! FBI! Open up!"

Inside the restaurant, three greeters, surrounded by 20 servers, prepared for the incoming crowd.

Hearing Tim's incessant pounding, one server remarked, "Some people will do anything to get in early."

The oldest of the group, a man who joined the team five weeks earlier, stood at the rear of the group. They called him "Wheezer" because by the end of the night, he was gasping for breath.

Cybil Rankin wasn't a server, as her neighbor suggested, but the assistant manager who oversaw the food stations. She was taking stock of the pans of food on the buffet when she heard the ruckus at the front door.

Seeing Barry Helms, the restaurant's manager walking from the kitchen, she called to him.

"He claims to be FBI. Barry. What should we do?"

"We only have five minutes until we open the doors. Let them wait."

"Wait! Are you kidding? It's the FBI!" snapped Cybil. "Don't you think it best we let them in? They wouldn't sound that distressed if something wasn't wrong."

"Okay. I'll check it out," replied Helms.

As he made his way toward the door, the oldest server was making his way toward the food lines where Cybil was performing a last check on each serving dish.

She turned around to see the man named Ed Gooding coming toward her. She often wondered why a man his age would take on such a stressful and exhausting job. Now, as he approached, she saw something she had never seen in him before. His eyes spoke of darkness. Her body trembled. She became afraid.

"Cybil."

"Yes, Ed."

"There's something I need to talk to you about."

"What's that, Ed?"

"It's about the Movable Feast."

"The Movable Feast? What about…?"

She remembered.

"That was an accidental punch, Ed."

"Nice try, Cybil."

Barry Helms opened the door and was about to ask to see credentials when Ron Lee pushed him out of the way, while yelling, "Cybil! Cybil Rankin!"

Tim, only a step behind Ron, closed the door. Turning, he looked Helms in the eye, saying, "Don't open that door until we tell you to. Do you understand?"

"Ye… yes," replied a shaken Helms.

"Where's Ed Gooding?" asked Ron.

"Who?"

"He's asking about The Wheezer, Mr. Helms," said a nearby server. Then, looking at Ron, she said, "He's right back here, mister."

She turned around to point him out, but he wasn't there. "Hey, where did he go?"

A scream penetrated the restaurant, and all eyes turned toward its direction.

They all saw Cybil Rankin, blood pouring from her right arm. A closer look saw that her right hand, the one that punched Ed Gooding in the mouth 15 months earlier, dangling from her arm at the wrist. Only a few ligaments kept it from falling off.

Of the 20 servers standing around the greeting desk, 14 were girls. All 14 screamed, as did the six male servers.

Ed now had Cybil around the neck, using her as a shield against the charging FBI agents.

"Let her go, Ed," growled Ron. "We know your endgame."

Ed, hearing Ron's utterance, put the boxcutter blade to Cybil's throat.

"Really? Tell me, Mr. FBI. What is my endgame?"

"We know, Ed. Let her go and we'll give it to you."

"No, you won't. I know how it is. You always try to take your man alive."

"But not the two of us, Ed. We hate going to trial. Ain't that right, Agent Pond?"

"Yeah, that's our motto, Ed. No trials for bad guys. We'd rather play golf."

"I must say, Ed, I never thought when it came down to the end, that you would turn cowardly," said Ron.

"I'm not a coward!"

"We expected you to go out like a man," Ron replied, while paying no attention to the man's denial. "I wouldn't have guessed that you would be a gutless fuck hiding behind a woman."

"You're just trying to egg me on, Mr. FBI," Ed said as he pressed the boxcutter against Cybil's throat to where it pierced the skin. A small stream of blood made its way down Cybil's chest until it disappeared into her cleavage.

"You cut me, you prick," screamed Cybil. "Don't think that just because you cut my hand off, I can't handle a pussy like you. Well, mister, you're dead-fucking wrong!"

Ron and Tim watched as Cybil raised her right leg and slammed her shoe's two inch heel down onto Gooding's right foot. The blow was so well executed that it broke a bone in his foot.

His scream sent shivers up the back of all those watching from 20 steps away.

Shocked by the pain, Gooding released Cybil from his grasp and in doing so, gave Ron and Tim their chance.

The volley of gunfire was deafening as every shot fired found its mark.

Each round drove Ed Gooding backward until he fell onto the buffet, displacing pans holding fried shrimp, littleneck clams in melted butter, and mussels. Those dishes, along with three or four others, would need immediate replacing.

According to the Culinary Institute, the FDA frowns upon garnishes, such as human blood and brain matter.

"Nice shooting partner," said Ron, with a high-five.

"Why thank you, sir. I believe I put two in his head and another half-dozen around the perimeter of his heart."

"I doubt the prick had a heart, Tim."

"Roger that, partner."

"Well," said Ron with an improvised sigh, "once again we avoided the need of having an unnecessary trial."

"Yeah, but, as you well know, partner, good shooting will do that," noted Tim with a wide grin.

"Amen to that," added Ron.

EPILOG

As medics carried Cybil Rankin on a gurney to a waiting ambulance, someone in the crowd heard her say, "I guess I won't be doing much housework for a while," as she waved her bandaged hand.

The Pawleys Island Chamber of Commerce honored Robin McCall as "Woman of the Year" for her bravery.

She also became a Grand Strand celebrity after spending weeks telling her story on both local and national television and radio shows.

When all returned to normal, Robin continued on the tradition of the Movable Feast in honor of her friend, Linda Ketron.

The next morning, before they had taken a single swig of coffee, or a single bite of a donut, Captain Jim Braddock had Ron and Tim called to his office.

The two agents arrived wearing gleeful faces, with expectations of hearing glowing commendations for their work.

Braddock melted away those smiles and the accompanying expectations when he uttered his opening statement.

"Don't be too proud of yourselves, fellas. The guy killed half the population of the Grand Strand before you put him down."

"Yeah, but Jim, we saved the other half," said a grinning Tim, while matching Braddock's exaggeration.

"Not funny, Agent Pond."

"Did you bring us in here to scold us, Jim?"

"Scold you? No. Put you on suspension? Yes."

"What the hell are you saying, Jim? We catch a guy killing women left and right, not to mention a bank robbing gang who killed a cop, amongst others. And for that you're putting us on suspension? Have you lost your mind!"

"Me! You're asking me if I lost my mind? What about you! You gunned that guy down in cold blood in front of two dozen witnesses! How stupid was that!"

"He had a boxcutter at a woman's throat and had already chopped off her hand! He had already killed more than a half-dozen people on that day alone, including one of our agents! Do you really think he deserved a pass!"

"You're both too volatile! You act like you're undisciplined and have no one to answer to! Well, I have news for you. You have me to answer to!" screeched Braddock. "I don't enjoy being fucked over. Now turn in your credentials and your weapons."

Standing, Ron removed his badge and weapon and slammed them down on Braddock's desk.

Looking at Braddock with total disgust, Ron roared, "When do we get these back?"

"If it were up to me, you'll never get them back," responded Braddock through clenched teeth. "We'll survive just fine without the two of you. There are plenty of worthy agents in this building."

Snickering, Ron replied, "What color is the sky in your world, Jim?"

Flustered by Lee's remark, Braddock responded, "From this point on, you'll call me, Captain Braddock! Now, get the hell out of my office!"

TUESDAY - SEPTEMBER 15, 2019

State Trooper Sergeant Harvey Little, with his cruiser parked in the exit lane of Long Bay's gated community, poured a cup of coffee from his thermos. He was working the midnight to 8:00am shift, and he had just gotten comfortable to enjoy his 4:00am coffee break. Everything was going fine until he spotted a cube truck, with only one headlight, heading west on Route 9.

"The driver may not know he's missing a light," said the trooper aloud.

Turning on his blue lights, Little pulled out and followed the truck for a half-mile. As he pulled into the left lane to wave the guy over, the truck swerved into the trooper's path.

Little avoided the collision by slamming on his brakes and steering his cruiser into the soft grassy median strip where he came to a full stop.

The truck took off and Little, stuck in mud, radioed the situation to troopers in the vicinity. Within minutes a roadblock, five miles up the road, was in place.

As the truck came upon the roadblock, it stopped some 200 yards away. Three men jumped from the cab carrying firearms and raced toward the woods that bordered the road.

Trooper Little, having freed his vehicle from the mud, came upon them as they were running.

Seeing the trooper, the gunmen turned their AK-47 weapons on him and sprayed his cruiser with multiple volleys. The state police would later announce they found

68 bullet holes in Little's cruiser. How Little escaped death, much less even being struck, was a miracle.

Moments before the trooper's windshield exploded into a thousand pieces, Little fell out the driver's door and onto the Route 9 pavement. He scurried to the rear of the vehicle on hands and knees to wait out the fusillade of hot lead.

Seconds later, as Little lay hunkered down, he realized he was no longer under attack. The gunmen's attention had turned elsewhere.

Hearing the crack of a sniper's rifle, he knew the troopers at the roadblock, seeing he was under attack, were retaliating.

The sniper's first shot took out the gunman closest to the woods. Two more head shots ended the conflict as he cut down the two remaining gunmen.

When the gunfire subsided, Little rose from behind his battered cruiser and made his way to meet the other officers. As he approached, trooper Ben Wilson asked, "What the hell is this all about, Harv?"

"I have no idea, Benny."

He took a half-dozen steps toward the truck, but stopped, asking, "Do I hear music?"

The gunmen had been listening to a CD when they abandoned the truck. Playing was a haunting Mexican ballad, called *"No More Boleros."*

"It's coming from the truck, Harvey," yelled a trooper who had checked out the cab.

Little motioned to a trooper to open the truck's rear doors.

"Let's see what the hell they have inside that truck that is so damn important that they found it necessary to get themselves killed."

The officer swung them open.

"Omigod!" whispered Little.

Inside the truck were a dozen or more bodies of men and women hanging from ropes attached to hooks in the truck's ceiling. With a half-dozen trooper flashlights shining on the interior of the truck, the scene turned surreal. The sight of bodies, some swaying, others twirling, and some just rocking back and forth, was too macabre to put into words.

"It looks like they are dancing to the music, Harv."

"Yeah, it does," agreed Little. "But they're dancing dead."

****

TUESDAY – SEPTEMBER 15, 2019

It was 6:12am when Ron Lee's phone rang. Still in sleep mode, Ron rolled over, retrieved his phone from the nightstand, and seeing the caller's name, answered, "Yes."

"You're reinstated," said Braddock as if his mouth was full of dogshit. "Be at the office within the hour."

Click.

Ron called his partner, Tim Pond.

A groggy Tim answered.

"Did you get a call?"

"Yeah, I did."

"See you in an hour. Oh, and Tim."

"Yeah."

"Don't forget the donuts."

I would like to dedicate this book to the ladies of

THE MOVABLE FEAST BOOK CLUB *whose members, as well as some non-members, enthusiastically offered to be "killed off."*

Thank you ladies and may you all, "Rest In Peace"